WHERE THE OGREKIN ROAM

WHERE THE OGREKIN ROAM

In a world where ogres are supposed to be extinct, one walks into a bar...

ELI RAINWATER

Eli Rainwater Books

Copyright

ISBN 979-8-9874-1681-5 (paperback)
ISBN 979-8-9874-1680-8 (hardback)
Eli Rainwater
www.elirainwater.com

Acknowledgments

Malachy and Casey for being incredible bosses, forcing me to take a much needed vacation (which was how all of this got started) and for supporting me every step of the way no matter how much I got inside my head

Sandra for being the reason why almost all of our regulars at Bull McCabes bought a copy and for being my biggest McCabes cheerleader (Beth is a close second)

Alicia for bringing home countless sticky buns and frittatas, wrangling the cats when I pulled all-nighters, and (still) making sure that I sleep and eat

Kim & Richard for being the most amazing brother and sister-in-law in the whole world

JD, Aron, Brandy, and the rest of the Wednesday night Metro 8 crew for coming to my events and always believing in me

Erin, Dave, and Ashley for all of your editing, proofreading, and sensitivity feedback

John for being the best unapologetic critic and helping me trust my gut

Most importantly, Brenda for continuing to be my rock, inspiration, and platonic soul mate

Contents

Fae & Cryptid Index   1

Character Index   9

1   16

2   27

3   34

4   46

5   52

6   66

7   85

8   105

9   119

10   131

11   148

12   159

13   168

14   187

15   206

16   224

17   234

18   241

19   249

20   257

21   265

22   276

Epilogue   294

Fae & Cryptid Index

This list consists of fae and cryptids either mentioned or who appear in the stories:

Banshee: Celtic fae, although there is speculation on whether they are actually cryptids, banshees are harbingers of death. They are always women who scream or wail to foretell the death of a member of an Irish family and are solitary creatures. Reports of their physical appearance vary.

Brownie: Brownies are Scottish and Irish fae and are classified as household spirits. They are known for cleaning and cooking in exchange for compensation (usually a bowl of cream, milk, or bread; no other gifts are considered acceptable).

Centaur: Greek cryptids with the body of a horse and torso and head of a human, these creatures are renowned for their wisdom, medical advancements, and fighting prowess, particularly with a bow and arrow

Dark Elf: Also known as Dǫkkálfar, dark elves live underground. Their skin is often dark gray or black, and some scholars believe that they are dwarves.

Dryad: Spirits of nature who originated in Greece. They are mostly commonly equated with trees and are tied to their trees and groves for life. They can manipulate wood and are typically wary of humans.

Fir Darrig: The Fir Darrig (pronounced "fear dare-ig") are Celtic fae. Also called Rat Boys, they are characterized by a ratlike appearance, red coats and hats, and living like rats. They are generally looked down upon and considered to be malevolent, but they can provide aid and protection when treated with respect.

Gargoyle: Gargoyles are stone during the day but appear human at night. Their skin and hair are dark gray like stone. They are some of the oldest cryptids in existence and are the keepers of the balance of good and evil in the universe. No one knows where they originated or how old they are.

Ghoul: Fae who haunt battlefields and cemeteries, ghouls feed on the dead, especially those who die violently. If summoned, ghouls will single-mindedly hunt their prey, and if their prey escapes, they will devour those who summoned them.

Hobgoblin: Celtic household fae, they can be helpful when rewarded, but mischievous, spiteful, and destructive when they do not feel appreciated. They love playing pranks and are related to pucks and brownies as well as goblins.

Huldra: The Huldra are Norse fae. Actually in the troll

family, they have the form of a beautiful, seductive woman with a cow's tail and sometimes hooves in place of feet. Her back can be covered in tree bark or hollowed out. They are forest spirits, but they can help humans when they so desire. They can also be malevolent and deadly when they choose. The males, or *huldrekall*, live underground.

Kalanaro: These spirit cryptids come from Madagascar and are characterized as being small and hairy with backwards facing legs and feet. They can be nasty and mischievous, but they are also protectors of children and will kidnap children if they feel the child is not cared for at home. They have the power to protect and heal humans and typically work with a "mosie", a Madagascar medium, to communicate.

Keiju: The Keiju are Norse fae. They are very small with beautiful wings, and they have the form of beautiful human-oids. They are shy by nature, but they will warm up to humans and dance around them.

Kitsune: Japanese fox spirits that originated in China as the huli jing, the Kitsune could be classified as fae. They can appear as beautiful women or men or as a fox, and they grow a new tail every hundred years until they have nine tails total. Their coats change from red to gold to white as they age. They possess magical abilities and great wisdom.

Lamia: The original Lamia is a Greek cryptid who was one of Zeus' many victims. She was a beautiful Libyan queen, but after Zeus became enamored of her, Hera, in jealousy, forced

Lamia to kill her own children. As Lamia went mad, she began to steal and eat other women's children until she became a monster, snakelike and bestial and living in shadows.

Leprechaun: Leprechauns are Irish fae, believed to be descended from the god Lugh, who was the god of the sun, arts, and crafting. Known to be skilled craftsmen, they tend to be solitary. They can be kind and helpful, but they are tricksters and can be malevolent. If captured, they can be forced or persuaded to grant three wishes.

Manticore: Persian cryptid with the body of an eagle, head of a lion, and tail of a scorpion. It can shoot poisonous darts that paralyze its prey, and it has multiple rows of sharp teeth.

Matagot: Matagot are spirit cryptids from France who typically prefer the forms of a cat, crow, or dog. They can sometimes appear human as well. They can bestow fortune and aid to those who treat them with respect or kindness, but they can also attack or ruin those who treat them unfairly or with disrespect.

Naga: The Naga are Hindi and Buddhist cryptids that are part human, part cobra. They can work on the side of good or evil, depending on how they are treated. They live in an underworld realm and are very wise and usually considered to be benefactors.

Nain Rouge: The Nain Rouge are North American fae from Detroit and are hybrids of French dwarves or goblins and

Native American spirits. They are said to be omens, appearing before disasters and with the power to strip fortune or luck from humans when attacked or antagonized. They are the same shape and size as dwarves but with red eyes and a disheveled appearance.

Nisse: A Norse fae similar to a brownie, the Nisse is a household spirit who takes the form of a small, old man and has one eye in the center of his forehead. They offer aid and assistance in return for payment.

Nuckelavee: Also known as the Orcadian Demon of the Sea. This is an ancient, malevolent Scottish fae with a man's torso on the back of a horse, a jutting snout like a pig's, and long dragging arms. It has no skin. Its only known weakness is freshwater, and it will destroy anything in its path at will.

Ogre: Ogres were once Oberon's Honor Guard until they disappeared right before the first cabal uprising; it was believed that they were extinct. They are over six feet tall and close to 300-pounds with grayish-green skin, humanoid faces, and horns similar to a bull's. They rampage in battle, at which point they grow to over nine feet tall, their eyes turn red, and their skin becomes diamond hard.

Peikko: Peikko are Scandinavian fae who are related to trolls and ogres. There are two types of peikko, hill and field. The field peikko lives in forests and often appears as an ugly, human man wearing clothes made out of bark. They are very strong and can't be defeated alone, but they are willing to provide assistance in return for aid or favors.

Pixie: Small, winged fae with a tendency toward theft and mischief. They have pointed ears and teeth. They are flighty and easily distracted, but they can be helpful when treated with kindness.

Puck: Old English fae, the most famous Puck is Robin Goodfellow, who serves King Oberon. The puck is a household spirit, known for being both helpful when properly rewarded for their work and destructive and mischievous when they feel they are not properly compensated with bread or milk. Unlike brownies, pucks prefer solitude.

Redcap: Subset of goblins, these Celtic fae are very malicious. Where most mischief causing fae do so in retaliation for treatment at the hands of humans, redcaps simply love to be mean. They frequently do the dirty work for other fae as long as they are compensated handsomely. They are small statured with matted beards, and they dip their hats in the blood of their victims.

Succubus: No one is sure whether the succubi are cryptids or fae. They are part demon and creatures of chaos but not necessarily evil. They are extremely attractive and are drawn to physical beauty as well as intelligence. They possess great powers of seduction which they use to attract lovers or stun and subdue prey and enemies.

Tuatha de Danann: Pronounced (tooth du dahnahn). The original rulers of Ireland, they are the predecessors of the Aos Sí. They are tall with red or blonde hair and blue or green eyes and worship the Goddess Danu. They were driven underground by humans where they lived in the fairy mounds known as the sídhe.

Vampire: Cryptids that were once human, they now survive off of blood for nourishment. Vampires are supernaturally strong, fast, can fly, and can shapeshift into different species of bats at night. By day they are weak and lose their powers of flight and shapeshifting. They are obsessed with wealth and prestige. They maintain a human facade, but their true form is almost batlike with gray, leathery skin, red eyes, large pointed ears, fangs, and talons.

Werepanther: Cryptids who can be created through birth or a bite from a fully shifted panther. Werepanthers travel in claws and have a leader, although they are not pack-like. They are great fighters, playful, and tend to keep to themselves.

Werewolf: Werewolves can be born or created through a bite by a shifted wolf. They are human/wolf hybrids with the ability to change at will. Their wolf forms retain their human intelligence and comprehension, and they are larger than wild wolves. They answer to a pack leader but don't necessarily travel or live as a pack in their every day lives.

White Lady: White ladies are spirit cryptids. They are essentially ghosts of women who died through some form of violence, usually at the hand of a jealous lover or husband. They are considered harbingers of death or doom, known to lead people to their deaths.

Character Index

Main

Jessie MacCaverty: Fire witch who was born somewhere around 960 AD in Scotland. She was named Jennet at birth, but due to her unnaturally long lifespan, she remade her identity many times, finally settling on Jessie.

Greta Schmidt: Earth witch who is Jessie's best friend. She was also born around 960 AD in what is now Germany. They met when Greta fled Germany during a French invasion and have been inseparable since.

Nicodemus: Also known as Nicky, he and his brother Mikael were originally from Greece and were turned into vampires almost 3000 years ago at the end of the Helladic period. Nicky is very close to Jessie.

Mikael: Nicky's older brother, he is frequently the more levelheaded of the two and close to Greta. He takes great care to dress in the most flattering and expensive suits and amassed great wealth over the millennia.

John Rossford: Local sheriff, leader of the werewolf pack, and Jessie's partner (once she got over her reservations about dating).

LaSalle: a Nain Rouge who showed up to warn them about an attempt to disrupt the Fae, Cryptid, Human, and Witch Alliance peace talks. Then he just never left.

Rupert: A Matagot who prefers the shape of a large black cat. He is also Madame Blanche's companion.

Supporting

Annie: A brownie in Mara's court who runs a cleaning service that caters to the fae, cryptids, and witches.

Astrid: Gertrud's daughter, very young and recruited by the cabal who preyed on her vanity and naivety to convince her to betray her mother. She is now a prisoner of the Witch Council.

Caroline Gregor: Jessie's apprentice and a water witch. She is a twin, which makes her one of the most powerful witches in a century.

Cassie Rodriguez: Caroline's human girlfriend and Jessie's tech support. Cassie worked to find ways to bring technology and advancements to the witch, fae, and cryptid communities.

Charlie: The ghost who died in the bathroom at Jessie's bar and now haunts it. He frequently helps her with inventory and can sense emotions and events.

Christopher Gregor: Caroline's twin brother and a fire witch. He is one of the most powerful witches in a century and is afraid of his power.

Emma: a hedge witch who runs the Night Market in south Atlanta. She also acts as the liaison for the hedge, hearth, and hood witches and the outside world.

Gertrud: A Norse witch called a *völva,* or a type of shaman who lost her powers when her daughter tricked her into making a necromancer. She now assists the Council where she can until her powers are restored.

Isabel: an air witch who was born in the same village at the same time as Jessie. She now heads up the Witch Council and is Jared's teacher in the arts of air magic.

Jared Daniels: Jessie's apprentice and an air witch. He is also a table top and role playing game developer and an athlete.

Madame Blanche: a White Lady and the European cryptid emissary to the Alliance. She was originally Charlotte de Valois, the original White Lady in France.

Mara Mac Gabhann: Duchess of Green Orchards and Oberon's great niece, she holds the lands in the Southeast on behalf of Faerie. She is a Tuatha de Danann and one of Jessie's greatest supporters and allies.

Matthias: a Fir Darrig Jessie and Greta met when they rescued Charlie and Madame Blanche. He became close friends with LaSalle and is glad to help out where he can.

Melodium: Tug's oldest brother and Oberon's general and head of his elite guard.

Riza: A fire witch and the head of security for the Witch Council. She is also a trusted confidant for Isabel.

Robin the Puck: Oberon's emissary to the Alliance who was the target of an attack by the cabal. He frequently acts as a liaison for Jessie and the Faerie courts.

Tug: An ogre Jared brought to the bar one day and who stuck around to become Jessie's tenant and security.

Won't Show Up Very Often, So It's Okay If You Forget Who They Are (aka the red shirts)

Annabelle: a water witch who died during the fight to rescue the ogres

Brigitte: a banshee who was turned into a necromancer and killed after she tried to kill John, Jessie, and Greta

Caliste: a shaman who helped Jessie and Greta rescue Charlie

Charlotte: an air witch who was killed by a Nuckelavee on the ogres' world

Crud: An ogre Jared helped heal

Dain: A Tuatha de Danann page in Mara's service who became good friends with Jared and joined his gaming group.

Frank: Emma's husband and a hearth witch. Feels that he owes Jessie a huge debt of gratitude for acting on his behalf when he was framed for a crime against the Council.

Fred: Sharon's husband and Jared's adopted father who is an earth witch.

Grubben: a hill peikko who was Astrid's prisoner and stayed to help on Gertrud's farm after Jessie, Greta, and Caliste freed him. Also helped them rescue Charlie and Madame Blanche.

Ingrid: A huldra in Gertrud's service who helps Jessie and Greta rescue Charlie and Madame Blanche.

Ivan: a water witch friend of Greta's who helps out from time to time and teaches Caroline the skills of water magic.

Marshall: a vampire groupie who was bewitched by the cabal to become obsessed with Nicky and kill Nicky's boyfriend.

Mary Jo Sutton: A local succubus who accidentally caused Charlie to have a heart attack and is now his girlfriend.

Nug: Tug's brother.

Oberon: The Fae High King who can appear as a beautiful dwarf or a blindingly regal elf.

Olav: A Nisse who serves Gertrud and came with her to the Witch Council to keep an eye on Astrid.

Renard: a vampire who originally went by the name of Hathus when he was a Visigoth; rescued by Mikael and Nicky and believes he owes them a life debt.

Ruth Ann Sutton: Mary Jo's daughter and a succubus.

Seanan: John's lieutenant and right hand, makes great cookies and transports the pack in her minivan.

Shania: a member of John's pack whose husband was killed during the battle to rescue the ogres. Jessie hired her to help out at the bar now that Caroline and Jared are growing up.

Sharaya: a keiju in Gertrud's service who helps Jessie and Greta rescue Charlie and Madame Blanche.

Sharon: Jared's mother and a water witch who was persecuted because of her brother's involvement with the original cabal.

Tabinda: A vampire from Persia who games with Jared.

Tam: a leprechaun who helped Jessie and Greta rescue Charlie and Madame Blanche.

Theodore: Jared's uncle and an earth witch who was trapped with the ogres after he kidnapped their entire race.

Victoria: a fire witch who was rescued from the ogres' world after being attacked by the Nuckelavee.

Zach: a human who began to follow Christopher after witnessing Chris's use of magic. Very rich and spoiled, he believes that magic can be siphoned and used by humans.

Warsaw: The gargoyle who stole Nicky's heart and was murdered to start the war between the cabal and the Alliance.

William: a human who's Jared's best friend and fellow gamer.

I

Jessie MacCaverty, owner of a small town bar in north Georgia and one of the world's oldest and most powerful witches, looked up from a spell book she read at the end of the bar as a swirl of late October autumn leaves preceded a chestnut-curled vampire through the door. Nicodemus paused for dramatic effect before he gave the bar staff and patrons a sweeping bow with an overly dramatic flourish of his wide-brimmed brown suede hat topped with a cluster of burnt orange-dyed ostrich feathers.

"What on earth are you wearing?" Jessie snorted as she tucked a long, silver curl behind one ear.

"What's wrong with my clothes?" Nicky demanded, looking down at himself and then back at his snickering friend with a tragically wounded face.

"Nothing if we were at the Met Gala," she giggled.

"Some of us believe in owning more than three types of clothing," he said in his most haughty tone, sitting down next to her and draping his floor-length, faux-fur, orange and brown striped coat on a stool. It matched his Italian leather orange boots, skin-tight brown leather pants, and orange silk shirt.

By contrast, Jessie wore her favorite pair of faded, broken-in jeans, that looked just like the rest of her faded, broken-in jeans, and a t-shirt from some bar in Atlanta that had closed years ago. The logo was almost illegible. Her long curls that, like all witches, had turned silver by the time she was thirty, framed her slightly oval, high-cheekboned face and piercing blue eyes. She was over a thousand years old but looked like she was in her mid-forties.

Jessie leaned closer and sniffed the vampire.

"Why do you smell like a pastry?"

"I do not smell like any such thing. It's Dior's Vanilla Diorama Fragrance, and it is an homage to Christian Dior's favorite dessert, the Diorama Gourmand," he stuck his nose in the air.

"So... a pastry," Jessie said. Nicky scowled.

"Hey, Nicky. Why are you dressed like a pimp at a pumpkin king's ball? I thought Halloween was next week," Caroline Gregor, Jessie's bartender and one of her apprentices, greeted him as she came out of the storage room with extra liquor bottles for the night. Her blue eyes sparkled with barely contained laughter, and she tossed her long, blonde, curly ponytail over her shoulder as she unloaded her precious cargo on the bar.

"Wow, Nicky. If I'd known I would see outfits like that around here, then I would have asked to move on instead of hanging around this place," Charlie, the resident ghost, added as he floated toward them with his succubus girlfriend, Mary Jo Sutton, by his side and trying to hide her smile.

When he was alive, Charlie had a heart attack in the bathroom while taking Mary Jo up on her offer to take him to heaven. She hadn't meant for the experience to be quite so literal. Now he was stuck in the bar for the foreseeable future and tried to make the most of his afterlife by filling the liquor and beer orders, listening to gossip, and complaining that Jessie didn't spend enough of her hard-earned money on sports programming for the TV over the bar.

"Haha. You're all so hilarious," Nicky glowered.

"You're going to give yourself wrinkles if you keep frowning like that," said Jared Daniels, Jessie's other apprentice and barback as he followed Caroline with cases of beer.

"Vampires don't get wrinkles, and I don't have to put up with this," Nicky drew himself up and tried to reclaim the tattered remnants of his dignity.

"Then don't dress like a pimp." Jessie grinned.

"Whatever," he rolled his eyes.

"How are you doing?" she asked in a softer tone, her blue eyes full of concern.

It had only been a few weeks since Nicky's lover, a sweet and serious gargoyle named Warsaw, was the first casualty in a plot to overthrow the tenuous Fae, Cryptid, Witch, and Human Alliance (or "ficwah" as Jessie and Nicky liked to call it). The Alliance was still in its infancy, and Nicky's brother, Mikael, was instrumental in its creation and development. Like other prominent leaders and communities, Mikael believed that the fae, cryptids, humans, and witches needed to learn how to coexist. After all, it wasn't like the supernatural community could hide its existence anymore now that it was out in the open.

Unfortunately for Nicky and Warsaw, only some agreed that peace was the answer. Most of the shyer and lesser-known fae and cryptids wanted to stay in the shadows, and many humans feared what they didn't understand. More dangerously, though, was the shadow group of witches who sought power and domination. Warsaw's assassination was one of the newly formed cabal's attempts to drive a wedge into the Alliance's peace talks.

Nicky had fallen for the thoughtful and brilliant gargoyle hard, and Warsaw's death devastated the flirtatious and mercurial vampire in a way Jessie had only seen a few times in her long life. She still felt that enough people had not paid for his pain.

"I'm okay," he shrugged and reached for the Manhattan that Caroline set in front of him. "I'll heal. I promise. It's just going to take time."

"I know, honey," she said with a gentle smile, reaching over to give him a side hug. "But maybe lay off the retail therapy. You really do look like a pimp."

He rolled his eyes again and changed the subject.

"Have you decided if you're going to talk to Tug?"

Jessie sighed, watching Jared out of the corner of her eye as he tensed up while pretending not to eavesdrop.

Jared, it turned out, was an air witch, much to their friend Isabel's delight. He spent a day a week at the Witch Council studying air magic with Isabel, who was the head of the Council.

Jared was a tall, dark-skinned young witch. Running and playing sports kept him in shape, and his impeccable fashion sense and good looks made him the object of interest to quite a few of Jessie's patrons— human and otherworldly. Sadly for his many admirers, his focus was on his budding career as an RPG game developer.

He had shown up at the bar with an ogre named Tug a few months ago. An ogre who shouldn't exist because they were supposed to be extinct. Jared had refused to tell Jessie where he got both the deep gash on his arm and the only ogre in the world, and then he informed her that Tug would be her new security guard and tenant in the apartment over the bar.

"I don't want to breach his or Jared's trust," she pitched her voice lower. "But John's right. We need allies, and we need to make sure that the other side doesn't get to the ogres first if they do, in fact, still exist somewhere."

"The first group that attacked us were, for all intents and purposes, just children, but we don't know how far this thing goes or if it's even just witches," Nicky said.

"That's also true," she agreed. "Yeah, I'll talk to Tug and Jared tonight, but I won't push it if he doesn't want to open up. We'll figure out another way."

"Fair. How's John doing?"

"Good," she smiled. "Lucky for him, werewolves heal quickly."

John Rossford, the local sheriff and leader of the neighborhood wolf pack, had been badly wounded when the cabal almost destroyed Jessie's bar. Greta, Jessie's best friend who spent most of her time traveling around the world doing research and development for the Witch Council, had to threaten to use her earth magic to crate him if he didn't stop trying to fight.

The process of transforming him back to a human shape

had been long, arduous, and dangerous after a broken rib punctured his lung. However, it had also been very eye-opening for Jessie; they had always cared about each other, but she had never been willing to let it go beyond flirtation. After all, witches could live for thousands of years, and no one was sure how long werewolves lived– they usually never made it long enough to find out. It was hard to want to be in a long-term relationship when you'll probably outlive your partner by a few centuries. She decided to take a chance on John, and now they were on their way to becoming the most nauseatingly adorable couple in town according to the regulars at the bar.

Jessie loved her bar. She had designed everything about the building to support the witches who called it home or needed a sanctuary. The fire-cured oak and the jars filled with candles along the bar top helped fire magic flare to life. Window beds of ivy grew in front of the old, stained glass windows behind the bar and cut-glass windows overlooking the front porch so that earth magic could blossom. The herb and flower gardens behind the building flanked a small pond that was sanctified under a full moon so water magic could flow, and Jessie always kept an assortment of incense and feathers to uplift her air magic witch friends. The bar itself had been a gift to Jessie from Greta, and Jessie frequently drew on it to supplement her own fire magic when she did tasks around the place.

The front door swung open, letting in another swirl of leaves and wind that caused the candles on the golden wood of the bar to gutter.

"Greetings, everyone!" LaSalle, their Nain Rouge friend and ally, belched spectacularly into his matted beard. His red eyes glowed with a mischievous gleam, and Matthias, the more uncertain rat-faced Fir Darrig, was right behind him.

They made quite the pair. LaSalle's gregarious personality, complete disregard for how much beer he spilled down his jerkin, and frequent cawing laughs were a sharp contrast to Matthias' shy demeanor, neat appearance, and rare smiles. Still, they had become instant and very close friends.

When LaSalle's clan sent him to warn the fae about an attempt to sabotage the peace talks, he stayed to help Jessie fight against the cabal. Then he just never left.

Ostensibly, he was only there to observe (and drink as much of the local beer as possible) per the standard Nain Rouge policy of "if it's not our fight, we don't get involved." In reality, his clan did not oppose the idea of him jumping in headfirst if Jessie and her friends needed someone to have their backs. More than one group of fae and cryptids had fallen victim to the original cabal centuries ago, and the Nain Rouge's memories were not so short-lived that they wanted to remain in the dark– or pass up the chance for a bit of revenge.

"Hi, LaSalle! Hi, Matthias," Jessie grinned with delight as she hopped off her stool and ran to hug them.

"Jessica, lovely to see you again," Matthias was still a little formal.

It had taken Jessie and Greta a lot of convincing to make the Fir Darrig believe that their offer to visit them whenever he wanted was sincere. Being one of the "rat people" and shunned by pretty much the whole world made it hard for him to trust. Like the Nain Rouge, the Fir Darrig were a race of fae with a nasty reputation for causing harm and mischief, but in reality, they only treated others the same way they were treated in return. Sadly, in the new cabal's amateurish attempt to overthrow the Alliance, one of Matthias' few friends had paid with her life.

The cabal had manipulated Brigitte, a banshee, into becoming a necromancer. Necromancers were fae or cryptid harbingers of death who were transformed into mortal witches and granted the power of the witch who completed the ritual. Necromancy was considered an abomination to the universe. Once the witch completed the ritual, both the witch and the harbinger had to pay a karmic price. Jessie still had no idea how many necromancers were out there with purloined magic working on behalf of the cabal.

In Brigitte's case, the price was too much to bear. Nicky had been forced to kill her, thus allowing the banshee to finally escape her fate after long years of suffering. Jessie was determined that not only would Matthias see justice brought to Brigitte, but he wouldn't be left alone in a world that tried to forget that he and others like him– those who weren't pretty and graceful– existed. Not that Jessie was motivated by pity. Matthias was intelligent and loyal, and his unlikely friendship with LaSalle added a dynamic to their little group that Jessie wouldn't give up for anything.

The door swung open again to let in more leaves, much to Jared's annoyance.

"Can everyone just come in at once?" he demanded, grabbing the broom for what seemed like the millionth time that night.

"But you sweep it all up so well!" Caroline teased him with

a wink at her girlfriend. Cassie laughed and took a sip from something electric blue.

Caroline's magical powers grew in leaps and bounds, shocking even Jessie and Greta. She had come into her elemental powers as a water witch, which was appropriate since she had a knack for making the most unlikely drinks. Cassie loved them. Nicky and his older brother, Mikael, were frequently appalled.

Cassandra Rodriguez was a human with a knack for technology that she used to help the local witch, fae, and cryptid communities. Most cryptids couldn't handle silver, and the fae were allergic to iron; both struggled to adapt to new concepts like cell phones and the internet. Witches had magical electromagnetic fields that shorted out pretty much everything they touched. Cassie's ability to insulate and protect equipment like cellphones and security system and her willingness to help the local supernatural community learn and grow with the times made her invaluable to many members of their small town.

"When I think about the centuries and effort and sacrifice to perfect distillation, drinks like that hurt my soul," Mikael shook his head as he took the stool on the other side of Nicky and eyed Cassie's drink with distaste.

Tonight Mikael wore a slate gray bespoke suit that was probably worth more than Jessie's bar. The crimson silk shirt underneath, like everything else he owned, brought out his gray eyes and complimented his athletic build. While vampires were known for being materialistic and vain, the brothers took it to a whole new level with wardrobes from the finest houses in Paris, only the best hairstylists out of New

York, and penthouse suites around the world. Jessie had never seen Mikael less than impeccably dressed. She didn't even want to think about what a pair of his or Nicky's shoes cost. She wasn't hurting for money by any means; she just couldn't wrap her head around the logic of paying a small fortune for a pair of footwear.

Rupert, the huge shape-shifting Matagot, accompanied the raven-haired vampire. Rupert had befriended them when his companion, Madame Blanche, Warsaw's employer and the European cryptid ambassador for the peace talks and all-around lovely White Lady, had been kidnapped by the cabal. He stretched before eyeing the bar to see if he should jump on it. After all, Rupert preferred the shape of a cat– including a cat's temperament and personality.

"Don't you dare," Caroline scolded him, tossing her long, blonde ponytail over her shoulder again. "We just got ready for service. It's bad enough that you shed all over the place when we're closed."

"Are you suggesting I do something as banal as 'shed'?" he demanded in his raspy voice.

"I'm not suggesting anything. I'm flat out telling you," Caroline glared at him with her hands on her hips.

"Actually, Rupert, do you mind watching the door with LaSalle and Matthias? I need to steal Tug for a little bit," Jessie interrupted their battle of wills. "Jared, I need you too."

Jared hesitated, trying to decide whether or not to argue. She returned his gaze without saying a word until he dropped his eyes.

"Yes, ma'am," he sighed, shoulders drooping in resignation as he headed down the hall toward her office. Jessie tried to fight the feeling that her apprentice was being led to his doom, but considering what they had dealt with already, it was hard. And if her gut was right, it was about to get harder.

Tug watched them without changing expression.

"Tug? Can I see you for a minute?" Jessie asked.

"Yes," he followed her down the hall behind Jared to her tiny office, which quickly became very cramped.

Jessie sat down at her beat-up, ancient desk that was held together by equal parts spellwork and duct tape. In her opinion, if something reached the point of absolute comfort, then why replace it? Shockingly, most of her friends did not share the sentiment.

She gestured to the decrepit-looking but very comfortable sofa opposite her desk. Jared sat down while Tug leaned against the wall. It wasn't that the big, grayish-green ogre didn't trust Jessie when she said the couch was safe. He just preferred not to be the one to prove her wrong.

"Look, I'm not going to beat around the bush here. Tug, you literally saved our lives when the cabal attacked us. They had pushed Greta and me to our limits, John was badly hurt, and Mikael and Nicky were about half an hour away from losing their strength at sunrise. Not to be melodramatic, but we wouldn't have made it in time for Cassie's charge," she said, smiling briefly at the memory of her IT guru bursting through the front door on the back of a centaur, screaming lines from *Die Hard* while leading a cavalry charge of local cryptids. Her smile faded.

"I never asked how Jared found you, and I don't want to pry. I'll drop it if you don't want to talk about it. But you need to understand something. The cabal knows about you now. Whatever reason you're not supposed to be here, whatever reason the world thinks ogres are extinct, whoever set that up knows by now that their deception failed. If there are more of you, we need to know, and we need to know where they are because, yes, it would be nice if they came and fought for our side, but more importantly, we need to make sure that they're not captured, tricked, or used to fight for the enemy. You saw what the cabal did to Brigitte. Don't let them do that to the ogres."

Tug looked at the ground, and Jared gave the ogre an encouraging smile.

"It's your call, buddy. But you should know that everything I learned about protecting and helping people, I learned from my parents and her," Jared nodded in Jessie's direction. "If she says she won't make you tell her where you're from, she means it. But she's not lying to you. These people are tricking the fae into doing unspeakable things and trying to capture witches like Caroline and me so they can use us without getting their hands dirty. They want to take over the world. At least let Jessie protect your family."

"I owe you my life. It's the least I can do," Jessie added. "Just think about it. I can take you to the Library where it's safe, and we know no one can hear you."

There was a long pause. Jessie almost gave up when Tug spoke.

"Can we go to the Library now," he finally asked, looking up at her and then nodding to Jared. "Both of us?"

"Of course," she said in surprise, rising from the desk. She had expected more of a fight— or, at the very least, a delay tactic or two.

"This might take a while. We probably should let Caroline and everyone know," Jared suggested.

"Good call. I'll be right back."

Minutes later, they were in front of the oak panel behind her desk as she pressed a knothole and whispered the spell that opened a portal in the wall to the Library she shared with Greta. She led them through the shimmering barrier and swallowed against the wave of vertigo and nausea witches felt whenever they crossed portals between worlds.

"Do you want me to ask Greta to stay away?" she asked once they were on the other side.

"Yes, please. Nothing personal, it's just that it's going to be hard enough telling everything to just you," Jared said, a pleading look in his dark eyes.

"Of course. I can fill her in on whatever she needs to know later. Make yourselves comfortable. I know the furniture doesn't look like much, but it's pretty reinforced. Does anyone want tea or coffee?"

"No, thanks," they said in unison. Tug's deep rumble startled the cats who shared the Library.

At some point in every witch's life, they needed a place of their own to study and store their artifacts, books, and, in Jessie and Greta's case, their cats: jet-black Aleister Meowley,

Lemur, a sweet and shy gray tabby, Spot the lap-hogging tortoiseshell, Lucy, a tiny but very bossy calico, sixteen-pound and perpetually starving to death orange and white Sunny, and now Ace, another elegant black cat with a penchant for tummy rubs.

The cats shared the massive room with its patched and mismatched comfortable furniture, walls of floor-to-ceiling shelves laden with books and artifacts, a cavernous stone fireplace, and windows overlooking a snow-capped mountain range lit by moonlight. Jared was pretty sure the mountains did not exist anywhere in their world.

"Okay," Jessie got comfortable in an armchair by the fire while Spot jumped into her lap. Tug and Jared sat opposite her on the sofa, and Sunny and Lemur disappeared wherever they hid as soon as strangers showed up.

Lucy jumped on Tug, who, startled, tentatively stroked the tiny cat's head while she purred thunderously. He winced as she started to make biscuits on his lap. His grayish-green skin could become diamond-hard in the heat of battle, but it was just as vulnerable to cat claws as anyone else's when he wasn't on a rampage. Aleister and Ace curled up on either side of Jared like twin jet-black statues, not quite on his lap but in reach of hands should Jared decide to start delegating scratches. Jared obliged them.

"Everyone comfortable? Start whenever you're ready," Jessie said briskly, seeing that they would drag this out all night if they could.

Tug and Jared exchanged a glance.

"Okay, I'll start," Jared sighed. "You've met my parents, and you know my dad adopted me because, you know, male witches can't have kids, and he and my mom have been really supportive about my working with you and about me making games and stuff for a career. Well, I found this old platform, like a disc, in their garage, and it seemed like the perfect thing to use for a portal into a world I want to build."

"Wait, you plan to build a world?" Jessie was startled. She knew her apprentice was talented, but she didn't know he was this ambitious.

"Well, not a real world. Okay, so role-playing games take place in game worlds, right?"

She nodded.

"Well, I want to make a sim world, like a holodeck kind of thing. You know, like in *Star Trek*," he explained. "The idea is that it will have everything a person needs to play a game in real-time: the quests, the NPCs, scenery, animals, raids, drops, everything. And the NPCs are just part of the game. If they're defeated, they disappear and respawn about ten minutes later."

"Jared, you know that's kickass, right?" Jessie was impressed. He grinned and ducked his head, embarrassed at the praise.

"Anyway," he continued "I built out the spell for a test region."

"Wait, you already did this? Without my knowledge and supervision? Were your parents at least involved?" Jessie demanded, eyebrows raised.

Apprenticeships had strict guidelines and rules about unsupervised experimentation for a reason. When a witch began to come into their powers, it was imperative that they find a teacher or get some type of education. A witch who didn't know what they were doing could hurt themselves or others or even, as it turned out, show up out of nowhere with an ogre. Jared looked guiltily at the floor.

"No, but I thought it wouldn't be that big of a deal! It wasn't supposed to be a real place," he defended himself.

"I see. We'll discuss that later, although I'm sure you learned the obvious consequences of experimenting with spellwork of this scope without the approval and supervision of your teacher or a full-fledged witch," she gestured to Tug, who was too enthralled with Lucy to notice. The little cat was upside down in his lap, purring while he rubbed her tummy with one massive finger.

Jessie turned back to Jared.

"So you built the spell for the region. Then what happened?"

"Well, I got my group together, and we went through the portal I made using the platform I found."

"Your group?"

"Yeah, William, Dain, and Tabinda. Robin played with us for a while, but he was too busy with Alliance stuff by the time I made the portal."

"Wait, Robin the Puck? *That* Robin? And Mara's Dain?" Jessie was startled.

While it didn't surprise her that Robin, Oberon's emissary for the peace talks, was into games, she had no idea that Dain and Jared had become friends. It made sense if she stopped to think about it. The young Tuatha de Danann page who served the local fae Duchess was probably close to Jared's age. Jessie imagined that standing all day in front of the decrepit cathedral that hid the entrance to the Faery Hill could get pretty dull.

"Yes, and William is a human I hang out with, and Tabinda is a vampire," he continued, getting irritated with all the interruptions.

"Hold on a second," Jessie said sharply. "You took a *human* into an untested world?"

"I had already tested it on myself. Jeez, Jess. I wasn't going to let him be a guinea pig!" Jared sounded downright insulted.

"Oh, that makes it so much better. We will have a serious talk about this later, young man! Now go on," Jessie crossed her arms and scowled. Jared bit his lip and looked at the floor again.

Tug was oblivious to their discussion. It blew his mind that this tiny, fluffy creature wanted to be his friend.

"Look, I know you're upset, and I know I fucked up. But I shut it all down once we realized what was going on. I promised not to tell anyone about that world, and I couldn't break my promise."

Jessie felt some of her anger dissipate. He had strong convictions and stronger loyalty, and she couldn't fault him for that.

"All right, just tell me what happened," she relented. "I'll try to keep the interruptions to a minimum."

"Okay, here goes," Jared took a breath and began the story that had stretched for what seemed like an eternity in Tug's life.

3

"Come on, man, aren't you ready yet?" I asked William, who just couldn't get it together.

"I'm coming! Give me a minute," William's robes were way too big for him, and he couldn't get them to hang the right way. He's this really tall and skinny white guy, and the robes were made for someone a lot bulkier than he is. It didn't help that his glasses wouldn't stay up and his hair kept falling into his face. He's trying to grow it out.

He was always more into books and learning stuff than doing anything active, which is why he was our healer. I don't know why he decided to go with the most over-the-top and impressive set of robes he could find unless he wanted to impress Tabinda. He's not a vampire groupie or anything like that, but he'd still had a crush on her forever.

Tabinda waited for us at my dad's garage with Dain. She's a pretty cool vampire, probably fifteen when she was turned. She was born in Persia a long time ago. She's our hunter. Man, that girl is deadly with a crossbow! She had on a sweet set of green leather armor, perfect for camouflage in trees.

Dain had leather armor too, but his was darker green and

black, and he had a brace of knives. He'd been practicing throwing them and gotten pretty good. See, he wanted to try out a rogue character. His armor looked more practical than ours, and my guess is that it was the real thing from Mara's armory. As the group's champion, I had this badass set of chainmail armor and a one-handed thin blade. I had a really nice, sturdy shield too.

Dain was excited because he got to hang out with people his age. Well, his age as far as how faeries mature anyway. We had already included him in a couple of tabletop campaigns, and he's surprisingly good at basketball. Don't tell him I said that. I'm tired of him kicking my ass and gloating.

"Took you long enough," Tabinda complained when we got there.

My folks were on vacation, so we knew we could get in some good game time without them finding out what we were up to, and before you say anything, I'm sure they're going to be just as pissed off as you are. You can all yell at me after I finish telling this story.

Anyway, a couple of months ago, I found the portal buried in the garage under what looked like a bunch of ancient junk, like old clothes and papers from when my uncle was still around. I hadn't seen any of that stuff before. I don't know; maybe my folks had it in storage or something. He disappeared right before the witch rebellion, and no one in my family really wanted to talk about him. From the few stories my grandmother and my mom told me, he was pretty much a piece of shit.

I figured it was safe to leave the portal there while I worked on it. Hell, the only time Dad goes in the garage is when he wants to smoke a cigar and have a beer and thinks he can hide it from Mom.

I had configured the spell using one of my dad's old spell books he gave me when I started studying with you. He had written a bunch of notes on porting, and I used some theory you taught us to get it right. I was pretty proud of it. It opened into this cool world with a clearing and some trees, and I plugged in some genetic traits for things like plants, birds, stuff like that. I even made goblins for us to try to fight.

"You're sure this is safe?" William asked again. I mean, I get it. Humans don't understand magic, so it's not like I expected him to act on faith. He's pretty brilliant too. He likes understanding exactly how things work.

"I tested it on myself," I tried to make him feel better. "Look, man. We don't have to do this. I just thought playing in a real setting could be fun."

"I think it's cool," Tabinda said. That's all William had to hear, and we were good to go. I activated the portal, and we went through into the sim world. Or so we thought.

At first glance, it was just a clearing in some woods. Our first clue that something wasn't right was Tabinda. See, it was night in the real world, but I had the sim set for daytime. As soon as we got through and came out in the sunlight, she could barely stand up.

"Dude, what did you do?" she yelled at me. "It feels like I'm in the middle of the Sahara or something. Did you have to make the sunlight so real and so strong?"

I was just as confused as she was.

"It's not supposed to be," I told her. "It's supposed to just be light."

Dain looked around, bewildered.

"Are you sure?" he asked. "I can feel the energy of the cosmos here more strongly than in our world."

"The cosmos?" William asked.

"Yeah, the fae use the universe's energy to fuel our magic. We don't use cardinal elements like witches," he explained. I know you told us that at one point, but I forgot it. I'm glad William didn't ask me.

"Jared, did you base this off of the real world? Because there are a lot of plants around here, and they need sunlight to grow. Maybe you incorporated more science than you thought," William pointed out.

"Tabinda, do you want to go back?" Dain asked.

Tabinda thought for a minute.

"Yeah. I'll go back and screw off for a while. Come get me when the sun goes down, okay?"

"No problem," I opened the portal for her. We figured we only had an hour of sunlight anyway.

She went back through, and we looked around. I hadn't gone very far the first time I had checked out the world on my own before I told my friends about it. I didn't want to get too far from the portal if something happened.

See, sometimes I think things through! You don't have to roll your eyes that hard.

We were in a clearing in the middle of some woods. I didn't recognize any of the birds who just sat in the trees and watched us. In fact, it didn't look very much like the world I had made at all. For one thing, it was a lot more... fleshed out. I don't know how else to describe it. It was actually kind of creepy.

The birds didn't sing, fly away, or do anything. They just stared at us. We explored the clearing for a while, checking out the plants and insects. I didn't recognize any of them, but I just chalked it up to plugging in some generic traits and letting the game compile the data to come up with the rest. The sky was brilliantly blue, like, bluer than I ever knew it could be.

"Hey, there's a path," Dain pointed at a little break in the trees that snaked away from us. He started to head for it, and William followed. I hesitated. I had a weird feeling in my gut.

"Guys, I didn't put that there," I told them. They stopped and looked back.

"Are you sure?" William asked.

"Yeah, man. I'm sure. I have all my notes and a very detailed diagram of exactly what I built into the spell for this game. I only made this clearing. We're supposed to be ambushed by some goblins, and that's it."

"Well, maybe the goblins left," William said, but there was already doubt in his voice.

"They're not supposed to. They're NPCs. They're only supposed to do what they're programmed to do. I didn't make these plants or the birds or insects either. I don't know, man. Something feels weird. I think we should go back."

Considering that I always pushed them to try new things, that got their attention.

"The sun will be down soon. Let's just look around until we can get Tabinda over here. Then we can all go down the path together," Dain is actually a pretty good voice of reason.

Yes, I'm sure he would have been more careful about building and exploring a sim world too, and you promised you would stop interrupting. Okay, so you promised to keep the interruptions to a minimum. Whatever.

We looked around the clearing. There was no sign of the goblins. Maybe they did wander off, but NPCs are supposed to be restricted to an area of movement. They're not supposed to develop sentient capabilities and go exploring.

"What kinds of plants are these?" Dain asked with a frown. The fae should know all about flora and fauna, so the fact that he didn't recognize them did not make me feel better.

"I don't know," I admitted. "I put in basic plant characteristics but didn't program anything specific. I wanted to see how this trial run went before I did more work on the sim."

Dain looked like he had doubts too.

"If you put in basic characteristics, then why don't they look like any of the plants on Earth?"

"Man, are you sure we're in a sim?" William asked, looking around.

"I don't think we are," Dain sounded even more doubtful than he looked.

"What else could it be?" I asked. I heard where they were coming from, but this was my baby. I wanted to make it work.

"What if we're on another world?" Dain lit up like that was the most exciting thing that could ever happen to him. "Imagine, we could be somewhere no one from our world has ever been! We could be real-life explorers!"

"Yeah, except we also don't know what's out there. What if something got the goblins? Can we take on anything bigger than we are? What happens if we die here? Do we die for real?" William sounded more nervous about being there.

"Maybe we should go back," I felt even more strongly like something was wrong.

"The sun's down enough that Tabinda will be okay if we get her," Dain said.

"Yeah, you're right. I'm going to do that."

Technically we should be able to defend ourselves if something attacked us. Even though we all started the game as low-level characters, the programming language I incorporated into the spell made sure that the NPCs were slightly weaker than we were. I planned to increase their difficulty levels if our trial run worked out and we decided to keep developing the game.

If any of us died in combat, we should, in theory, respawn at the portal. The NPCs would respawn about every ten minutes or so. But with that weird feeling in my gut, I didn't want to risk it. What if we really were on another world, and one of us died? Or worse, what if we killed a real inhabitant? Having a vampire at full power with us was smart.

I opened the portal, and Tabinda looked at us in surprise.

"What are you doing here?"

"What do you mean? We said we'd come for you when the sun went down," I knew it had been at least an hour, so I had no idea why she looked so confused.

"How can the sun be down already? You just sent me through the portal."

We all looked at each other, completely lost.

"No, we sent you back here about an hour ago," William told her.

"Dude, it's only been a minute at the most," she argued.

"Come on," I grabbed Tabinda by the arm and dragged

her through the portal. It was now completely dark in the clearing.

"Jared, look," Dain pointed at the sky.

Two moons were coming up, you could see more stars than I ever knew could be in the sky, and none of our constellations were there.

"I definitely did not do that," I told them. "Believe me, I would love to take credit for this because holy hell, that is an amazing view, but it's not from me."

"Um, what's that?" Tabinda sounded... not scared, but she had an uncertain tone in her voice for the first time since I had met her.

I looked where she pointed and froze. Something huge blocked the path. Then it walked into the moonlight, and I recognized it from some of the frescoes at the Hill the few times I had hung out there with Dain. We stood there and looked at a real, not extinct, ogre.

"Please tell me that's not one of the goblins we have to fight because if you made goblins that look like ogres, then you and I need to have a very serious conversation about expectations versus reality, my dude," William said in a remarkably calm voice, considering what we were up against.

"Ogres are extinct," Dain sounded dazed. "They disappeared over three hundred years ago."

"Guys, extinct or not, I think that is an actual ogre, and I didn't make it. We need to get out of here. Now," I was very proud that my voice stayed steady because I was pretty sure I was one step away from pissing my armor.

"That is a great plan," Tabinda agreed. We backed slowly toward the portal while I cast the spell to open it.

"Any day now, Jared," Dain's voice was tense.

But nothing happened. The portal wouldn't open.

"Why won't it open? Get it open!" William started to panic.

"William, calm down! Lower your voice! We can't show fear," Tabinda snapped. She had been an assassin in her past life. If anyone could get us out of this mess now, it was her.

"There are two more!" William could barely keep his voice under control.

"Why aren't they doing anything?" Dain stopped backing up and looked at the ogres, puzzled.

He was right. They just calmly watched us, and that's when I realized they didn't have any weapons. In fact, one of them held what looked like a giant guitar.

"Fuck it. It's not like they can kill me," Tabinda decided, putting her crossbow on the ground in a universal gesture of peace.

She took a deep breath and marched across the clearing toward the ogres, who watched her come toward them like three giant statues. It's not like we had a choice. The portal wouldn't open, and the path was the only way out of the clearing. We couldn't stand there all night.

Tabinda reached the ogres, and we watched as she bowed. We could see them talking, but we couldn't hear what they said. Finally, the biggest one bowed back to her, and they turned around and headed down the path as she walked back to us.

"They're really nice and very intelligent," she said, astonished. I know I was. Sorry, Tug, but there were some pretty nasty stereotypes about ogres for a long time. Well, there still are, I guess.

"What did they say?" William still sounded nervous.

"They welcomed us, asked where we came from and how we got here, and said that if we can't get the portal open, then we can spend the night in their village."

William and I looked at each other. We'd been best friends since we were kids, so I knew what he was thinking. Now that we knew that we weren't in danger, the scholar part of him wanted to head for that village so badly he could almost taste it. The sensible part wanted to go home and get an adult to come back with us.

"What do you think? Try the portal one more time?" he asked.

"It can't hurt. Then we can go from there," I shrugged, but the portal was already open when we turned around.

"What the hell?" Dain sounded as stunned as I felt. Oh, by the way, it's hilarious to listen to him swear. You know, because he's so proper.

"Come on, before it closes again," Tabinda grabbed her crossbow in one hand and William's sleeve in the other, practically dragging him through the portal and back into my garage with the rest of us right behind her.

I'm glad my friends are who they are because anyone else would have cussed me out and walked out forever, but they just looked at me, waiting for an explanation.

"Well, I think it's safe to say that's not my sim."

I was so disappointed. I thought I had made a world that had never existed before, and no, it just turned out that we went somewhere else.

"What do we do with it?" Dain asked.

"I don't think we should explore it until we have a better

understanding of that world's limitations," William said. "Maybe the ogres can give us more information."

I stared at him.

"Wait, you mean you want to go back and talk to the ogres?" I couldn't believe it. I mean, it wasn't all that surprising that he wanted to learn more, but I have to admit that I figured he would want to get someone older and wiser first.

"Of course! Are you kidding me? Dude! You found another *world!* And there are ogres! Think of the possibilities of study!" I hadn't heard William this excited in years.

"Of course we have to return! There are ogres! I can't wait to share this with Mara," Dain squealed. I was surprised he didn't start jumping up and down and clapping his hands like a little kid.

"Before we do anything, we have to figure out why the portal didn't work," Tabinda cut them off.

Something kept nagging at me that I couldn't put my finger on, and even though we were back in our world, I still had that wrong feeling in my gut.

"I think it was the ogres," I said.

"What do you mean?" William asked.

"They're supposed to be extinct, but then we find them on a whole different world. What if they aren't supposed to come back here, and the portal closed itself to keep them out?"

Everyone was quiet for a moment.

"I think we need to ask Robin," Tabinda finally said. "Ogres are fae. If anyone would know, he would."

"Yeah, you're right. Okay, I'll try to track him down. But no one says anything about this to anyone else, understand? Including Mara, Dain."

"Yeah, of course. Are you okay?" Dain looked worried.

I led them out of the garage and locked the door behind me.

"I have a bad feeling. Something's not right. That's not the world I made, and I don't know where it came from. And why were there ogres there? I don't know, man. I just feel like something's wrong. I'll let you know what Robin says, okay? Let's meet back here tomorrow at sundown."

"Works for me," Tabinda shrugged and headed toward her motorcycle.

"See you tomorrow, guys," Dain waved before he opened his portal and disappeared.

"Want me to stick around while you call Robin?" William asked me.

"Yeah, but let's go back to my place. I don't know why, but I feel like we shouldn't do that around the portal," I said as we got in my car and pulled out. I thought I saw a light in the garage. I should have checked, but when I looked again, it was gone, so I thought it was probably just my headlights on the window. Man, I really wish I had checked, though. Things would have been so different if I had.

4

✱

Jared stopped talking and exchanged glances with Tug. Jessie waited.

"I think maybe you should tell her what happened with you and your tribe at the same time, man," Jared leaned forward and propped his elbows on his knees.

He had always been gentle and protective over Tug. Jessie had never fully appreciated the extent of his protection until now when she began to see the two of them in a new light.

Lucy looked up at Tug and chirped a comforting sound before she began to groom his finger. Jessie smiled.

"She's telling you that it's going to be okay. She won't let anything hurt you," Jessie told him. "I don't know how a spiky fluff ball the size of a small loaf of bread will stop anything from hurting you, but there you are. Are you okay? Can you do this?"

"I can do it," he said, steeling his resolve.

"Okay, take your time."

She got up and walked over to the tea table where she dumped sage tea in a mug decorated with llamas and the slogan "no drama llamas." She poured water over the tea from

Greta's dented cherry red kettle on the old table and heated the cup with her natural fire magic before nestling down in the arm chair once more.

Tug sighed and shot Jared a doubtful glance.

"I'm right here," Jared smiled.

"I have to give you some back story to make you understand things better," he told them, gently rubbing Lucy's ears.

"Okay, we're ready," Jessie said as Spot jumped in her lap again.

"There were six clans throughout our village, all male. My clan was just my two brothers and me. We did not know our parents. In fact, there were no parental units in our village."

"So your village was all young, male ogres?" Jessie asked. A nasty suspicion began to dawn on her.

"Yes. My brothers are Nug and Melodium," Tug explained.

"What?" Jessie was startled by the incongruity of the names.

"Every clan had names that rhymed in that manner. For instance, there was a clan named Mud, Bud, Hud, and Sud. But in ours, Melodium refused to go by his name, Lug. He insisted that it was not his real name and that our names were also not ours. He swore that his name was Melodium, and he would rid us of the curse that forced us to live in a simple village where we worked from sunrise to sunset every day to survive."

"Why was he so certain of this?" Jessie frowned. "I mean, it's a safe assumption that he was right, and you and your kinsmen were among those who served Oberon before all of the ogres literally vanished overnight, but why wasn't he affected like the rest of you?"

Tug shrugged his massive shoulders, disturbing Lucy, who batted at his finger until he went back to rubbing her behind the ears.

"You will see as I tell my story. In the end, he was, as you point out, right. Not that it mattered."

"I'm sorry. Please, go on," Jessie encouraged him as Jared patted the ogre on the arm.

"Now that I no longer live that life, I see that it was odd that none of us questioned where we came from or why there were no others with us— no elders, children, or women. Any time one of us, other than Melodium, began to question our existence, we would experience great pain in our heads, sometimes until our noses and eyes would bleed."

"Magical aneurysm," Jessie snarled. "It's a fail safe really shitty witches use when they enchant someone. If the enchanted being starts to break the spell, a little bomb goes off in their head. I hate it when magic users become bullies."

"I agree," Tug murmured, looking down at the little cat who batted at the necklace that fell out from under his t-shirt. Jessie knew he wore it, but she had never seen it up close. It was a strand of gold chain links with an amulet at the end: three circles interlinked around an oak tree with a sleeping dragon at the base. She leaned forward with a frown.

"Tug, where did you get that necklace?"

"It was Melodium's. He gave it to me when he sent me to this world."

"I have to ask, do you know what it means," she was gentle but insistent. She *knew* she had seen that somewhere before, but where?

"No," he seemed surprised at her interest. "It's just a thing we had."

"I want to take a picture and send it to Greta. Is that all right?"

He glanced at Jared again for reassurance. Jessie had never realized how much Tug depended on her apprentice. She mentally kicked herself for not trying to get to know Tug better.

"It's okay," Jared encouraged the ogre. Jessie leaned forward and took a picture of the emblem with her phone, sending it to Greta with a message that said:

Important, find out what this is fast. Don't come to the Library until I tell you to.

A second later, her phone pinged.

Okay, winner of the most cryptic witch ever award. I know that emblem. I can't remember where I've seen it. I have a terrible feeling.

So do I. Let me know what you find out. Ask Robin.

She put the phone away and turned back to the boys. Jessie and Greta were each over a thousand years old. Anyone younger than eight hundred would always be a kid in her eyes.

"Okay, continue," she ordered, crisscrossing her legs in the chair.

"A magic user, a witch, lived among us there. He came down from the mountain at the end of each summer and took from our harvests and meat stores. He chose the finest cuts of meat and the best vegetables and grains. We carried them on our backs to his cave in the mountain, and then he left us alone for another year. This went on as long as we could remember."

"A witch?" Jessie's jaw dropped. "Who?"

Tug hesitated and looked at Jared, who looked at the floor.

"That is not for me to say," Tug said.

"I see. Jared?"

"Can it wait until we get back to my part of the story?" Jared mumbled, still looking at the floor.

"Of course. What else?"

"That was our life, day in and day out."

"Did Melodium ever confront the witch?" Jessie asked.

"He did the first time the witch arrived. After that, the witch threatened Nug and myself with death or worse if Melodium ever spoke against him again."

Jared frowned as something occurred to him.

"How did you make enough food to support him for an entire year and feed your village, too?" he asked, looking up at the ogre.

Tug paused.

"I do not know," he admitted. "But now that I think of it, I do not think the witch took a large portion of our food. I do not know much about how you sustain yourselves, but the amount he took would probably sustain an ogre for a month, maybe a little more."

"My guess would be that translates to three or four months in witch metabolism," Jessie said. She could see where Jared was going. "You think there were other villages, and the witch did the same thing at each one."

"Exactly. It doesn't make sense that the entire ogre race consisted of five or six clans, all male, and all in the same age range."

"One witch controlling an entire race takes a lot of power

and work, and witches can't cast glamours on the fae," Jessie frowned.

"We were glamoured?" Tug asked.

"Yes. In a nutshell, glamour is the art of making someone believe in something that is not real," Jessie explained. "It's also the province of the fae. Air witches can cast illusions well, but that's about the extent of any witch's glamour capabilities. This has pretty bad implications because someone else had to have helped the witch set it up. Sorry, Tug. Go on."

Tug sighed, growing still as he gazed in the distance. Lucy wrapped herself around his finger and started to doze off. He came to himself and looked down at her with a gentle smile.

"This is what happened the day we found Jared and his companions," he began the next leg of the story.

5

It should have been another typical day— sun in the morning, rain early afternoon, sun in the late afternoon. Tend the fields, hunt the wildlife, dress the kills and store them in the smokehouse for winter, tan the hides to make clothing, repair a roof on this hut, replace a warped door on that one, all of the usual things we did every day.

Our village was a simple one. We had built our huts from the stones we uncovered in the fields. We had uprooted and split tree trunks for the doors and frames and gathered grass and straw to thatch our roofs.

Our huts circled a square where a bonfire burned next to a deep well. Our crafting tables and a long table we used for our meals were also in the square. A dark forest smudged the horizon in the distance past our eastern and northern fields, but we had no desire to seek it out. Some tamer woods edged our fields at the southern border, and here we hunted and foraged at the edge of the tree line; the magic user forbade us to go any further.

A single mountain loomed in the distance to the west, and on that mountain lived the magic user who ruled over us. A narrow path led to his mountain through a boggy marsh, but no other paths or roads stretched to or from our village.

Every day was the same with life marching on from season to season. But it all changed on this day when Jared discovered entry into our world. It started with Melodium's usual rants about how this wasn't our true lot in life. He was always so confident that we had a life none remembered, a purpose we were meant to serve that was greater than our simple existence. He believed we were not in this place of our free will. None of us paid him any heed, choosing instead to continue our daily toil.

On that day, his rants died off earlier than usual, and he brooded in uncharacteristic silence. He sat on a rough-hewn stool in a corner of our stone hut and scowled at his amulet. The amulet had been in his possession for as long as we could remember. He never took it off; it usually remained under his leather jerkin, out of our sight. I had never cared to look at it as it was not of my perceived lot in life. Looking back now, I see how often we quickly dismissed those thoughts or curiosities that would have made us examine our lives more closely.

You have to understand something about my brother. He was a born leader. Even with his incessant ravings that we lived a lie, he still led us with confidence and ease through times of hardship, conflict, and peace. He planted and harvested more crops, made more kills, took the least amount of food during winter when stores ran low, the least amount of water in summer when our well began to dry up, and we all looked to him for guidance and advice. We could not understand why he believed our existence was a lie, but he kept us sheltered, clothed, and fed, and he settled disputes, and that was what mattered.

So for him to look at this amulet and do nothing, we were certain he suffered from a fever. He brooded, refusing food and drink. Indeed, it was as if our brother, Nug, and I were not present at all. As the sun climbed the heavens and the morning gave way to the afternoon, we became more worried.

"What should we do?" Nug finally whispered to me.

We had just come back to the hut from a morning of working the fields and performing duties that would keep our village fed and warm when winter clasped us in her chill embrace once more. I had hunted and cleaned a deer, preparing the hide to be tanned, and Nug had salted and filleted the venison for our smokehouse.

Melodium had not left the hut. This lack of action was most unlike him, for he oversaw and assisted in all labor throughout our village.

"Lu–, I mean, Melodium," I stepped forward. He hated his given name, insisting that his real name was Melodium. Of late, he had gone so far as to openly refuse to acknowledge that Lug was his name at all. "Is all well with you, brother?"

"Brother," he laughed, but the sound was bitter. "Yes, I am your brother. They did not take that away when they stole our identities and purpose. What is the point anymore? Oberon will not come for us, no matter how we fought for him in the past."

Now, none of us knew Oberon. Melodium had never uttered his name before. In fact, we had no awareness that the king of all Faerie even existed, much less that we had once been in his service. Yes, that is how deeply the enchantment held us.

I do not know what magic was at work that made Melodium speak Oberon's name that particular day. I suspect that when Jared linked his portal to our world, he inadvertently began to weaken the enchantment that had been placed on us.

It felt as though a shock wave blasted through me, stirring something profound and potent deep in my very core, and I suddenly realized a fog that I never knew existed surrounded my mind. I became sharply aware of myself in a new way, as if I were a stranger.

I fell to my knees next to my brother.

"Melodium, say that name again," I demanded. I needed to know what I felt. I needed to feel it again.

My brother looked at me, his eyes bright and eager as if he had waited for that command his whole life.

"Oberon! Our king. Our ruler. The Lord and High King of the Fae, who we fought to protect for centuries. Oberon. Say it!"

I stared at him, shaken.

"Say it!" he screamed, spittle flying across his face.

He lunged toward me as I scrambled to get away. He knew. He knew something changed within my mind; he could see it upon my countenance. The fog was disturbed. It had not lifted, but it was no longer a heavy blanket, lulling my senses into a stupor.

I fled from the hut and ran through the village, pelting blindly toward the forest. My fellow villagers watched me run, startled from their daily work. Nug ran behind me, calling for me to stop, and I could hear Melodium scream Oberon's name to the skies. All around me, the members of my village stopped what they were doing, staring in confusion and fear. Some dropped to their knees and clutched their heads in agony. I could see it as I passed; their fog stirred too.

I ran until I left the village behind and could no longer hear my brothers' cries. I ran until I reached the edge of the forbidden forest just past our southern fields. The witch had told us it was cursed, and we would bring a terrible plague upon the village if we entered it. We had never thought to question his word.

A path I had never seen before appeared in front of me, leading into the woods. I stumbled along the narrow trail as the trees beckoned me onward beneath their boughs. I became aware that the forest, once terrifying in its foreboding darkness, was now softly inviting. I felt no reluctance as I dove into its safe embrace.

Just as the trees began to thin and I saw a clearing ahead of me, new creatures blocked my way. They looked like smaller versions of my brethren and me, but they wore armor for battle. I do not know how I recognized their garb. We had always been peaceful farmers, yet somehow I recognized the armaments of war. They stared at me, as startled as I was, before the leader lunged forward, yelling, "Attack!"

"Tug!" My brother Nug cried as he reached my side. He saw the creatures too. Then, to my amazement, he began to change. His eyes became as red as burning embers, and he grew taller and bigger. His shoulders became so broad that they stretched and tore his jerkin with a mighty rending sound. His skin glittered like a diamond; when he charged at the creatures and they tried to attack him with their swords, the blades broke off in their grips.

But when I saw the creatures attack my brother, something changed within me as well. I felt an overwhelming surge that I later recognized as the rage all ogres feel before they rampage, as you call it. I felt my bones, muscles, and skin all stretch and expand in response to this primal urge. I felt the itch as my skin hardened. I felt as though I were encased in a diamond that could move as I did, and I knew exactly how to attack these creatures. I knew what they were. Goblins. I do not know how the name came to be known to me, but my brother recognized them too. We knew how to destroy them and made short work of it.

When the fight was over and their corpses surrounded us, we stared at each other.

"Brother, I do not understand," Nug said in wonderment as he held his hand up to his face and watched the late afternoon rays of the sun that sifted through the trees play across his diamond skin.

"I do not either, but I begin to question our existence in this place. What if Melodium was right all along? What if we are under a spell?" I pondered, realizing that it took no effort to speak Melodium's name as if it were his true name and the name Lug had never existed at all.

"We will take these to our village. All of our brethren shall feast upon the fruits of our victory," Nug gestured to the scattered corpses on the ground.

"Yes, I do not understand how I know that it is in our nature to dine on the flesh of our enemies, but I know it to be true," I said, feeling more and more like the fog both lifted me up and weighed me down at the same time. "After we feast, we can return and examine the clearing up ahead and see where else this path might take us."

We gathered together the bodies and carried them to our home, where we stopped in the village square. Our brethren stood, mouths agape at the strange sight before them, for Nug and I were still as mighty as we had become in the forest.

"Brothers," Nug bellowed, awesome in his towering, glittering form. "Come close and listen, for the words Melodium speaks are true. We are not only farmers, set to toil day in and day out in fields. We are also warriors! We battle, and when we do, we adapt and grow. Look upon my brother Tug and myself. We bring you the flesh of our enemies that we may dine well tonight!"

We threw the goblin carcasses at the feet of our brethren who gathered around us. They looked upon us in amazement. Understanding and recognition dawned in the eyes of some, while others shook their heads in disbelief. The fog began to lift from us all. How peculiar that one name, the name of Oberon, could have so much power. Melodium came to the door of our hut and watched, eyes gleaming. He knew that we began to know the truth now, and nothing would stop us from finding out the rest of the story.

It was early evening by this time. My size and shape began to dwindle, and I felt my skin soften. I became more aware of sensations upon it than before– the fire's heat and the cool breath of the wind. I could see Nug return to his natural state, and our brethren gathered around us, whispering to each other and touching our arms and hands with tentative fingers as they witnessed the transformation.

We made short work of preparing the goblins for the feast. Somehow our hands knew what to do. As we worked, we set aside their broken weapons and armor so that we could reshape them and craft weapons for ourselves. You see, we knew what our next steps had to be. It was time to see where the forest path would take us, and then we would hunt down the witch and make him give us the answers we desperately needed.

We worked as the sun dipped below the horizon and soon had a hearty meal prepared. We ate of our enemies with relish, raising steins of ale so that we might toast gods we could not yet name who granted us this victory and full bellies. The words of the toast came unbidden, but they were right.

After we dined, Nug handed me my mandolin, and I played for our brethren. I played until the moons rose, and Melodium knelt by my side.

"Brother, it is time. We must go back to the path and see where it leads," he said.

"Yes, brother. Come. Gather Nug. We will show you the way," I agreed.

I carried the mandolin over my shoulder as we led Melodium to the path. The polished, carved wood felt right in my hands, and I was not ready to put it down yet.

It was fully night, but for the first time, we could see as clearly as if it were daylight. This was another thing the fog that once clouded our minds took from us. Our senses had been dulled and stripped until they were no better than a human's. We had stumbled about in the dark, as lost and afraid as babes.

Now the night was warmer and sweeter than any sun.

A whole world we did not know existed stretched before us under the tree limbs, dappled in shadow and moonlight. We often stopped along the path so that we might revel in the forest's glory: a doe amongst the trees, the sweet song of night insects, the silver play of light on the forest floor as the moonlight sifted through the leaves.

Melodium led the way as we wound through the trees that welcomed us with gentle touches from their leaves and sighs from the wind among their branches. They beckoned us further into the forest's depths. After perhaps a quarter of a league, we reached the clearing. A strange disk lay upon the ground, and a group of what appeared to be children faced us. Somehow we knew they were not a threat despite the weapons they carried.

The newcomers espied us and conversed amongst themselves before one lay her weapon on the ground and approached, bowing as she came close. We could see that she was a vampire, the term arising unbidden in our minds.

"Noble ogres, please allow us to trespass for a moment longer," she said with great respect. "Our way home is blocked, and we seek another path to our world."

Melodium nodded in acknowledgment of her words. I had many questions. Of what world did she speak? Where did these strange beings come from, and how did we recognize this female as a vampire? I could see the curiosity written over Nug's face as well, but we kept silent.

"We will not interfere with your quest," Melodium said. "But how did you come to find this place and from whence do you hail?"

"We come from a place known as Earth. One of my

companions created a bridge between our world and yours. It is this bridge we seek to reopen so that we may return to our home."

"Then we wish you success. Should you need shelter for the night, our village lies at the end of the path," Melodium said and bowed his head to her.

"I give you our thanks, O great one," she said. "It is truly an honor to meet one of your kind."

And before we could ask what she meant by those words, she turned to rejoin her companions. Melodium gestured for us to go a little way from the clearing. We followed and stopped to face each other in the clear, silver moonlight. Melodium frowned.

"The vampire knows of us," he said. "We should investigate further."

"Yes," I said. "Perhaps she and her companions can tell us how we came to be here and shed light upon the mystery of our existence."

"I also feel that this plan has merit," Nug agreed.

"Then let us return to these wanderers and seek what knowledge they can give us," Melodium decided, and he led the way back to the clearing.

However, the strange visitors were gone, leaving only the disc in the clearing. We approached the disc, but it did not respond to our presence, nor did it seem to be a threat. It lay in the grass, cold and black. We were baffled and returned to our village to share our news with the rest of our brethren.

But when we arrived back at our village, we were shocked to discover that we could not find our brethren. The great fire at the center of the village no longer burned in its pit, and the stone huts sat empty. The remnants of the feast lay in cold bowls upon the ground. It was as if our brethren had never existed. We looked at each other in confusion. We had been gone perhaps half an hour– certainly not enough time for our entire village to vanish so completely.

"What do you think happened? Where could our fellow clans have gone" Nug asked, shifting back and forth on his feet, a gesture I knew from old to mean he was uncertain.

Melodium looked at us, the moonlight glittering in his eyes.

"I fear that the one who bespelled our people sensed that the spell became unraveled and took our brethren prisoner. Come, we must search carefully so as to divine what has happened to them."

Nug relit our fire, and I got to work. As I was the best tracker in the village, I searched for any sign of our brethren's passing along the village's edge and in the fields. I had just discovered the faint edge of a footprint leading away from the village and toward the mountain when I heard Melodium cry out behind me.

"Brothers! To me!" he bellowed.

We ran to his side. The amulet, which he grasped in his hand, glowed with an ugly red light as he dangled it over the fire.

"Witchcraft happened here," he growled, his eyes beginning to glow red to match the emblem. "I sensed an unnatural vibration around our fire, for it would take a great act to extinguish such a blaze. Our amulet shows the truth."

"I found a footprint toward the witch's mountain," I told

him. "There must be more. Someone attempted to conceal the print, but their effort was insufficient."

"Very good, brother," Melodium clasped my shoulder before pushing past me toward the dark, winding path leading to the mountain. "Come, let us visit the witch and settle this once and for all. Stay by my side and in the light of Oberon's talisman, for it will protect our minds."

We walked single file toward the mountain, the amulet glowing like red fire. Melodium led the way through groves of trees and untended fields with confident steps. Our vision remained as clear as it was when the night first fell, and we could easily see the traps set to try to dissuade us from our quest.

"Primitive," Melodium sneered in disgust as he sliced through a tripwire with his hunting knife.

He was right. The traps looked almost childish and hastily put together. It was obvious that the creator had counted on us being as night blind as we had always been, which would explain the error in judgment when we reached the rope bridge that crossed the chasm separating the mountain pass from the road to our village. The enemy we followed had attempted to hack through the ropes, but ogres had created the bridge, and we are skilled craftsmen. It only took minutes for Nug to reinforce the bridge, and we were soon on our way to the other side.

We climbed the steep mountainside with confidence and determination, navigating the narrow, winding trail. Once we reached the entrance to the cave, we stopped in dismay, for the cave stood abandoned. It was not a deep cave. We could see the back of it, and all it held was an old fire and some scraps of food scattered across the floor. Melodium bellowed, raising his fist to the sky, the amulet shining between his fingers.

"We will find and avenge you, my brothers! I swear it in Oberon's name!"

I felt the power of that oath to my core. The mountain trembled beneath us as if it sensed Melodium's conviction and resolve.

"Come, let us return to the village," he said. "We must search for any other paths leading outward. Perhaps we will stumble upon more of our kind, for I am certain we are not alone in this world."

But we found no others. We searched for days, and no matter where we turned, our path always ended at our village. The clearing, which grew more and more overrun as it lay abandoned except for daily goblin attacks, and the mountain were the only places we were able to reach.

We never knew how the goblins continued to find us or from whence they came, but we were grateful for the meat as our food supplies had mysteriously vanished. The forest animals were nowhere to be found, and our fields became barren. Our well began to dry up, and even the wood from the forest would not burn to sustain our fire.

After perhaps a fortnight, we were startled one evening by the sounds of shouting. We hurried down the path to the clearing to investigate the cause of the commotion. The goblins had again returned, but so had the mysterious visitors. They fought the goblins valiantly, but we could see that of the four of them, only the vampire had true skill and mastery over her weapon. We remained at the edge of the clearing and observed the battle, respecting the code that is the warrior's way of allowing the visitors to win the honor of victory on their own.

Why do you snort, Jared? We spared you and your friends the humiliation of being unable to procure your victory in battle.

After the visitors defeated the goblins, their reaction was most peculiar. The one known as William felt a need to vomit, while the one called Dain could not stand. The one known as Tabinda, the vampire, was a true warrior, for she cheered most heartily after the last goblin fell. And you, Jared, you fought well, even if you were reluctant to deliver the final killing blows.

We approached them once more.

"You fought most bravely," Melodium said diplomatically. After all, it was not their fault that Tabinda was their only trained warrior.

We examined each other. They were older than we thought. We could see they were, indeed, adults, even if they lacked training in war arts. My brothers and I exchanged a glance, and I could see we had the same thought. Perhaps these strange people could tell us where we came from and, more importantly, assist us in locating our brethren.

If it is permissible, I would like Jared to take over the telling of our tale now. I believe he can best explain what came next.

6

No problem, Tug. I got it from here.

The night after we came back from Tug's world, William and I met the others at my folks' garage. The portal was still where we had left it. We looked at each other. The only light was from the streetlight coming through the window, which, if we're going to be honest, isn't the cleanest thing in the world. So it was already kind of creepy in there. I could tell even Tabinda had some doubts.

"I tried to get in touch with Robin, but I couldn't get through," I told them.

"Neither could I," Dain said. He fidgeted nervously in his armor. I couldn't help but see that it was solid black and looked a little more utilitarian. He saw me looking and grimaced.

"The armorer noticed when a suit of ceremonial hunter's armor went missing. He told me that a rogue would never wear hunter's armor with green in it because they would want to stick to the shadows, and if I really wanted to be a good sneak thief, I should consider all black in a softer leather that doesn't creak."

I tried to hide my grin.

"That sounds like something Jessie would say. The softer leather probably won't chafe as much if we walk around for hours too."

His eyes got really big, and he looked down at his armor with new appreciation.

"I did some research into ogres," William told us in the voice he gets when he's about to start a lecture. He's going to make a great professor one day.

"They used to be Oberon's honor guard and the elite fighting force of the Fae. Almost nothing could stand up to a fully grown ogre in battle, much less a battalion of them. They disappeared right before the witch rebellion in the 18th century."

"Didn't your mentor fight in that?" Tabinda asked me with a frown. She may have only been fifteen when she was turned, but that was long enough ago that she remembered the rebellion.

"Yeah. I wonder if Jessie knows about the ogres," I said.

"I doubt it," William shook his head. "Even then, the different factions of the world pretty much stayed away from each other. The fae wouldn't have come to the witches with their problems."

"True," I conceded. "Well, the ogres seemed friendly enough. Maybe they can tell us more. Are we ready to do this?"

"Yeah, let's go," Dain said, hooking his thumbs in his knife belt.

I opened the portal, and we stepped through. Luckily for Tabinda— and us, as it turns out— it was dusk. We stepped through and came to a dead stop. The first thing we noticed was that the clearing was completely overgrown.

"How long were we gone?" Dain was baffled.

"Probably a couple of weeks in their time," I shrugged, which was when we noticed the second thing. Pointed ears like a bat, helmets, and really ugly faces. The smell was horrible, like sewage and rotten fish. Unfortunately for us, we were downwind the whole time.

"Jared, what's that?" William pointed.

"Aw, fuck. It's the goblins. I guess they aren't dead after all. Well, we wanted a real battle. I guess we got it."

"Hold up," William turned on me. "We wanted a real battle when we thought this world was a sim. What happens when one of us dies here? Because this place is real, man!"

We didn't have time to figure out an answer to that because the goblins attacked, screaming in rage. Tabinda got one with her crossbow, but they were on us before she could reload.

"William, look out," I shouted. He froze, and I realized he didn't have a way to defend himself. He was supposed to be a healer in our game. He wasn't a fighter. He should have been behind us. I heard Tabinda's crossbow go off again, and she took down the goblin charging at William with a bolt through the neck.

Dain rolled out of the way and tripped a goblin, who went down hard. Tabinda got it between the shoulder blades with a throwing knife. The last one bore down on Dain fast. He ducked, but he had brought a knife to a sword fight, and he couldn't get under the goblin's blade to attack. His training was definitely not against anything like this. I did the only thing I could think of. I struck my shield with the flat of my blade, tried to make as much noise as I could, and started to yell.

"Hey, you ugly piece of shit! I bet I can kick your ass blindfolded!"

The goblin snarled and whipped around. It moved fast. I had enough time to get my sword and shield up before it hit me like a ton of bricks. I almost lost my balance, but I pushed it off with the shield and parried its attack.

Don't look so surprised. I learned how to fence years ago.

Its weapons were pretty weak, and I had it on the ground in no time.

"Kill it, Jared!" Tabinda yelled. I couldn't do it, though. It saw my hesitation and launched off the ground at me again, but she took it out with another knife. If the world had been a sim, it would have been different, but now that we knew it wasn't, how did we know if these were really alive or just characters in the game? Even though it tried to kill me, I couldn't just take a life like that.

William threw up, and Dain sat on the ground, visibly shaken. He had a cut on his forehead, and I could see a gouge on his armor's leather chest piece. Knowing that he could have been seriously hurt or worse made my blood run cold. This was more than we bargained for.

Tabinda and I looked at each other. I could tell she was thinking what I was thinking, that maybe we should send William and Dain back. William didn't have the skills for this world, either with magic or fighting. Not that I'm the best fighter in the world, but I can defend myself. I didn't know enough about fae anatomy to know if Dain's injuries were serious or not, especially the cut on the head.

Then I noticed that the ogres were back and watching us.

"Guys," I pointed. William got to his feet, wiping his mouth. Dain stood up too. He was still pretty shaken up.

"They couldn't have shown up ten minutes ago?" William muttered.

"They were here the whole time," Tabinda told him. "I think they wanted to see if we could do it ourselves."

"We wouldn't have if you hadn't been here," Dain said. I noticed the bleeding from the cut on his head stopped, which made me feel a little better.

"Nah, you would have figured something out," Tabinda brushed off the thanks with a wave.

I shuddered. I didn't want to think about what that would have looked like. To be honest, I never killed anything before—other than mosquitoes. I don't think those count. I mean, I had nightmares after we cleaned up the bar after your fight with the cabal, and I wasn't even there for that. I thought it would be okay if they were just NPCs I made up, but none of us except Tabinda could actually kill someone. It was a shitty situation.

Anyway, the ogres walked up to us. They wore some kind of leather clothing and looked, well, kind. We weren't afraid of them. The biggest one made some comment about how we fought bravely, which was a bullshit line if I've ever heard one. He might as well have given us a trophy for participation. I thanked him anyway because it didn't hurt to be friendly, and also, if we had that much trouble against some goblins, then we absolutely would not have stood a chance against one of the ogres, much less all three of them. Even Tabinda isn't that good.

I also couldn't help but notice that the portal wouldn't open again. The ogres must have seen how nervous we were because the biggest one gave a half bow and said, "Do not concern yourselves, young ones. We will gather your enemies for the feast and hold it in your honor. Our home is open to you all."

"Wait, what feast?" William asked, looking green in the moonlight from the two moons overhead. I honestly didn't know that was an actual thing until that moment.

"Do you not feast upon the bodies of your enemies?" Tug asked. He looked even more confused when William threw up again.

"Ah, no. No, we do not," I stepped in at this point. "I'm Jared. These are my companions, Tabinda, Dain, and that's William over there. Sorry. We're having a little bit of a hard time right now."

The ogres looked at each other for a second and then back at us.

"We will be happy to aid you in whatever way we can. Regretfully our situation requires that I ask a boon of you in our time of need. Please understand I take no pride in making our burden your own. Would you perhaps be able to assist us?" the big one asked. I did not expect that question. The third ogre eyeballed the goblins.

"Um, sure, I guess. I mean, yes. We would be happy to be of assistance," I said as Tabinda elbowed me. I felt it through my chain mail armor. She has some pointy ass elbows!

"We are in your debt. These are my brothers. For now, you can call them Tug and Nug. I am Melodium," he bowed again and gestured toward the path.

The "for now" confused me, but before I could ask what he meant, Nug stepped up.

"Forgive me, for I realize that my actions will be distasteful. We have no food except these goblins that appear each day. I regret bringing additional discomfort to you and your companions, but we need sustenance. I shall stay behind to gather the goblins and follow at a distance so that I do not expose you to our unfortunate circumstance."

By the way, as I'm sure you already figured out from listening to Tug's story so far, they all really talk like that. Whatever you know or think you know about ogres, you are dead wrong.

"Wait, do the same goblins show up each time?" William got excited.

"We believe so, for they appear at the same time each day and have the same appearance and behaviors," Melodium said.

"Jared! They must be your goblins! I bet that's why they weren't here when we came through the first time!" William yelled.

"Your goblins? Are they your pets? But how could that be?" Melodium looked lost.

"No, see, I thought that I had made a new world for a game. A simulation, if you will. It wasn't supposed to be real. I don't know how we got here or what world this is, but it's not the one I made– or tried to make. Anyway, I made these goblins for us to fight, but when we realized this world was real, we weren't sure if the goblins were too or what would happen to them or us. That's why it was hard for us to kill them," I tried to explain.

"Ah! I see. You showed restraint because you were uncertain

of the consequences of your actions. Very wise, young knight. But come and we will take you to our village. I would like to hear more about this world you tried to create, and we have many questions for you. I wish to explain our predicament as well. Perhaps you have wisdom and guidance we lack."

"Lead the way," I said.

What's that saying? In for a penny, in for a pound? We had come this far, and I knew that the way time moved here versus our world would be different enough that we could probably safely explore without anyone missing us for a while. Everyone else seemed on board too, and we fell in line behind the ogres as we followed them down the dark path. Only Nug stayed behind to collect the goblin bodies. None of us wanted to be there for that.

I gave the ogres the run down on the world I had tried to make as we walked until we came to what looked like a stone village. It was in pretty good shape. There was a well and a massive fire pit in the center with a bunch of long tables covered with crafting tools and materials. It wasn't big; maybe five or six homes. There were fields on one side, but everything in them was dead. I didn't see any other roads or paths except one on the opposite side that went into dark woods. It looked like it might lead to a mountain in the distance. The mountain struck me as odd because it was the only one in a very flat land. I didn't even see hills.

"Where are the animals?" Dain looked around.

It dawned on me that he was right. There were no other creatures anywhere. The birds we had seen in the forest the first time were gone, and we hadn't seen deer, squirrels, raccoons, possums, or anything on the way back to the village.

"That is part of what we wish to speak to you about," Melodium gestured for us to sit on a log by the fire pit. "The night of your last visit to our world, we returned from the clearing to discover that our kinsmen were gone– taken, we presume, by an evil force that dwells upon that mountain. Our fields became barren, and the animals of the forest vanished overnight. Our well dried up this morning. We have survived this long by defeating and consuming the goblins, or we would have surely perished by now."

"For how long? In our time, it's only been a day," I said, looking uneasily at William. I don't know why, but I remembered the weird light I thought I had seen in the garage when we left the night before.

"A fortnight," Tug said.

"That means two weeks," William whispered.

"I know what it means," I glared at him.

"Just making sure."

Melodium leaned closer to me, looking at my face like he was trying to figure something out. He made me really nervous.

"Did you try to go to the mountain?" I asked him. The bad gut feeling I had the last time was back, and it was very strong.

"We did, and the cave at its summit appears abandoned. But this does not ring true to me, for I sense a veil that I cannot see," Melodium said as he and Tug sat opposite us. I heard metal banging and what sounded like a knife slicing through wet meat behind us. None of us wanted to turn around, except for Tabinda, of course, who drifted over to watch.

"We also sought out the magic user who lives in the

mountain but to no avail, for he vanished as well. All ways we try to take to leave our village come back to this point except for the path to your disc," Tug said.

"Wait, there's a magic user here? Like a witch?" I asked more sharply than I meant to. My gut cramped up even more.

"Yes, he resides in the mountain. Forgive me young knight, but your resemblance to the witch is uncanny," Melodium said, still looking at me like he had me under a microscope.

"Jared? Do you really think a witch is here?" William was as startled as I was.

"Well, if an entire race that's supposed to be extinct wound up here, why not? Maybe that's who brought the ogres here in the first place," I pointed out. "I don't know why he would look like me, though. Do you remember anything about our world?"

"Your world? Why would we know your world?" Tug asked. I could tell the question surprised him.

"Because I'm pretty sure that's where you came from. Ogres lived on our world until about three centuries ago, and then they vanished. You were just gone. But this village doesn't look big enough for all the ogres who were supposed to exist. Did you raise your families here? Are there any other villages?"

They looked totally lost.

"Of what families and villages do you speak? It is simply our five clans, all brothers to each other," Melodium said. "We have never seen another village."

"What about sisters and mothers?" Dain asked.

"We have no females of our kind," Melodium answered slowly, but it was like he was trying to work through a confusing puzzle. "And yet I know that a sister and a mother are female. How could this be?"

"Perhaps the amulet has more to awaken within our minds, brother," Tug suggested.

"The amulet?" Dain and I asked at the same time.

Melodium pulled it out from under his jerkin.

"This has been mine as far back as I can remember. I know it bears a link to one we protected named Oberon and that we come from a faraway land, and I know whoever banished us to this world took our names and memories from us."

"*The* Oberon?" William's voice went up an octave. Humans are, unsurprisingly, still pretty leery about the Fae.

"You know of Oberon? Please speak to us about him!" Melodium leaned across the fire, as eager as a child. For a minute, I thought he was going to burn himself. Even Nug stopped slicing up goblins to listen.

"He's the Faery King," Dain said. "The ogres were his honor guard long ago before you all vanished."

"I bet if we can get Robin the Puck to come here, he would know more," I added.

"I think he would too. I don't know as much since it was before my time, and now ogres are a thing of legend." Dain nodded.

"Yeah, but the ogres don't have food," William pointed out.

Dain and I looked at each other, lost. I didn't get the connection.

"Jared," William said in this annoying voice he uses when he thinks the rest of us don't get something really obvious. "In the time it took for us to be gone a day, two weeks passed here. What if it takes longer than that to get Robin and bring him back? They can't live off of goblins for a month. We need to help them now."

"Oh, yeah. You're right. Sorry," I felt stupid.

I looked at Melodium and Tug, and I swear they looked like they were about to start crying.

"You would help us? Truly?" Melodium asked as if we held out the world's biggest lifeline.

"Well, yeah. I mean, you're obviously under some kind of spell. Jared's a witch too. He can break it," said William, thus proving that humans don't know jack shit about how witch-craft works.

"Can we not get ahead of ourselves?" I cut in before he committed me to something I couldn't do, and we pissed off about two tons worth of apex predators. And yes, I know. This is why you don't experiment with crazy spells when your teacher's not around.

Still, I felt like maybe there was something in the air. I mean, now I know it's because I'm an air witch, but I didn't know then. I just knew that the air felt wrong like someone forced it to do something it didn't want to do. The more I thought about it, the worse my gut felt.

"Hey, Jared, are you okay?" Dain asked. "You don't look so great."

"There's something here. I can feel it. The more I think about it, the more my stomach cramps. Like I literally have a bad feeling in my gut," I tried not to double over.

"Can you speak more to us of this 'feeling' you experience?" Melodium sounded concerned.

"It's like the air is wrong. I can't explain it more than that. I don't know, but the more I think about it, the worse I feel."

The ogres gave each other that look people get when they're hiding something.

"So, now would be a good time to tell us whatever we don't already know," I tried not to snap at them, but it was getting hard.

"Forgive me, young knight," Melodium stood up. "Please, follow me."

Dain and I followed him and Tug, and William caught up after we'd gone a few dozen feet. Something about staying behind to watch Nug butcher goblins wasn't all that appealing to him. Tabinda, on the other hand, was fascinated. I could hear her as we walked away.

"Their organs are so different! Oh, their blood is blue! That's so neat!"

"I think I'm going to puke," William muttered.

"Do you even have anything left to throw up?" Dain asked, curious.

William decided not to dignify that with a response.

Melodium and Tug led us further away from the village across the barren fields. Dain frowned as we walked across the dead fields, finally stopping to pick up a handful of dirt and handing it to William.

"Hey, William. Does this look right to you?"

William leaned in, squinting as he grabbed a tiny pinch of soil. He held it up and looked more closely, finally very tentatively tasting it. He spat it out.

"Salt. Someone definitely fucked up your fields, man. Nothing's going to grow here for a long time."

We stepped back in alarm as Tug's eyes started to turn red.

Melodium put a hand on his brother's arm before looking back at us.

"I suspected foul play. Come, let us continue, and you will see why I am suspicious."

So we kept going toward the distant tree line. When we got to the edge of the fields, the ogres stopped.

"We can go no further, young knight," Melodium said. "One more step and we find ourselves facing our village once more."

I started to walk forward and felt like someone shoved a knife into my stomach. The air felt so *wrong*, like it screamed in pain.

"Sir Knight! Are you unwell?" Melodium sounded worried, probably because I doubled over and hit the ground. I know I definitely freaked out William and Dain.

"Something's very wrong here," I tried to tell them.

"Can you fix it?" William asked me.

At that time, I didn't know if I could or not, but I knew I had to try because it was like the air begged me to help it. I got my feet back under me, and I squinted. I could see a shimmer in the air like pollution on water. It went all the way down to the ground, but I could see the edge of it. I reached out and kind of hooked my fingers under it and pulled. There was this feeling like a bubble popping, and the pain was gone. Melodium and Tug almost fell over backward because the distant tree line was gone. Instead, we were suddenly right in front of a forest full of really old, massive trees. We could see a little path under the trees.

"What was that?" William sounded impressed and a little scared.

"Someone made a weird cloaking bubble over the village. Did you guys ever feel anything when you tried to come this way?" I asked the ogres.

"No," Melodium shook his head and rubbed the amulet hard. "As I said, we would try to walk this way and then discover ourselves facing the village once more."

"So someone probably tuned the spell to ogres to get you turned around without realizing it."

It was pretty obvious that another witch was involved, and they probably weren't an air witch. An air witch would have been able to cast the bubble that was over the village without creating that sense of pain in the air. Whoever was responsible was also strong enough to imprison a whole race of fae creatures. The worst part is that the ogres hadn't even realized they were prisoners.

"Do you know any witches capable of such a feat?" Melodium asked.

"Most witches are capable of a cloaking spell like this when they're at full power, but if there's a way for a witch to control an entire race, I haven't learned about it," I told him. "The real question is who would do it. I don't know anyone that shitty, but my teacher probably has some ideas. I want to tell her if that's alright with you."

They looked at each other.

"We beg that you keep our secret for now," Melodium finally said. "We are uncertain who to trust in these matters as it is clear that the witch who frequented our village is responsible for our current misfortune."

I didn't like it, but I didn't see what choice I had at the moment.

"Fair enough. Do you want to see where this path goes?" I asked.

"No, there is another path we should take," Melodium decided, leading us back across the field and through the village to the path heading toward the mountain.

"Great. Climbing. My most favorite thing ever," William muttered.

"You can always go back and hang out with Tabinda and Nug," Dain pointed out with a little smirk.

"No, thanks," William almost tripped over his ridiculous robe while trying as fast as he could to catch up with everyone. I think the memory of the goblin butcherfest was still pretty strong in his mind– I know it was in mine.

I felt fine going all the way up the path to the mountain, but not gonna lie, I never want to do that in a full suit of armor again. That was brutal. Stop rolling your eyes, Tug. You weren't wearing half your body weight in metal.

We made it to the suspension bridge, and I thought William was going to tap out. It didn't look like it would support any of us, much less three ogres at one time. It held up well, though. We were about halfway across when my gut cramped up again.

"Hold up, guys. I think there's another bubble. My stomach hurts again," I warned them.

"I believe that you are correct. In fact, I count upon it," Melodium sounded pretty pissed. Somehow it made the whole experience feel even more ominous than it already was.

By the time we reached the cave, I could barely stand up straight. This time I didn't even wait. I just ripped through the bubble with everything I had in me. I would rather have food poisoning from bad sushi than feel what I felt when the air was forced into a spell like that again.

"Holy fuck!" William almost fell backward into Dain. My jaw was on the ground.

When I ripped off the bubble, the whole cave opened up, and it was full of ogres. I mean, they were packed in there. The smell was horrible. Like, if you look at Melodium and Tug and Nug, they were clean and neat, even if their jerkins were a little worn out. These poor guys, though, had been shoved into this cave for weeks. They were filthy. There were some food supplies at the back, but they looked moldy.

For the record, I know you saw Tug rampage when you had that fight at the bar, but never, and I cannot stress this enough, stand within six feet of an ogre when the rage hits him. When Melodium roared, I actually felt the shockwave—like all the way through my bones. I swear he doubled in size and height. It was like standing next to a pissed-off bipedal elephant. His eyes were blood red, and his skin glittered like diamonds covered it. I heard another roar behind me and didn't even have to turn around to see that Tug was probably just as big and just as pissed off. The squishy ones of us in the group got out of the way as fast as we could.

"Brothers, who did this to you?" Melodium roared again, charging into the cave. The ogres stared at him in shock before stumbling out of the back of the cave. Everyone tried to talk at the same time.

"It's Melodium!"

"Melodium has returned!"

"But the witch told us that he perished. How is he here?"

They swarmed around Melodium and Tug like they

couldn't believe their eyes. I realized very quickly that we needed to get out of there. If there was a witch in the area who was strong enough to hide that many ogres and warp an element that wasn't theirs, then I probably wasn't strong enough to fight them. The problem was wading into the middle of about twenty ogres and trying to get that point across. I settled for the next best thing and beat the absolute fuck out of my shield with my sword to get their attention. Damaged the hell out of it too. That was a nice shield.

Yes, Tug, I know. If it dented that easily then it probably wasn't that nice. You know, I don't need the two of you ganging up on me like this.

Anyway, they all stopped and stared at me, which totally did not make me want to run away or piss myself or anything like that.

"Hey, guys, we should continue this back at the village, you know, where we can get everyone cleaned up and regroup. Melodium and Tug are the only ones who look like they're in any condition to fight, and anyone who can bespell a group of ogres this big is going to be stronger than I can take on without help."

And then I cringed, hoping they would listen to me and not squash me like a bug. Luckily for me, they decided to listen.

"The knight speaks the truth. Come, brothers. We have a feast of goblins and stories to share," Melodium said. He started to shrink, but his eyes were still red, and his skin still looked like it was covered in diamond dust.

"We must hurry, for the magic user returns at dawn each

day," one of the ogres said. That was our cue to get the hell out of there, and let me tell you, we couldn't do it fast enough.

7

We made it back down the bridge and to the village as the sun started rising.

"How are we going to get them cleaned up? They don't have water," Dain whispered.

"I bet the path in those woods Jared uncovered leads to a river somewhere. The witch couldn't have hidden them for this long without water," William whispered back.

We met up with Tabinda and Nug at the center of the village. The ogres we rescued looked terrible. Some looked exhausted and others seemed confused, but most of them were just really pissed off. The amulet still glowed in Melodium's hand.

"Brothers, we have been deceived," he bellowed, although I'm pretty sure they had already figured that part out. "The night you were taken from us, the night the truth was revealed through the light of this amulet and Oberon's name, these young travelers came to our world for the first time. They have returned with wisdom and knowledge of our kind. They believe that once we held places of honor by a king's side on another world far away from here. We need to listen to what they have to say."

One of the rescuees came closer.

"How do we know they truly mean to help us? Did we not already put our faith in one of their kind, and for what? To be held prisoner and stripped of our dignity and means to live? This one resembles the one who held us captive for so long," the ogre pointed right at me.

Honestly, it was a valid point. The ogres didn't know anything about us, and if another witch was involved, then I couldn't blame them for not trusting us. The thing about the witch looking like me started to make me nervous, though. I didn't understand how that was possible. I just hoped they would at least let us leave.

"I hear your words, Hud. I understand your mistrust, for it is well placed. However, this one," Melodium put his hand on my shoulder, which did not make me nervous at all (that's sarcasm, Tug), "led us to you. He freed our village and destroyed the illusion of isolation that covered it like a shroud. Look there, upon the forest. Without him, you would remain a prisoner."

I decided now was as good a time to speak up as any.

"Excuse me, noble ogres. If I may be so bold as to provide some insight, my companions and I found this world by accident, but we know of your kind. You once lived on our world and served Oberon, the King of the Fae as his honor guard. Your allies looked upon you with respect, and your name made the blood of your enemies run cold in fear."

Yes, I really said it like that. And my mom said playing D&D would never pay off.

"I don't know how you wound up here, but it was centuries ago, right before a rebellion took place on our world," I kept going and tried to stand tall under all those angry eyes. "I understand your trepidation, and I beg you to let me prove my worth. Please give us a chance to help you."

"What's going on?" Tabinda whispered. I forgot she wasn't there for everything that had just gone down.

"Jared just committed us to saving the ogre race," William whispered back.

"Wicked! When do we start?" She was way too excited.

"We have bigger problems," I said as I realized the sun was about to come up. "The witch comes back at dawn, and you can't handle the sun here. How are we going to get you back to the portal?"

"Shit, I didn't think about that. I need a place to go to ground," she was worried.

We realized the ogres were watching us with a very healthy degree of skepticism.

"Ogres, I have a request and proposal," I really hoped my friends weren't about to kill me for what I planned to do.

"You may speak," Melodium nodded.

"My companion is a vampire and needs to find shelter before the sun rises. Please allow my friends to return to our world for the day, and I will stay with you as a token of good faith."

"Jared, what are you doing?! We can't come back here without you, remember? You're the only one who can open the portal. You can't stay here. This is crazy!" William was, predictably, freaking out.

"Time moves faster here, remember? It's fine. I know what I'm doing," I lied through my teeth.

"But you even said you can't take on this witch by yourself," Dain argued.

"Wait, what witch?" Even Tabinda sounded alarmed.

"Guys, trust me. I have a plan."

Meanwhile, the ogres had their own discussion.

"We accept your proposal," Melodium said in a voice that kind of implied that he was the one who accepted it and didn't care what anyone else thought.

We got all our stuff together and started back to the clearing with Tug escorting us. He hung back and waited on the path so that I could open the portal. I pulled my house keys out of my pocket and cast an identity spell on them.

"Listen," I told them. "Here is my key to my folks' house. William, I spelled it to recognize you as being allowed to enter. They have a bookshelf in the living room. Grab all the books you can find on breaking enchantments and bring them back here. Dain, stand on the disc in the garage to hold the portal open. Try to be as fast as possible."

"You got it," William grabbed the key and ran to the house with Tabinda right behind him. It was already daylight, but the sun wasn't as bad in our world. I mean, she was weakened, but she wasn't incapacitated. I heard her motorcycle roar as she sped off. Dain stood on the disc and stared at me.

"This is nuts, Jared. You know that, right? We should be getting Jessie or Mara right now."

"I know, but we promised not to get anyone else involved. If you don't hear from me in one hour, you can get them, but please let me try to fix this first."

"No, *you* promised, but fine. I'm not happy about this, though."

William ran back faster than I expected and thrust an armful of books at me.

"We're coming for you in an hour, our time. That should be fourteen hours in yours unless time is even weirder between these worlds than we think. Don't be late, or I'm getting the cavalry," he snapped at me. The two of them glared while I struggled not to drop the books.

"Understood. See you in an hour," I released the spell on the portal and let Tug know he could come out into the clearing. I dropped the books on the ground and looked at what William had grabbed, trying to figure out where to start.

The sun was up by now, and I had a day to figure out how to free a bunch of ogres from an unknown witch, and I'm not gonna lie, I was definitely in over my head, and I knew it. But I had to help the ogres, and I didn't know if I could leave this world, get help, and get back in time to save them. I didn't even know if we would be able to get back through. What if the witch could dismantle the portal?

"Brother and Sir Knight!"

It was Nug, running toward us and looking extremely freaked out.

"The witch has returned! He seeks the knight and claims that our young friend is the cause of the evil in this world that afflicted our fields and dried up our well and led the animals to vanish."

At least I was still their young friend.

"Brother, these accusations are serious," Tug said. "What of our brethren? Do they believe these lies?"

"They are uncertain. Melodium holds the amulet aloft to clear their heads, but not all of our brethren were healed from their false lives as quickly as you and I."

They looked at me, waiting for me to weigh in.

"Okay, here's what we're going to do," I said. "We'll sneak back to the village under a small cloaking spell. I want to get a look at this guy. Then I'm going to find a spell in these books that will let me get rid of whatever makes it so you can't get through the portal and back to our world, and then we just have to lay low for a day until my friends come back."

"Sir Knight, your plan has merit, but I fear we do not have a day. The witch's words are powerful, and his magic is strong," Nug sounded doubtful.

"Okay, new plan. Give me ten minutes to try to find a spell, and then we'll sneak back."

They looked at each other, and then Nug nodded. Unfortunately, William had grabbed the densest, driest, most complex books on enchantment breaking that have ever existed. I knew almost immediately that we wouldn't have time for me to find a spell that would work. I was going to have to wing it. I hid the books by the portal, and we started back down the path.

As we got closer to the village, we heard shouting. I cast a cloaking spell, and then something weird happened. It was like the air told me that because I had helped it before, it wanted to help us now. I knew that, somehow, the spell was more potent than it should have been.

We got to the edge of the village, and I saw Melodium facing off against a witch. The witch had his back to us, but I could tell he was Black, probably close to my height.

Melodium held the amulet up higher, and it glowed so brightly that it hurt my eyes. The ogres looked awful. They held their heads and rolled around on the ground with blood coming out of their eyes and noses.

"Our brethren!" Nug hissed.

"I see them," I said. "His spell has a fail safe, a way to hurt the bespelled if they fight it. If we don't do something, they'll die."

"What is your plan, Sir Knight? How may we assist you?"

Something about having people put their unquestioning faith in you is both rewarding and terrifying, especially since I had no clue how we would pull this off. Then I noticed that the ogres closest to Melodium weren't bleeding, and I realized the amulet was protecting them. Then the idea popped into my head that light waves travel, and maybe the air would like to help the light from the amulet travel farther and faster to reach all of the ogres. I don't even remember saying or doing anything to make the spell go off. I wanted it to happen, and it happened. The amulet was like a sun in Melodium's hand, and beside me, I heard Tug roar.

"In Oberon's name, I banish you and your foul sorcery! Begone, witch! Go back from whence you came and leave us be or suffer our wrath!" Melodium roared.

The effect was electrifying. The ogres reacted almost immediately, bellowing so loudly that it felt like an earthquake. The witch and I both lost our footing and fell, but right when he did, I saw his face and felt like I had been sucker punched.

Jessie, it was my uncle Theodore. The same guy who spied on the Witch Council for the cabal and disappeared right before the war. He had been the one who kidnapped all of the ogres, and he saw me, and he *knew* me.

He must be an earth witch because he tried to make the ground open up under me, but luckily, his aim was way off. Either that or the air still had my back. I was too shaken up to tell the difference. He took off running toward the mountain, and then he did something that made the earth swallow him up so that he disappeared.

The amulet stopped trying to replicate a supernova, but I still made sure that the light reached every ogre. We all stood there for a minute, staring at each other. More than one ogre looked at me like he wanted to kill and eat me. Honestly, I didn't blame them. When Melodium said I looked like the magic user from the mountain, I figured it was an all-humanoids-look-alike thing. I didn't realize that the guy really did look like me. It had been like looking in an older mirror. I'd only ever seen one picture of him from when he and my mom were kids, and he'd looked like me then too.

"Before you all say anything, I know what this looks like, and I swear on whatever you want me to swear on that I did not know he was here. He's supposed to be dead. Everyone on my world thought he *was* dead. But I'm the one making sure all of you can see the light of the amulet right now, and I'm stopping you from having your brains explode because of whatever he put in his spell."

"Can you break the spell he placed on our minds, young knight?" Melodium asked before anyone else could say anything.

"I'm willing to try, but I'm just an apprentice. I want to

bring my teacher back here, but I'm afraid we'll be too late. Time moves a lot faster here than in our world."

"Then prove your word and release us of this foul bond," someone yelled.

"We have faith in you, young knight," Melodium smiled.

"While I'm working on this, I think you can find water down the path on the other side of your fields," I told him. "There's no way a forest grows that well without a water source."

"You speak the truth," he agreed. "Tug, travel to the forest our young friend revealed to us before *he* rescued our brethren. Take the water skins and weapons and seek out water and food."

I liked how he put a slight emphasis on the word "he" so they would know who to thank later. The water skins could probably fill a bathtub, and I was thrilled not to be part of that little trip.

Tug meant it when he said that Melodium was a born leader. He had the amulet around his neck again, but it still glowed. He went around to all of the ogres and checked on each one. He passed out bowls of what was probably leftover goblin, and when Tug came back with water and a deer, he made sure everyone else got to drink before he did.

I mostly just asked the air if it would help the light from the amulet keep reaching everyone as a favor to me and then started thinking about the enchantment. When I broke the bubble at the edge of the woods, I found an edge close to the ground and pulled until it popped. What if this worked the same way? If I squinted at Tug just right, I could see a kind of tattered shimmer around him, but it didn't seem to be a complete spell. But Nug had more of a shimmer, and maybe it was something I could work with. Plus, he was probably the least likely to try to smash me if something went wrong.

"Hey, Nug. Can I borrow you for a second?" I asked. I really hoped I was right about the smashing.

"Of course, young knight. How may I be of assistance?"

Man, I was glad ogres are pretty accommodating and very intelligent. This would have gone south so quickly if they weren't.

"I think I can get rid of the enchantment on you, but I don't know if it will hurt or even work."

"I put myself in your most capable hands," he said.

"Glad one of us has faith," I said. "Hold still."

It was harder than trying to pop the bubble at the edge of the village. The bubble over the village was thinner, so there was less surface area, whereas the spell over Nug was much more concentrated. I started peeling it off of him. I could tell it hurt, but he didn't say anything. He just winced a lot. But it finally worked. The problem was it took at least half an hour, and I felt like I had run a marathon when I finished. I was not going to be able to get to all of them before either I passed out or my uncle came back, and when he did come back, he probably wouldn't be alone.

"You look troubled, young witch," Nug observed.

"That was harder and took longer than I thought. I honestly don't think I can save the rest of the village before my uncle returns with reinforcements."

He frowned. That wouldn't sound good to the already hostile ogres scrutinizing me, waiting for me to betray them so they could take me out.

"Can you perhaps draw on the power of my brother's medallion?"

I thought about it. The medallion seemed to help me do everything else. Maybe it was just as desperate to get the ogres back where they belonged and just as tired of existing in a place where my uncle had twisted and warped magic against its will. The thing was, I didn't know anything about it and where it came from, and by this point, I had definitely learned my lesson about messing with things I didn't fully understand. I just didn't see what other options I had.

"I guess it's worth a try. I need another volunteer, though, and no one looks too thrilled with me right now."

Nug eyed the rest of the ogres.

"Wait here. I shall consult with my brother," he said as if I had anywhere else to go. I was pretty sure I couldn't outrun the ogres, even if I had been willing to leave them behind. And I still had about twelve hours until the sun went down and my backup arrived.

"Can I get the books I left back at the portal? Maybe I can find a spell that will work," I asked before he walked away. He obligingly took me back to the portal and even let me carry all forty pounds of spell books to the village by myself.

Nug and Melodium put their heads together while I looked through the books again. There was nothing on magic amulets that looked like the one Melodium carried and nothing about what to do when you find yourself in a strange world with an entire species that's supposed to be extinct. Just when I was about to give up, I finally stumbled on exactly what I needed to get us all out of there– a really complicated portal spell my uncle must have used. There were notes in what I can only assume was his handwriting on how to modify the spell so that he could use it to trap beings in another realm. I always knew this guy was a dick, but this was a whole new level of assholery. The problem was that it was going to take a while for me to figure out how to reverse engineer it so that I could get all of the ogres back to our world.

"Young knight," Melodium interrupted me. I looked up, and he was in front of me with a very nervous-looking ogre standing behind him. The ogre looked smaller than the rest of them, so I guessed he was probably an adolescent in ogre years. Melodium gestured to the ogre.

"This is Crud. He has agreed to allow you to try to lift the spell with the help of my amulet."

"Hi, Crud. Thank you for volunteering. I have to warn you that this might hurt, and if you want me to stop, just say so. I won't keep going if you don't want me to."

"I appreciate your concern for my well-being, young knight, but I wish to be freed from this accursed spell and feel its burden no longer," Crud was very emphatic.

If we can get the rest of the ogres back to this world, they will make a fortune in the greeting card and Shakespearean theater industries.

"Okay, let's try it," I said with a lot more confidence than I felt.

Melodium held up his amulet, which still glowed. I looked at it and how its light seemed to turn into fractals in the air, and then I looked at Crud. In the amulet's light, it was much easier to see the edges of the spell and where they were the weakest, so I started there. It was like peeling an orange. With Nug, I sort of dug in and tried to pull off the spell piece by piece, but with the amulet's help, I was able to make one smooth, gentle pull that peeled the spell right off of Crud. When I finished, the rest of the spell fell apart in my hands, and he stood there blinking and staring down at his body. Then he roared and grabbed me in a bear hug that I'm pretty sure crushed my armor and cracked a few ribs.

"Brothers! The knight is true to his word! I am free!" he yelled at the rest of the village. They started cheering with this deafening roar that made my ears ring. Did you know that's a real thing? It's not pleasant.

What was more alarming was that the whole group started to rush me. If Melodium, Nug, and Tug hadn't stepped in, I might have been trampled by a bunch of overjoyed ogres. It was what I imagine would be like if a toddler walked into a pack of Saint Bernards.

No, Tug, I don't think ogres are dogs. Saint Bernards are great! What's wrong with being a Saint Bernard? They're the best thing ever.

Anyway, I realized that as I helped them, I didn't feel magic exhaustion. I think that because the amulet provided the energy, it absorbed the magic cost, too.

I was down to the last five or six when we heard angry shouting from the other side of the village. It came from where the ogres I had already healed stood congratulating each other and looking around like they saw the village for the first time.

"What troubles our brethren?" Nug asked.

"I know not. Tug, go and find out," Melodium said with a very uneasy note to his voice.

Tug didn't have to go far. My uncle was back, and he

wasn't alone. He had another witch with him, and they brought something Fae that I didn't recognize but looked like a shorter, meaner goblin.

"Redcaps," Tug snarled. His skin went diamond hard again, and I realized the ogres began to grow. Not a lot scares me, and you know that, but being the only human in the middle of a village of nine-foot-tall ogres getting ready to rampage is not on my list of things I ever want to do again.

"What's a redcap?" I asked.

"A creature of evil," he growled. "Redcaps are the worst of the goblins. They feel no remorse, no kindness, only greed and cruelty and hatred."

Something else interesting about ogres is when they start to change, their voices do too. They get even deeper and more guttural like they're chewing granite.

The witch and my uncle hadn't seen me yet. They were focused on trying to get the ogres back under their control. The witch did something with his hands, and I know this sounds crazy, but I swear I could feel the air scream. Like you know how when a jet flies at supersonic speed, and you feel the sound wave? It was like that, but it was the air. I knew without a shadow of a doubt that my uncle had brought an air witch with him, and I was definitely way out of my league. I decided right then and there that If I was going down, then I would go down fighting.

Rolling your eyes like that is really rude, you know.

I tried to think of every spell I knew that might help us, but my gut hurt more and more every time I tried to focus. When I gave up, the pain went away. Somehow I knew I needed to stop trying, and it would come to me. So I did. I stopped trying, and I started looking and feeling. I felt what he was trying to do, and I told the air in front of him to make a vacuum. Everything he tried to do got sucked into the vacuum. He looked more and more pissed off because he couldn't figure out where the vacuum came from. See, I don't think it occurred to my uncle that I might help the ogres fight back or that I was an air witch. To my knowledge, there aren't any air witches in my immediate family, and you taught us that elemental magic is usually genetic. There probably was one down the line somewhere, but none of us knew who it was.

It didn't take long for the ogres to take matters into their own hands. Every attack my uncle did to them just bounced off. Their skin pretty much repelled everything. When the air witch gave up trying to get them back under his control, he tried to make this net thing out of the air to hold them captive. I overplayed my hand and gave myself away when I tried to get his net away from him. I felt a mad sting, and when I looked down, there was this huge gash where the net had wrapped around my arm and and sliced through the armor. The armor is probably the only reason why the cut didn't go all the way to the bone. It was enough to get his attention, though. He found me in the crowd of ogres and grabbed my uncle, pointing at me.

"There he is! Get the boy!" Theodore yelled. The redcaps looked at me, looked at the ogres surrounding me, looked at my uncle, and started to back away.

"*You* get him if he's so important," one of them yelled.

"Yeah, we're outta here. Tell your buddies all the freedom and riches they promised us isn't worth it if we get trampled by a bunch of ogres," another one said. They all turned and started to run back to the mountain.

"Fools! You will never escape, for I now control the portal! I will punish you for your treachery," my uncle screamed. They didn't stop running, though.

So you know that thing I do when I open my big mouth? Yeah, this next part's going to piss you off. I mean, even more than you are now.

"Hey, jackass," I yelled, really hoping that all of the ogres around me would protect me. "Funny that you're the one talking about treachery after you turned your back on your whole family. How about you go fuck yourself, and I'm just gonna go back and tell my mom, your sister, that I watched you get killed by a bunch of creatures the whole world thought were extinct just so I can see her smile."

He froze and then gave me this smirk that made my blood boil and run cold at the same time.

"Ah, yes. My dear sister. Her home is quite lovely, is it not? I must thank you for opening my portal and giving me back the access to her world that I so richly deserve. Much has changed, but one night was not enough to enjoy its spoils. I am eager to take what is rightfully mine."

Before I could attack him, and believe me, I had every intention of doing it, the air warned me that the air witch was about to do something really bad, and I had seconds to defend myself. What I was not prepared for was that the air witch was able to force out every other element until the air was pure oxygen, and my uncle was somehow able to set the whole thing on fire and fling the fireball at me. Melodium lunged forward and grabbed me, hunching over until he was on top of me. The fire moved along his diamond skin without leaving so much as a blister, but I would have been dead if he hadn't been there. When he stood up, my uncle and the air witch were gone.

"That was foolish, young knight," Melodium reproached me. "You played a game with all of our lives without knowing the consequences. If our skin was not impenetrable in this state, you would have been responsible for our brethren's serious injury and possible death."

Yeah, see, you don't have to yell at me anymore because he made me feel like the biggest asshole in the world.

"I'm sorry, Melodium," I said, feeling worse by the second. I could feel the reproach in the air too. "What he did to my family, especially my mom... I just saw red and snapped. She lost everything when he betrayed them. Her work, home, friends... she and my grandmother were forced into camps and had to go through so many inquests trying to prove that she wasn't part of the cabal too."

He patted me on the back. I don't know how I didn't fall on my face.

"I take back my rebuke, young knight, for I understand how it feels when rage over an injustice against your family courses through your blood. If such a thing were possible, I would suspect that ogre blood runs in your veins. But you must get to safety. I have one request. You must take one of my brothers with you and find a way to free us from this prison."

"I'll try, but I still haven't figured out how to get an ogre through the portal," I told him.

"Then you must try harder," he shrugged like it was the simplest thing in the world.

The rest of the ogres had joined us by then.

"My leader, the witches and the goblins are lost to us. The path to the mountain has vanished, and we cannot see their trail," one of them said.

"There is more," Crud added. "Our brethren who you did not save from the foul witch's spell could not resist his summons and joined his side in the skirmish. We were forced to take them prisoner. Fortunately, they cannot achieve their true battle state as long as the spell has them in its power."

"Thank the Goddess for small favors," I said. "Where are they? I want to get them freed and then try to open the portal."

"This way, young knight," Crud pointed at the biggest hut on the other side of the square. Two ogres flanked the door.

Thanks to the amulet, lifting the spell from the remaining ogres didn't take long. When I finished, I got all of the spell books together, and Melodium, Tug, Nug, and I started back to the portal while the rest of their village cheered. It made me feel uncomfortable, like I was being put on the spot—especially since I couldn't guarantee their freedom. It was also very loud.

"We have decided that Tug shall accompany you to your world. We need Nug's skills as a forager and hunter here if we are to survive until you return and grant us our freedom," Melodium told me.

"Makes sense. Before I go back, is there anything you can remember or tell me about my uncle? I'm willing to bet he is either an earth witch or a fire witch. I was positive it was earth until he set fire to the sheet of air that air witch made."

"The fire was not of your uncle's making," Nug said. "He used a device that produced the flame."

"Huh. Okay, so they planned that attack, then. Good to know. Then he's probably an earth witch, and that's how he got the paths to all disappear or lead you back to your village. I bet he used the earth to kidnap the rest of the village too. It wouldn't be hard to sink them into the earth and have the earth transport them to the cave in the mountains. That also explains why the air felt so wrong when I found the bubbles over the village and cave. He tried to manipulate the air so that you couldn't tell there was anything beyond your village, but he did a terrible job and hurt it because he's not an air witch."

"How are you certain of this?" Tug asked.

"I don't know. I just felt it. It was like the air screamed every time I got near one of his illusions, and then my gut cramped up."

"Perhaps you are an air witch," Tug said with a nod.

I paused, thinking about how easy it had been to help the air.

"Yeah, I bet you're right."

We had reached the clearing by now. Melodium and Nug stopped at the edge of the path.

"Take this, my brother, for protection," Melodium gave the amulet to Tug. "With our minds restored and our eyes open, we will be safe as we look for more of our kindred."

"Are you certain, brother?" Tug asked, clearly worried about leaving his kindred unprotected. "If you discover more villages, it is likely that they are ensorcelled. Without this talisman, how shall you free them?"

"We'll do it together," I told them with a lot more courage than I felt. "It took my magic to make the amulet's power reach the whole village, and I'm not going to abandon you. This is all my uncle's fault. I know he will never fix it, so I will. You scout for villages. Every night Tug and I will come back and see if you found more. I'll also figure out how to help you cleanse your soil so you can start growing things again."

"Your honor does your kind much credit, young knight," Melodium said gravely, bowing to me again. "I must ask for yet another boon. Please keep our world a secret. We do not know who to trust, and I fear my brethren will look at more of your kind with great trepidation."

"As they should," I admitted. "I'll do it, but I really wish I could change your mind. My teacher can help us. She's honorable and powerful. She helped a lot of persecuted races during the Witch Wars."

"I will ponder on this and consult with our village. I will not make that decision for my brethren without their consent. Meanwhile, Tug shall determine your mentor's character himself," Melodium said with that definite note of finality that all adults use when the discussion is over.

We said goodbye and left them on the path while we walked to the portal. I opened the book, which had somehow miraculously escaped a fiery death, and looked at the portal spell. Whatever else he may be, my uncle was meticulous in his notes. I couldn't reverse the entire spell, but I could modify it enough for one ogre to get through. So Tug took the amulet, I brought him back through the portal, and here we are.

8

Jessie got up and made another cup of tea without saying a word. While she added the water, she stared into the fireplace for a moment, collecting her thoughts. Jared's blatant transgressions could wait– it was clear that his heart was in the right place, and he felt remorse. His tendency to act first and think later was a problem though; she knew she would have to address it before he got in enough hot water to land in front of the Witch Council.

"How many times have you been back?" she finally asked, turning to look at the boys. Lucy was still passed out in Tug's lap, and Spot had taken over Jared's, leaving Ace and Aleister to fend for themselves.

"We go back every night," Jared gently rubbed Spot behind the ears. "We found three more villages. One was more male ogres around Tug's age, and two were villages of female ogres. One of those villages was in the same age range, but the other was older, like the age his mom would be. They're one-third of the Elders. We haven't found their counterparts."

Jessie frowned.

"What do you mean," she asked.

"We believe that male and female are two sides to the same genderless coin," Tug answered, looking up from Lucy, an infatuated look still on his face. "Our council elders are equal parts male, female, and those who choose no gender. They must work together for all solutions. Regardless of what gender an ogre prefers to be or to be with, all decisions must benefit all ogres, and the way we achieve that goal is through equal votes and representation."

"Wow," Jessie blinked in surprise. "That's very progressive."

"No, it's very practical," Tug shrugged.

"Okay," she put her mug on the table and ran her hands through her long, gray curls before pulling them over one shoulder. "So we can pretty much safely assume that the cabal knows you're here, Theodore failed, and the ogres are still on the table. Also, if Melodium's real name wasn't Lug, then what is yours? Because it can't be Tug."

Tug glanced at Jared for reassurance again.

"It's okay," Jared nodded.

"I do not know," Tug said, looking at Jessie again. "There are still spaces where my memory has not returned. I fear that perhaps part of the spell still has me in its grasp."

"Do you mind if I take a look?" Jessie asked gently.

"I do not mind."

He sat very still as she walked over to him, bent forward, and peered at him closely. She used the illuminating power of fire to find the places where the spell clung to his skin like pieces of a tattered rag, but the remnants weren't enough to cause the kind of memory loss he described. She sighed.

"I think you're right, but it's inside you, in your mind. I can purify you with fire and burn it off, but I'd rather have

Greta do it because she can remove it while it's intact. I don't want to risk reactivating the failsafe."

She straightened and picked up her mug again, returning to a spot in front of the fireplace.

"We need to think about the next steps and get more people involved, starting with Greta, Isabel, Mara, and Robin," she continued as her phone buzzed. She grabbed it and pulled up Greta's text.

Robin and I are in your office. We need to see the amulet right now. Robin knows it and knows that it's vital, but his nose started bleeding when he tried to remember.

"Fuck. Robin and Greta are outside. They want to come in and see the amulet. Greta said Robin's nose started bleeding when he tried to remember how he knew it."

"Let them come," Tug said before Jared could protest.

"Thank you," Jessie crossed the room and opened the panel that revealed her office. Greta and Robin burst through from the other side.

Tall with a silver pixie haircut, and dark brown-green hazel eyes, Greta was Jessie's counterpart in every way. They had been best friends for longer than anyone could remember. She gave Jessie a quick hug and immediately started to pace in front of the fireplace while chewing on her thumbnail and staring anxiously at Tug and Jared.

If Jessie could figure out how to harvest Greta's nervous energy, the world would never face an energy crisis again.

Robin the Puck, Oberon's emissary for the Alliance peace talks and apparently a gamer to boot, made a beeline for Tug. His hair and eyes had begun shifting in color from autumn red and gold to winter black and holly green, and his normally impeccable waistcoat was unbuttoned over a ruffled shirt and leather trousers.

"Please, I must see it," he begged.

Tug held up the amulet. The flash when it seemed to catch fire in Robin's presence blinded them all and made the cats bolt. Robin fell to his knees and howled in pain, clutching his head. A trickle of blood seeped from his nose, and Jared had a flashback to the ogres under his uncle's spell having the same reaction in the village.

The flare dimmed, and the amulet hung from its chain, still glowing a deep red. Robin shakily came to his feet.

"I remember," he gasped. He reached out and tentatively took the amulet from Tug's fist. "I remember the ogres. I remember everything. How did I forget? Who could wipe my mind so cleanly of an entire race so integral to the protection and foundation of Faery? How could Oberon forget you? How did we all forget?"

He looked up at Tug.

"I know your name. Elisian. You and your brothers led Oberon's Honor Guard. You were tasked with the protection of the king of all Faery."

Tears streamed down his cheeks unchecked.

"You were gone, and we never knew you were supposed to be there at all. I am deeply sorry, my friend. We failed you."

Tug gently took the amulet back and slipped it over his head.

"No, you did not fail us. We were under the same spell. We did not know from whence we came or our purpose in this world. Until Jared found us, we did not even know we were under a spell. We knew the magic user who came to us each year was a witch, but only my brother Melodium believed we were at odds with our true purpose. He held the amulet and passed it to me for protection when I escaped the realm which yet holds my people prisoner."

"A witch?" Greta stopped pacing and stared at Tug.

"Oh, yeah," Jessie said with a curt laugh. "Not just any witch either. Remember our good friend Theodore? Turns out he's not as dead as we thought."

"Melodium was Oberon's first general and right hand," Robin said, his voice so low that it was almost a whisper. He rocked back on his heels and looked awestruck. "You were his tracker, and your brother, Lucidia, was his hunter. The three of you led the Guard."

"I'm guessing Lucidia is Nug," Jared said.

Spot came out of hiding and returned to her place in Jared's lap. Lucy jumped in Tug's lap, hissed at Robin, and began furiously cleaning her tail to show her disapproval of the whole situation. She calmed down when Tug stroked her head.

"What now?" Greta looked from Jessie to Robin. "You know as well as I do that a witch, especially Theo, can't cast that kind of spell over the fae. Theodore was never more than mediocre at best."

"Knowing Robin was under the spell too changes everything," Jessie agreed. "We have to go to Oberon and Isabel as soon as possible. A cloaking spell cast by a witch can affect the fae, but this goes beyond cloaking. This is glamour. Someone tampered with your memories and created a false reality. Only the fae can do that."

"A witch and a fae working together to remove Oberon's

strongest form of defense and hide the ogres from the world opens up some rather grim possibilities, my dear," Robin shook his head. He moved to the hearth where he stared into the cheerful fire without seeming to really see it.

"We could never prove to our satisfaction that the original cabal was only witches," Jessie reminded him.

"Yes, I am well aware."

"Why didn't they kill the ogres?" Jared asked with a frown.

"That is an excellent question," Robin turned away from the fireplace, brows creased in thought. "Tug, what communication did you have with your captors in that world?"

Tug, choosing not to comment on Robin's use of his false name, shook his head.

"Very little. The witch appeared to us once a year, took what he wanted from our stores, and was gone again. He preached to us on the virtues of providing for our community and reminded us that he was our ruler and deserved our lives, blood, sweat, and tears."

"How noble and cliche," Jessie rolled her eyes.

"And typical Theo. It sounds to me like he planned on keeping you as his slaves," Greta mused. She gave Tug a sympathetic glance.

"Perhaps," Tug shrugged, surrendering his finger to Lucy as she wrapped around it and started bunny-kicking the palm of his hand.

"He must have had a lot of power to be able to keep that going," Greta resumed her circuit around the room.

"The air was cleaner and stronger than it is here," Jared told her. "I bet the earth was too. I think he was alone in the beginning because he did all of the illusion spells, and they were really bad. But we know that at some point an air witch joined him. So that's at least two witches, probably more, and however many fae were involved. Robin, how many ogres were there before they left?"

"I would have to go back and double-check the census, but my guess is around thirty families. Children were very rare, and they were considered adolescents until they reached the end of their first century of life."

"So we probably found about half of them," Jared looked at Tug.

"Assuming the rest are still alive," Greta pointed out. "Not to be harsh, but no matter how great the elements are, trying to maintain spells like that on approximately a hundred and fifty beings is a lot, especially when they're spread out."

"What else can you tell us?" Robin asked.

"Redcaps helped my uncle attack us," Jared told him. Robin stopped, staring at Jared in surprise.

"Redcaps? Are you certain?"

"Aye, very," Tug said grimly.

"If we had any questions about the involvement of the fae, those doubts, unfortunately, have been laid to rest," Robin shook his head and sighed. He ran a hand through his thick hair and straightened his vest.

"Why? Aren't they basically just thugs for hire?" Greta asked.

"A common misconception, but no. Many mistakenly believe that the term 'redcap' is a designation for groups of fae who might cause mischief or trouble. For instance, the Fir Darrig, like our friend Matthias, are sometimes called redcaps because they look and live like rats, and, well, they wear red caps. They also attack anyone who treats them with disrespect or ill will.

"But in reality, redcaps are a species in the goblin family. They are murderous, thuggish brutes who delight in inflicting pain and dip their hats in the blood of their enemies. However, they are not mercenaries. In fact, they deeply distrust the high fae, witches, and humans. If they are involved, it's because someone promised them something they want. And make no mistake, they will stick it out until they get what they were promised."

"Like what?" Jared felt uneasy as he remembered the ugly grins on the redcaps' faces before they realized that the ogres wouldn't be so easy to take down.

"Power, riches, an end to Oberon, those are the first things that come to mind," Robin gave a little shrug.

"Great," Jared leaned forward and put his head in his hands, only to hastily straighten up when Spot squawked in protest. "Sorry!"

She went back to sleep, only slightly mollified.

"Wait, but they ran away when they realized the ogres were ready to rampage," Jared frowned as the memory came back to him.

"They're not stupid," Robin gave a wry chuckle. "They will run away to fight another day, as I believe the saying goes. Very few things in this world can take down a rampaging ogre, much less a village of them. A mob of witches with access to a leyline can slow one down, as Tug found out when you had to battle the members of the cabal in the bar, but trust me when I say that he would have freed himself in the end. And redcaps will never sacrifice themselves for anyone's cause, not even their own."

"We also have to consider that redcaps are probably not the only fae involved," Jessie added. "Mara told me about them once. According to her, redcaps are unpredictable and hard to control, and Theo would have wanted a way to keep them under his thumb. The redcaps were probably the enforcers for the real fae power."

"I fear you may be right. Redcaps also do not have the magic or powers of persuasion necessary to cast anything stronger than very basic glamour spells. At best, a redcap can convince humans that their eyes played tricks on them. But redcaps, as a whole, would never have been able to ensorcel the ogres and myself, much less the High King of Faery," Robin shook his head before turning back to the two on the sofa. "Jared, what do you know of your uncle?"

"Not much. I knew he was bad and caused a lot of problems for my mom and grandmother, but we thought he was dead. My mom and her mother had to do a lot of work to make the Council believe they were innocent. My grandmother eventually moved off to the middle of nowhere where no one knew who she was, my mom lost her house and her job, and a lot of people she thought were her friends turned their backs on her. Jessie and Greta were pretty much the only ones in town who stuck by her until she proved her innocence to everyone's satisfaction," he couldn't keep the bitterness out of his voice.

He hadn't been born when his mother dealt with the fall-out from her brother's actions. Still, his grandmother had told him the stories to make sure her grandson remembered how fickle the world was for a family that fought the battles of racism on one front and guilt by association on the other.

"She wasn't guilty," Jessie shrugged.

It still made her furious to think about what Sharon had suffered at the Council's hands. The relentless McCarthyism-style persecution of anyone unfortunate enough to be related to a member of the cabal, especially if that witch was a minority, was unforgivable. When it was all over, she and Greta had stepped down from their Council seats to focus on advocating for the people in their communities, although Greta still traveled around Europe researching artifacts and lore for Isabel.

"We remember Theodore," Greta said. "He was a slimy asshole. I would apologize for that statement, but I think Jared already agrees. He was manipulative and greedy and entitled, and he didn't care who he hurt when he tried to get his way. I am not surprised that he's behind this, but I know there's no way he's the only one. He would never work this hard. He always looked for the easy way out."

"How has no one seen him since then?" Jessie frowned. "The ogres disappeared a little over three hundred years ago."

"That is an excellent question," Robin said. "Perhaps he had no way to leave the world once he brought the ogres there."

"We confiscated all of his artifacts we could find and put them in secured vaults at the Council," Greta told him. "If Theo had used any of the items we took to get to and from that world, then he would have lost access as soon as we locked them up. The vaults are lined with wormwood and iron walls that are six feet thick."

"We also can't discount the possibility that he used Jared's portal to get back into this world," Jessie added. "Although the timing seems a little circumspect. How did he get reinforcements back to confront Jared and the ogres so quickly?"

"The fae can travel between worlds and realms. He easily could have communicated with the cabal through a fae messenger," Robin said. "We must find a way to break this spell and rescue the ogres before Theo regains control of their minds."

"What about the amulet?" Jared asked. "It lent me its power so I could break the spells Tug and his kindred were under. And when Melodium wielded it, it protected the ogres from the failsafe. It was like the amulet knew that his role was their leader, and he needed to be able to protect them by setting them free. Maybe if Oberon holds it, it can break the spell on the rest of the fae too."

"It appears there is more to this story that I would very much like to hear," Robin whistled. "Another time perhaps—for now, I think you're right. Tug, may I take the amulet to our King? I swear on the Tree and the triple Goddess who governs us all that I will return it as soon as possible."

Tug hesitated, casting a doubtful glance at Jared, who gave an encouraging smile.

"Here, please find the answers you seek so that we may free my kindred."

"I will be back before you know it," Robin gave Tug a bow as he took the amulet from Tug's hand. It flared red again before Robin popped out of sight.

They looked at each other in silence before Jessie curled up in her chair. Greta leaned against the mantle and looked at the boys.

"Well, the next step is to talk to your parents," she said to Jared.

"Do we have to?" he groaned.

"Um, yeah. You opened a portal to another world in their garage while they were on vacation. Theodore was in their *house*. I mean, protecting Tug is one thing, but how could you not think to warn them, Jared? Sharon's life was almost destroyed because of her brother. If he showed up at her house again and someone saw him, then there is absolutely nothing we could do that would prove her innocence," Jessie's snapped.

Jared looked at her, stricken.

"I didn't think one time would matter. We moved the portal, hid it, and put a security spell on it. I'm the only one who can use it now. No one else can go through it unless they're with me."

"Jared, you're an apprentice. Do you honestly think you know any spell right now that is strong enough to keep your uncle out? That you're strong enough to pull off?"

Jared looked down at his hands and squirmed. He didn't speak. Jessie's eyes narrowed.

"Jared, what did you do?"

"I promised–" he started to defend himself, but she cut him off, her voice rising sharply.

"No! No more secrets! I am your teacher, and you are in an extremely dangerous situation right now! What did you *do?*"

"I had help," he muttered.

"Help from whom? And if you make me drag it out of you, then your parents won't have to punish you because you will be magic grounded for the next millennium."

He had never heard of being magic grounded, but it did not sound like something he would enjoy. He looked down at Spot for a long moment. The silence grew uncomfortably heavy as Jessie and Greta waited.

"It was Caroline's brother," he finally said, right when Jessie was ready to blow up at him.

Jessie stared at him in shock.

"I'm sorry, Caroline's *what?*"

The memory of them in the garden behind the pub after they rescued Charlie came rushing back to her. She had told her apprentices to seek out young witches and let them know they could come to her for mentorship after learning that the cabal recruited witches who had just come into their power to be nothing more than cannon fodder. Jared and Cassie had agreed, but Caroline wouldn't meet her eyes.

"Look, we can deal with that later," Greta cut in. "We have more important things to take care of right now. Jared, where is the portal?"

"It's in the bathroom at my apartment," he said, still looking at his lap.

Greta dug her phone out of the back pocket of her jeans and clicked through the contacts.

"Hey, Sharon. Yeah, great! How are you? Uh-huh. So, look, I'm calling because your son is in a huge amount of trouble with his teacher right now, and he's about to be in even more trouble with you, so I need you to meet us at his apartment so you can get first dibs on punishing him. Great! See you there."

She hung up and turned to Jessie, who still stared at Jared in shock. Jared gave Greta a wounded look while Tug tried not to laugh.

"Jessie, honey, you can magic ground him later. Right now, we need to get to his apartment, and since you know what it looks like, I need you to grab your portal key and take us there."

Jessie's eyes narrowed dangerously.

"This is not over," she pointed an accusing finger at Jared before slamming her mug back down on the table. She stormed over to an old desk in the corner that looked like it could barely stand and dug around in a drawer before pulling out a massive, gaudy toy ring. She put it on, concentrated, and twisted the ring around her finger three times. A portal to Jared's living room opened, and Greta waved Tug and a very reluctant Jared through.

9

"How did Caroline and Cassie not notice a portal in the bathroom when you all hid out here while the bar was under attack?" Greta asked once they stood in front of the brown, second-hand sofa and beat-up coffee table. It was covered in game controllers, a stack of Dungeons and Dragons books, Warhammer miniatures, and an empty Mountain Dew bottle. Jared heaved an internal sigh of relief that the mountain of dirty laundry was safely out of sight.

"I have it hidden under an illusion spell," he was able to mostly keep the note of pride out of his voice as a second portal opened in his living room, and his parents stepped through.

Sharon and Frederick Daniels were settled in for the night before Sharon got Greta's call. Fred had replaced the blazer and nice jeans he wore when he taught economic classes at West Georgia with sweatpants and an ancient UGA T-shirt that was so old, that its logo had almost disappeared. He wore his gray hair short, and he kept his trim build in shape by running every day, rain or shine.

Sharon stayed in shape by chasing preschoolers around all

day. She had tied up her gray locs at the nape of her neck, and she had a smudge of flour on one high cheekbone that matched the flour on the front of her Atlanta Zoo t-shirt. Her eyes, so much like Jared's, twinkled with suppressed laughter as she looked down at herself.

"If anyone can teach me how to make a pie crust without getting flour everywhere, I would greatly appreciate it," she said with a little laugh.

"I'll let you know as soon as I find out," Greta returned her smile and gave her a warm hug, ignoring the immediate transfer of flour to her black tank top. Jessie was right behind her. Sharon's hugs were magical. Even Tug came forward for one, and Jessie had never seen him voluntarily touch another creature except for her cat.

Jared felt a rush of guilt as he looked at his parents. Sharon suffered for so long after what his uncle did. Now, Jared himself had almost destroyed her peace. Sharon met his gaze and raised an eyebrow.

"What did he do this time?" She sounded amused. Jared was brilliant, but he also had an unfortunate tendency to rush headlong into trouble. Her smile faded as she looked at her friends' somber faces and the guilt all over her son's.

"Mom, I'm so sorry. I didn't know he would come back," Jared stumbled on the words, unable to meet his mother's eyes.

"Who?" she whispered.

But she knew. She knew exactly who had come back. She had known since they returned from their vacation and found the garage suspiciously cleaned up by a son who couldn't even remember to put his dirty clothes in the hamper. She had known when she saw that her favorite bowl for practicing water magic was moved a millimeter to the right. She had known when she touched the back of a chair and felt *his* energy. She had hidden from that knowledge, refusing to accept that after sleeping for three hundred years, the nightmare was awake again.

She knew, and now her son– *her son*– stood in front of her, telling her that somehow he let the monster who had once been her little brother back into her world.

"Jared, son, tell us what happened," Fred moved between Jared and his mother, creating a wall Sharon could hide behind. He had made the same gesture countless times over the last three hundred years while she tried to pick up the pieces of her life from a world that kept shattering them until they were too small and jagged to hold without slicing her open. She saw Greta move to her side, ready to give support. Jessie had moved to Jared's, ready to show that, as his teacher, she shared the responsibility for his actions.

"Wait," Sharon held up her hand. "Before we go any further. I know what you're all trying to do. I knew something was wrong when we came home from our trip, and I didn't want to believe it. Greta and Fred, I can stand up on my own. I appreciate the support, but I don't need protection from this. Not anymore.

"Jessica, I want to know how this happened under your watch, and Jared, when I tell you that you are in big trouble, I can promise you that you have no idea how much trouble you're in. You will tell me everything, young man, and you will tell me why you felt that I did not deserve to know that you let the man who destroyed our lives back into this world, and you will tell me how you plan to fix this."

"It's not Jessie's fault, Mom. She's my teacher, not my babysitter. She can't be on top of me every second of every day. She didn't know I had tried to do something like this. She never gave us permission to experiment with spells on our own. I did this to myself," Jared tried to push past the lump of guilt and shame in his throat.

"Yeah, I could be more involved in everything Jared and Caroline do during their time off, but I wanted them to get a chance to live their lives without having to answer to me every second," Jessie added. "I had no idea Jared would blatantly break my number one rule: they cannot create or perform spells without my supervision. This is a perfect example of why that rule exists."

Jessie knew it wasn't really her fault, but she couldn't help but feel the burden of responsibility. They all listened in silence as Jared told his mother the story. While he talked, Sharon leaned against the arm of the sofa, arms crossed across her chest, her face unreadable. When he finished, she turned and walked to the glass sliding doors that opened up to the balcony. She looked across the parking lot and to the trees beyond.

"Where is the portal now?" she finally asked.

"In my bathroom," he said. She whipped around, ready to strike, ready to run.

"It's *here*? You chose to keep an interdimensional portal in your *home*? One that leads to a dangerous criminal who could bring Goddess only knows what back through it? Child, I know you didn't learn to be this reckless from Jessie or us!"

"I didn't know what else to do! I promised Tug and Melodium that I wouldn't tell anyone about their world in case the cabal found out! I'm sorry, Mom, but we're talking about a whole race trapped on another world. A bunch of people either want to control or destroy the ogres. We have to help them. And what if they were bespelled again and forced to fight for the cabal? Tug alone took out most of the people who attacked Jessie's bar that night. What if twenty ogres showed up here and attacked us? Or all of them? There are still at least seventy-five or eighty out there that we haven't even found yet!"

Sharon's face didn't give away the pride she couldn't help but feel at the conviction in her son's words. Yes, he did something idiotic and was in *so* much trouble, but he had turned it into a chance to help someone else because it was the right thing to do– not because of heroics or fame. But he still had an interdimensional portal that a very dangerous criminal was desperate to use in his bathroom, of all places. Did he just never *think*?

"Son, show us the portal," Fred said in the voice he used when he was very interested in something but trying not to let it show because his interest was probably very inappropriate at that moment. Like now.

"It's in here," Jared led them to the bathroom halfway down the hall of his apartment.

The apartment was standard: prefab with beige carpeting, white walls, faux granite countertops, and a garden tub in the decent-sized bathroom. In the tub was a black disc that Fred immediately recognized as one of Theodore's last magical artifacts. Theo's magic signature was all over it. Fred and Sharon tensed, and Sharon looked at her husband in a panic.

"This was Theo's. I thought Sharon and her mother were past dealing with his betrayal. Jared, how did you find it?" Fred asked, anger rising in his voice. Sharon slipped her hand in his and tucked her head on his shoulder, and the familiar gesture calmed him down.

"It was with a pile of junk in the garage," Jared said nervously. The older witches froze and looked at each other.

"We turned it all over," Sharon pleaded. "I swear, we didn't keep any of it."

"I know. I cataloged the collection," Greta replied, locking eyes with Jessie. "Jess, Isabel had told me she was worried that a spy was in the Council and asked me to keep a record of everything we confiscated from all of the cabal members. I still have my records. Sharon gave us this portal, and I can prove it."

"What does that mean?" Jared looked from one witch to another.

"It means someone stole this from the Council's vaults and planted it in your parents' garage. Who knew you were trying to build that sim world?" Jessie asked. She crossed her arms while Greta started chewing on a fingernail until Sharon made her stop. It was a miracle that Greta's fingernails still grew after all this time.

"A lot of people," he admitted. "Everyone at the gaming store, some of the regulars at the bar, my gaming group, of course."

"Well, that doesn't narrow it down," Greta sighed. She turned away and leaned her palms on the edge of the sink.

"Did anyone seem more interested than everyone else or ask about your progress?" Fred asked, leaning next to Greta.

Jared thought for a minute, brows furrowed.

"Yeah," he said slowly. "A witch at the store. Some quiet guy who's been coming there forever. His name is Greg, I think. He mostly buys collectibles and keeps to himself. He seems nice, I guess. It's not that he asked me a lot of questions. It's just that he never talked to me before then."

"What kinds of questions?" Jessie asked, fixing her apprentice with a piercing blue gaze.

"Just what kind of world was I trying to build and what kind of portal did I plan to use," he shrugged. "That was it. Then I found the portal when I came over to help fix that shelf in the garage a couple of months ago. I just saw it underneath a bunch of junk in the back corner. That was when I decided to try to build the spell."

"We need to track this Greg down," Jessie said to Greta.

"Agreed. Sharon, I hate to bring up bad memories, but can you tell us anything about Theodore that might help?"

"Well," Sharon thought for a moment. She had never wanted to revisit this topic. "His element is earth. He was especially good at manipulating landscapes. When we were kids and would play games like hide and seek, he could move the landscape around so that I never found him."

"Wow, that's impressive," Jessie grudgingly admitted. Most witches were in their early twenties before they truly connected with their base elements on that level.

"That's the problem. He thought he was better than everyone else because he developed his elemental connection so early. It didn't help that Mama spoiled him rotten because he was her baby. But, and please understand that I do not say this out of jealousy or bitterness, when he became an adult, he wasn't as good as he could have been because he never applied himself and truly studied. He just thought it would come as naturally as his connection did. So by the time we were adults, he was a mediocre witch at best, and his pride couldn't handle that. He was ripe pickings for the cabal."

"Do you know exactly what he was supposed to do for the cabal?" Greta asked. "What would force him into exile on another world with ogres?"

Sharon shook her head.

"No, I didn't even know he was working for the cabal until the Council came to arrest him. He was long gone by then. We honestly thought he was dead, although I suppose, deep down, a little part of me knew he wasn't."

"He left a journal behind," Fred pushed off from the counter and moved to his wife's side, where he put an arm around her shoulders. "Maybe that will help you. I think it was with the stuff we turned over to the council."

"It was, but he wrote it in code. We all thought he was dead too. None of us had the time to decode a dead witch's journal," Greta admitted, wishing now that she had pushed for the project to go through. But at the time, the Council had been stretched thin, and the ravings of a man no one cared for and everyone thought was long gone were very low on anyone's list of priorities.

"Well, Jared's about to have a lot of free time when he's grounded for the next century. He can work on it," Jessie decided.

"Why, I think that's an excellent idea," Sharon grinned.

"Oh, come on!" Jared started to object and stopped when Jessie raised her eyebrows.

"We put quite a few of those in storage. I'm sure Isabel would love to get them out for us and see what Jared can find," Greta examined her nails.

"Stop biting them," Sharon scolded her. Greta sighed and tucked her hands in her pockets.

"What do we do now?" Tug spoke from the doorway where he stood watching.

"Well, the portal can't stay here. We need a safer and much more secure place for it," Jessie said. "I vote for a cell at the Council. We can modify the security protocols to recognize Jared and Tug, but anyone else who tries to go through or come back would be captured."

"I like that plan except for the part where we have to assume that someone within the Council was able to get the portal out and put it in my garage," Fred pointed out. "As long as we know that to be the case, we can't guarantee Jared's or Tug's safety or the safety of the ogres left in that world."

"True. The Library, maybe?" Jessie shot Greta a questioning look.

"Yeah, as long as one of us is there. At least with our wards, if anyone tries to come through with ill intent, they'll..." Greta blew a raspberry and motioned with her hands like something blowing up.

Whenever someone tried to violate a witch's Library's defenses, attack the Library's owner, or had malevolent intentions, the wards activated, spectacularly disintegrating the person into a fine spray of gore. Nicky was quite bitter that he'd had to clean up the mess from attacks on Jessie and Greta's Library twice.

"That's one way to deal with it," Jessie considered the possibilities. "Plus, we wouldn't have to clean up the mess for once since it would be on another world."

Sharon wrinkled her nose.

"It gets everywhere," she shuddered. "And you can't get it out of cracks. I would rather have a tub of glitter dumped over my office than go through that again."

"Mom!" Jared stared at his mother in shock.

"Yes, son?" she raised an eyebrow as she returned his stare.

"Your mom's a badass," Jessie grinned. "Where do you think I learned how to fight dirty?"

"I didn't know you fight dirty, and can we please change the subject? This is very disturbing," Jared scowled.

"Fine," Sharon reached over and pulled her son into a hug. "So you're going to take the portal. What about the faeries and witch council?"

"We have to figure that out. I'm sorry, Sharon. I wish this weren't happening to you again," Jessie scuffed the toe of her Converse on the floor and looked down.

"Well, you tried to protect me before, which counts for something. If it's anyone's fault, it's all of ours for teaching my son to respect all forms of life and help those who couldn't help themselves. Tug, don't look like that. No one blames you, honey," Sharon pulled Tug into the other side of her hug.

"Come on, let's get this out of here," Fred looked down at the portal.

No one was eager to touch it. In the end, Greta and Fred cast a combined earth shield around it while Jared floated it out of the tub and through the portal Jessie opened to the Library.

"Do you want to come through for some tea?" Jessie asked, waving at the cheerful fire and curious cats who peeked around the edge of the portal.

"No, we'd better head home. I want to go over our house and garage to make sure nothing else showed up we don't know about," Fred replied.

"Let us know if you need help," Greta told them while Jessie closed the portal. They all exchanged hugs before Sharon and Fred left.

"Now what?" Jared asked his teacher.

Before she could answer, her phone rang, and she was surprised to see Mara's name come up on the caller ID. Cassie, with the ingenuity and perseverance only humans possessed, had been able to make her phones work in the Faery hills. The various fae were either thrilled at the new toys or horrified at what they viewed as human encroachment on their realm. Mara was one of those who was fascinated by these new methods of communication and made sure to let Jessie know by calling her. A lot.

"Hey, Mara, what's up?"

"Jessica! How lovely to hear your voice. I have a rather urgent request. Can you come to my court and bring Jared and Tug? Oberon wishes to speak with them immediately, if not sooner. Preferably sooner."

"Sure, we'll be at the cathedral in thirty seconds," Jessie exchanged a surprised look with Greta. "See you soon."

She hung up and looked at her student and the ogre.

"I sure hope you're ready. You're about to meet the King of Faery. Greta, coming?"

"Oh, I *absolutely* would not miss this for the world," Greta cackled.

10

The portal let them out in the courtyard of an abandoned, seemingly derelict cathedral on the outskirts of town, surrounded by ancient oaks, sycamores, and holly. The wards around the cathedral discouraged trespassers, and the property's illusions hid a lush and thriving Faery Hill and the home of the Court of Mara Mac Gabhann, Duchess of Green Orchards and Oberon's great-niece. She was also one of Jessie's dearest friends.

Dain waited for them at the top of the steps, standing rigidly at attention and resplendent in a doublet of the ducal colors, grass green and sky blue. His wind-tossed wheat-blonde hair was the only thing that moved. He offered Jessie a deep bow as she approached.

"Milady Witch, the Duchess offers you greetings this eve and wishes for you to know that you are her guest in this establishment and under the mantle of her hospitality."

"Hello, Dain. It's a pleasure to see you again. We came as soon as we could," Jessie bowed her head in acknowledgment of the greeting.

A witch, especially one as old and well-known as Jessie,

was under no obligation to bow or show fealty to another being, but it never hurt to be polite. Besides, it made him happy to feel like he had done an excellent job– which he had. Like most young Tuatha de Danann in service to the nobility, Dain was eager to please. He took his role as Mara's page very seriously and was cherished by everyone at Court.

Greta always had an almost uncontrollable desire to ruffle his hair just to make him a little less serious. Jessie told her in no uncertain terms to leave him alone. And, of course, Jared, master of making friends wherever he went, couldn't resist the chance to enthusiastically befriend the young fae. Jessie hoped Mara wouldn't be too pissed when she found out that Jared had dragged Dain to a new world.

Jared and Dain exchanged an elaborate handshake when they thought Jessie wasn't looking.

"Are we still on for a game Saturday?" Jared asked in a low voice.

"Of course," Dain whispered back. "I am quite eager to try my hand at being a knight this time."

"Sweet," Jared grinned as Dain hurried to the front of the group so he could properly lead them into the Hill.

Dain escorted them down a hallway carpeted with a green runner trimmed in sky blue. The local dryads worked their magic each day to decorate the stone walls with everchanging wooden murals that depicted scenes from the Court's history.

Throughout the hall, Jessie could hear the sounds of laughter and music. The music tore at her heart and worked its way into her thoughts with tantalizing imagery of wild dancing on a Scottish moor; a human could never withstand the music's lure. It was hard enough for a witch to resist its call–

and on that note (no pun intended), she reached back to take Jared firmly by the arm.

"What?" he asked in a slight daze.

"Just come on. I don't need to hunt you down while you try to chase the music and whoever is playing it."

"It's not like it's my first time here, you know," he muttered under his breath, but he followed obediently behind her, arm still clutched in her grasp, as Dain led them to a small alcove just off the main hall.

"If you would be so good as to wait here, Her Grace will be with you shortly," he instructed them with a bow.

"Of course," Jessie gave him a nod of dismissal.

The receiving room was pleasant, with a bench on one side underneath a mural showing a faun chasing some nymphs through apple trees. Purple cushioned chairs flanked a small table on the other, and Jessie gave the chairs a wide berth. Mara's subjects weren't known for making practicality a priority. She still vividly remembered sitting in one of those chairs and feeling like she would never stop sinking into its cushiony depths.

A small balcony overlooked the herb and rose gardens, glistening in the moonlight, across from the entrance to the alcove. Jessie felt a pang as she looked at the herb gardens and thought about Brigitte, the doomed banshee. Mara had told Jessie that the gardens were one of the few places where Brigitte found solace.

Jessie heard a startled squawk behind her and turned to see Jared struggle to escape the clutches of one of the chairs. It seemed determined to make him sink into the seat until nothing was left but a pair of Vans sticking out the top.

"Tug, can you give him a hand?" She grinned.

Tug didn't try to conceal his grin either as he hauled Jared out of the chair and deposited him on the floor. Jared glared at them before moving to the much safer bench.

He was saved from any further embarrassment when the door opened, and Dain announced Mara's presence. Mara swept into the room with all the aplomb and grace that a Tuatha de Danann Duchess should carry. She was beautiful in the alien way of the fae with sharply planed cheekbones, emerald green cat eyes, and hip-length hair the color of ripe plums, and she wore a forest green crushed velvet gown that swirled around her ankles as she swept Jessie and Greta into a warm hug.

"My dears, it has been too long! What news do you bring today? And greetings to you as well, Tug and Jared. It's always a pleasure to see you again."

"Hello, Mara. It's good to see you too," Jessie felt a twinge of guilt. She had made herself scarce after the Courts emerged from their seclusion for Brigitte's burial rites. It wasn't that she had been avoiding the Hill. It was more that she felt that the fae needed some space after the events of the last few weeks, especially the part where Nicky killed one of their own. She herself wasn't too eager to relive the memory.

"I couldn't help but notice that you don't visit as much as you used to. I certainly hope you haven't removed yourself from our presence over Brigitte," Mara gave Jessie a shrewd look. "She made those decisions on her own. You and Nicodemus did what you had to do."

"I know, but that doesn't make it easier," Jessie shrugged

before changing the subject. "Does Oberon think he can help us rescue the rest of the ogres?"

"I'm not sure what my uncle thinks, only that he sounded very urgent and excited when he contacted me and told me he needed to speak with all of you immediately. Come, I'll take you to him," she led the way to a small door on the other side of the alcove, Dain moving right behind her.

They followed her through to a small room with more dastardly purple chairs, which they all avoided much to Mara's amusement, and a scrying mirror set up along the opposite wall. The room lacked the frescoes of the main hall and alcove and only had one window overlooking the grounds. Jessie expected to see Oberon's throne room in the mirror; instead, they saw a plain, round, windowless stone chamber with a simple but elegant wooden desk and beautifully woven rug as the only decoration. Robin's face popped into view.

"They're here, my lord," he gestured to someone off-mirror. Oberon stepped into the frame, and, as always, Jessie caught her breath. His beauty was legendary. He appeared to them today in what Jessie called his forest dwarf guise: golden yellow cat eyes, dark green hair cascading down his back from his antlers, and cloven hooves like a deer's in place of feet. He was the same height as the Puck. She was secretly glad he chose this over his tall, regally elegant elven court persona.

"Your Majesty," Mara curtsied, and Tug and Dain bowed. Jessie, Greta, and Jared gave shallow half-bows of their own.

"Mara, my dear child. And Greta and Jennet! Or no— you go by Jessica now, if I am not mistaken," Oberon greeted them with a smile.

"Yes, your Majesty, I do. It's a pleasure to see you again. I would like to take this opportunity to present my apprentice, Jared Daniels. He is responsible for locating the missing ogres and has been able to return the one you know as Elisian to our world," Jessie gestured to Jared, who looked like he wanted to be anywhere but there, especially when Oberon turned his golden gaze on him with intense scrutiny.

"Your majesty," Jared stammered.

"Relax, child. There is no need to be nervous," Oberon tried to be soothing, but even for a seasoned witch like Jessie, his presence was overwhelming.

"Yes, your majesty. Do you think you can help us save the rest of Tug's– well, I guess it's Elisian's family?"

"That is our goal, but we need to know more about this world you discovered. How did you come to find it?" Oberon's gaze shifted from warm to stern in a heartbeat. Jared wondered if this was what it was like to be under interrogation.

"I found the portal in my parent's garage. Someone planted it there. I thought I could use it to make a simulation world for a game, not realizing that it was actively set to the world where the ogres had been exiled."

"My lord, we think someone gained knowledge of Jared's intentions to build this game and planted the portal somewhere they knew he would find it in hopes that he would reopen the path to the world with the lost ogres," Jessie added. "His uncle, a malevolent witch who had worked for the original cabal, is responsible for capturing and imprisoning the ogres and is trapped on that world with them."

"His uncle," Oberon's tone was flat, and it had a dangerous undercurrent.

"Yes, however, the Council absolved Jared's family of all knowledge and involvement. He himself never met his uncle. Plus, Jared has been my apprentice and friend for the last five years. I vouch for him myself. We wish to share this information with you because we feel it is vital to be as open with you as possible about the circumstances behind the ogres' disappearance and their discovery."

"We acknowledge your transparency and are willing to continue hearing this child's story without further judgment," Oberon regally inclined his head.

Jared wondered at precisely what point in his life he would stop being called a child. Probably when he was five hundred, he glumly mused to himself before Jessie elbowed him in the ribs to go on.

He managed to get through the gist of the story without losing his nerve or cool.

"I swear to you that while Theodore may be related to me, I do not now, nor have I ever, considered him to be my family. I will do whatever I must to make this right, and so will my mom and dad. He destroyed my mom's and grandmother's lives, and most importantly, he destroyed the lives of every ogre he transplanted and subjugated. I'm not going to let him do it anymore. I just ask that you give the ogres back their rightful place by your side. I plan on taking care of the rest," he finished, standing tall and looking Oberon in the eye. Jessie barely managed to keep from gushing in pride.

Oberon regarded Jared thoughtfully.

"Your conviction does you credit, child. That the ogres would be restored to their rightful place was never in doubt. However, you cannot stand alone against faery magic. Even if your teacher accompanies you, you will need the assistance of the fae. Robin will assemble a team to accompany you when you return to free the ogres from their unjust imprisonment."

"Thank you, Your Majesty. I think we should plan to return tomorrow if that's okay with you," Jared said with an anxious glance at Tug, who stood by impassively. Only the tightness of Tug's shoulders gave away his nervousness and unease. "It's too late tonight to be able to get the necessary teams and provisions together on such short notice."

"I agree. I will begin the preparations at once. I believe we already have the necessary fae on hand to help with the rescue," Robin said. "An honor guard from your court will give us the rest of the support and fighting power we need, Your Majesty."

There was no question that LaSalle and Matthias were going with them, and Jessie wasn't upset by that. She would rather have fae who weren't afraid to fight dirty and had her back by her side than a group she didn't know who might find themselves honor-bound. Sometimes being a magic user grounded in neutrality and not good had its perks.

"Very well," Oberon nodded to his emissary as he stood in front of the mirror with his hands clasped behind his back. "Jessica, Jared, Elisian, I shall await word of your triumphant return and ready the ogre village for the return of its denizens. Mara—"

But before he could finish, Mara went sprawling to the floor when Dain barreled into her, shoving her away from the window. She came to her feet like a cat and stared down at her page in shock.

"Forgive me, Your Grace," he fought to get the words

out before he collapsed face down on the rug. A dart with fletching Jessie didn't recognize quivered between his shoulder blades.

"Dain!" Mara shrieked as she scrambled to his side.

"Niece! What has happened?" Oberon thundered, eyes filling with storm clouds and his skin turning dark gray.

"Someone tried to shoot Mara, and Dain pushed her out of the way in time. But the dart got him instead. I think it's poisoned! He's not breathing," Jessie tried not to panic. She could do a lot, but knowledge of the fae was still relatively new to witches, and she didn't even know how to begin poisoning one outside of iron, much less come up with an antidote. Greta fell to her knees by Dain.

"Mara, we need your healer. Robin, I need you to find a tracker and start searching the grounds immediately. Jessie, see if you can pick up a magical signature or any evidence outside the window. We need to find who did this."

"Go," Oberon snapped at Robin, pacing in front of the mirror like a caged animal.

As Jessie ran to the window and began casting for any kind of magical evidence, she spared a thought for how he must feel. He had just discovered that an entire species of fae he had magically forgotten about existed, and now he had to watch his niece's page fight for his life. He couldn't even help Mara or Dain for fear of leaving the High Court unattended in these uncertain times.

And Dain still did not breathe.

"What can poison a fae other than iron?" Greta looked from Mara to Oberon.

"The juice of a citrus fruit," Oberon snapped, still pacing.

"Very little else could cause such an immediate reaction. A lemon is more vile to us than iron itself."

"Tug, I need a basin of water from the heart of this Hill. Get someone to show you where it is," Greta began snapping orders. When there was a crisis, she did not give a flying rat's ass who was nobility and who wasn't.

"Mara, honey, I know you want to stay here, but I need you to find your healer for me *now*. They have to be here somewhere. Jared, get someone to take you to the gardens and find hawthorn and foxglove for me. I need the blossoms from both."

She closed her eyes and held her hands over Dain's prone body, fervently hoping that she could counteract the poison and that healing poisoned fae wouldn't become normal every time something went wrong. Dain still did not breathe. Oberon watched, helpless to act on his niece's behalf.

"We're losing him. I can feel it in his blood," Greta said, sweat beginning to form across her forehead. "I'm trying to force the poison to move to one area so we can get it out, but it's fighting me. It weakened his natural magic and defenses. I need that water and those flowers, now! *Where is the healer?*"

"BRING THE WITCH THAT WHICH SHE HAS RE-QUESTED IMMEDIATELY OR FACE MY WRATH!" Oberon's voice blasted throughout the Hill, scaring Greta so badly that she fell over backward.

"Thank you for that, Oberon," she scrambled back to her knees as Tug burst through the door, spilling water from a basin across the floor. Annie the brownie followed him.

"Here," Tug thrust the basin at Greta. She grabbed it and

poured half of its contents over Dain's inert body. Dain still wasn't breathing. She felt the pulse in his wrist grow weaker.

"What took so long? We're losing him," she tried to keep the panic out of her voice.

"We couldn't reach the fountain. Someone hid it," Annie wrung her hands, worry laced through her voice. "Who would do such a thing?"

"There's a fae signature outside the window that doesn't fit the rest of the Hill," Jessie started to warn them, but she was interrupted as Mara ran into the room with an arm full of hawthorn and foxglove flowers.

"Here, what can I do?" she gasped.

"Where is your *healer?*" Greta couldn't keep the frustration and fear out of her voice. She crushed the flowers and dropped them over Dain's body.

"I can't find her," Mara desperately wrung her hands together. "I sent the courtiers throughout the Hill."

"Give me your hand and magic," Greta snapped, grabbing the Duchess' hand as she tried to force the water into Dain's body, trying to reach his faltering heart.

It was too late. She felt it the moment his heart stopped.

Mara screamed, and it was a sound Greta never wanted to hear again as long as she lived.

Annie wailed, collapsing into Tug's arms.

Jared sat down heavily and buried his face in his hands, not trying to hide his sobs.

Oberon stared at Greta, stricken.

"Is this how it is always to be? When the witches are involved, will one of my own pay the price?"

"I'm going to pretend you didn't say that," Greta looked

up at him, blind fury seeping out of every pore, blackness bleeding into her eyes. "Particularly because *this* was done by one of your own. One of your own who wishes to harm you so much that they helped hide your entire honor guard. A guard you forgot ever existed. So don't you *fucking dare* point fingers, Oberon! I don't give a flying fuck who you are! Your fae are in this as much as the witches, and if you think you're the only one paying the price, then you can go fuck yourself and kiss my ass in the process."

"*Enough,*" Jessie's voice cracked through the room like lightning with all the fury and heat of her fire behind it.

"But–" Greta started to protest.

"No! This is not the time or place! I cannot believe that I have to stand here and scold the High King of the Fae and one of the oldest witches in the world instead of taking care of our friend, *your niece*, Oberon, who just lost someone dear to her and suffers."

Mara's heartbroken sobs continued behind Jessie as Greta and Oberon looked at her guiltily and then at each other.

"I apologize, milady witch. My accusation was baseless and spoken out of pain and anger."

"I apologize too, Your Majesty. Dain means– meant– a great deal to all of us. We have already lost so many to the last war. I shouldn't have lashed out."

"Great. Now that we're back to behaving like adults, we need to go," Jessie snapped, turning on her heel.

"You're leaving? Just like that? After everything you just witnessed? After Dain?" Mara lifted her tear-stained face and looked up at Jessie in shock. Jessie paused and looked at her friend, nonplussed.

"Well, you need to start the mourning rites, so we have to figure out how to rescue Tug's family as soon as possible without the fae. If someone tried to assassinate you and get you out of the way, then they're probably coming for the ogres next if they haven't already."

"No," Mara snarled, a guttural, ripping sound that made the hair stand up on Jessie's arms. "We will mourn our precious boy after we stop the ones who took him from us."

She looked down at the limp body in her arms and gently brushed Dain's hair back from his pale face.

"I will find the ones responsible and destroy them," she said in a deadly, quiet voice.

"Then we need to see if we can find more traces of them on the Hill. Greta sent Robin to find a tracker, and hopefully they can give us news soon. It's no coincidence that we couldn't find your healer or that the fountain was buried," Jessie said, kneeling by Dain's side and gently laying her hand over his. Tears finally began to fall down her face. "Does he have family here?"

"No, he is– was– an orphan. His parents died long ago in one of our wars, and he was fostered by me at a young age."

Jessie felt a pang as she realized Mara was the closest thing to a mother Dain had.

"I'm so sorry, Mara," she bowed her head.

Whatever Mara was about to say was interrupted when the door flung open. Robin stood in the doorway with John right behind him. They paused as they took in the scene in front of them.

"John? What are you doing here?" Greta asked, puzzled.

"We needed a tracker, so I got a tracker," Robin said, his

voice as cold as the North wind. "The fae are good, but nothing gets past a werewolf's nose."

"Did you get anything?" Jessie looked from one to the other.

"Yes," John bared his teeth, canines already elongating into his wolf fangs, eyes turning golden as he stared at Dain on the floor. He pushed past Robin and thrust the crumpled form of a redcap onto the floor. They stared at the goblin, who glared defiantly back.

"Who sent you," Oberon thundered.

"You'll never get it out of me," the redcap cackled. "Your reign is ending, and we'll all be free from you soon enough!"

Oberon's eyes glowed an almost incandescent green, and Jessie winced as she felt the power of his compulsion spell build. She grabbed Jared and thrust him behind her. If Oberon was about to cast anything truth related, then she really did not want to hear what her apprentice did on his days off.

But before Oberon could act, the redcap gasped and clutched his chest as his face turned blue. He fell to the floor, screaming in agony before the scream cut off. Blood trickled out his mouth, and he lay still, staring sightlessly at the ceiling.

"A failsafe," Greta said in disgust. "I should have known."

"As should I," Oberon was equally disgusted. "No matter, I have those among my court who can speak to his blood and make it sing. Niece, my resources are yours to command. We will end this on the morrow, and then we will mourn your loss, for Dain's absence will be felt by all."

"Thank you, uncle," Mara's voice was numb.

"Jared, we need more information," Oberon looked at the apprentice. "Where did the goblins who attacked the ogres each night come from, and how did they continue to re-appear?"

"I'm not sure," Jared said, wiping his eyes and coming to his feet. He squared his shoulders and set his jaw as he faced the mirror. "Our theory is that my game-world spell somehow overlaid on Theodore's portal spell, so whatever elements my spell contained that his did not bled through into the ogres' world."

"That is a sound theory," Oberon mused.

"Melodium came up with it. He's a really smart guy," Jared said, looking at Tug, who nodded in agreement.

"Aye, that he is. He was my right hand and the general of my armies. I did not realize the hole left in my life by the loss of him and his brothers until you showed me. For that, I deeply apologize, Elisian."

"It is the fault of none but the witches and fae who conspired to break our bond asunder," Tug acknowledged the apology with a deep bow.

"But a witch can't cast a spell that affects the minds of the fae like this one, right?" Jared continued. "I mean, from what I learned, there are some things we can do with cloaking, and if a witch is powerful enough, then they can put a fae under a spell like what happened to Robin a few weeks ago. But we can't do something like make an entire species forget the existence of one race or make an entire race forget their whole life. But according to Melodium, some faeries can."

"Which ones?" Jessie asked.

"The rulers," Oberon admitted. "Myself, Titania, Mab, the Erlkönig, the Morrigan, to name a few. There are others throughout the world. Our power over the fae allows us to cast our spells in a far-reaching manner such as this."

"From what Jared said about his uncle and the air witch showing up right before he escaped with Tug, we already know that the witches behind the cabal are done hiding behind apprentices and children. Fae rulers add a whole new level of crap. We're going back to the bar and rallying our troops," Jessie said in a voice that brooked no argument.

Greta came to her feet.

"I'm going to go tell Madame Blanche what happened and make sure Rupert stays with us for this. And Mara, I am sorry for my outburst earlier," she hugged Jessie and Mara. Mara stared at Dain, unaware that Greta had even touched her. Jessie and Robin exchanged a worried look.

"I'll walk you out," he said as he led them to the front door.

"Is she going to be okay?" Jessie asked once they were in the parking lot.

"I don't know. She loved Dain like a son. We all did," Robin admitted with a helpless shrug. "But if she goes into deep mourning, then the Hill will go into mourning with her, and it will be defenseless."

"Talk to Oberon and see if you can get the most vulnerable fae a temporary place in his Court," Jessie said. "We'll figure out what we can do to help bolster the defenses on our end."

"Thank you, Jessie. You're a true friend to the fae. Both of you are, no matter what happened back there. What *did* happen, by the way? I can't remember the last time I heard Oberon apologize to anyone, much less someone who wasn't fae."

"We were both upset. He accused the witches of being

the reason for the recent deaths of the fae, and, well, I kind of have a hot temper," Greta hastily interjected before Jessie could say anything.

"Oh, dear. Yes, I can see how that wouldn't go over well," Robin grimaced. "Well, at any rate, I will be at the pub at–what time are we going?"

"Are we bringing vampires?" Jared asked.

"It would be preferable," Jessie said, weighing the value of Mikael and Nicky at full strength against a possible army of ogres.

"Then we need to go around nine o'clock. That's about when the sun will set in the ogres' world.

"Understood. Tug, I am going to retrieve the amulet from Oberon. I will meet all of you at the bar tomorrow evening," Robin bowed and disappeared into the depths of the cathedral, leaving them in the parking lot with their grief.

I I

Half an hour later, they were seated around the bar with the rest of their friends after Jessie finished yelling at Greta— again— for getting into a fight with Oberon. Greta, suitably chastened, took a seat between Mikael and Nicky.

"I let Isabel and Madame Blanche know what's going on," she told them. "Rupert, Madame Blanche brought up the point that if these are the same witches who were part of the original cabal, you may be in danger too. They know how to hurt the Matagot. Are you sure you want to come with us?"

The giant cat regarded her with his emerald gaze.

"While I appreciate your concern as well as the concern of my companion, I will not be left behind if my presence can help Tug in any way."

Apparently, doubling as Jessie's security had created a bond between the Matagot, Tug, and LaSalle, who pounded on the bar and roared enthusiastically while raising his glass in a toast and sloshing his beer everywhere. The kitsune on his other side indignantly rescued their drink and glared at him.

"Come on, man, I have to clean that up," Jared complained as he trudged to the back for the mop. Jessie couldn't figure out why he didn't just leave it closer to the bar whenever LaSalle was around. And Goddess forbid Renard, their vampire friend, pop in for a night of drinking! Cleaning the spillage was a lost cause at that point.

"While he's getting the mop, I'll fill you in," Jessie said, and she and Greta told the group what happened on the Hill.

"I knew it was bad before we even made it back to you," John shook his head. "We heard Mara's scream all the way at the edge of the woods on the other side of the Hill."

Jessie tucked herself under his arm and wrapped her arms around his chest, and Cassie wiped tears from her eyes.

"Poor Dain," she said as Caroline came out from behind the bar to hug her. "He didn't deserve that."

"Aye," LaSalle's boisterous demeanor sobered. "He is a true casualty of this war. But as much as it pains me to admit this, his death did the one thing nothing else could have done. It guaranteed that the fae who are on your side will fight for you."

"This is not how I wanted that guarantee," Jessie shook her head, remembering Mara's vow of vengeance.

"What now?" Nicky asked.

"Now we get the ogres back," Jessie told him. "Oberon is preparing a place in his kingdom for their arrival now."

"Isabel said she would send someone over here to see what we need for tomorrow night," Greta slid off her stool. "And we need to make sure the portal is anchored to the Library's wards so nothing nasty can follow us through. I think Frederick can help. He's been working on some kind of portal tunnel concept. I want to check in with him before I head home."

"Sounds good. Get some rest too, and be back here by

about eight tomorrow night," Jessie called after her. Greta gave them a little wave over her shoulder and disappeared down the hall to the Library.

Jared watched Jessie nervously. She could tell he was working up to something, and she didn't have to wait long before he marched up to her and John.

"Hey, Jess," he said, squaring his shoulders and lifting his chin.

"What's up?" she asked as she stirred her sweet tea with a straw.

"I'm not getting left behind."

Jessie stared at her apprentice, perplexed.

"Why would you be left behind?"

"Because it's dangerous, and you always make Caroline and me stay behind whenever dangerous stuff happens."

"Okay, that was one time when we had no idea what we were really up against. You can't stay behind. You have to get us into this world and act as a liaison between the ogres and us. From what you told me, they're already pretty distrustful of witches, and for a good reason. I don't think they will welcome us with open arms without you. Plus, based on what you told me, you already proved that you can stand your ground in this situation. But Caroline, you and Cassie are staying here."

She cut off their protests with a wave.

"Someone has to be here to run the bar," she pointed out, ignoring Caroline's scowl.

"The pack's coming too," John added. "I'm splitting them up. Most will act as security on the bar, but my lieutenant and four top fighters will be with us."

"Good, that will help a lot," Jessie felt some of the tension go out of her shoulders.

He hugged her close and kissed the top of her head.

"We got this," he reassured her.

"Yeah, but this isn't a fight with a bunch of inexperienced witches. These are at least two full-powered witches, a group of redcaps, and any ogres Jared couldn't save who could turn against us. That's the part I'm really worried about."

"I will speak with my people," Tug rumbled. "I will go through the portal with Jared tonight so they know you're coming. We will assuage my peoples' doubts and then summon you forth."

His little speech startled most of the bar's patrons, who had never actually heard Tug speak in a complete sentence.

"Yeah, ogres are smart," Jared smirked. "Deal with it."

"Am I too late for the party?" asked a rich, alto voice behind them, and Jessie smiled in delight as she turned around.

"About time you showed up," she said as she tackled the new witch in a hug. "Everyone, this is Riza, the captain of the Witch Council security force. She's a total badass, so don't mess with her. You have no idea what a fire witch's true potential for destruction is until you piss off this one over here."

Riza gave the group at the bar a cocky grin as they eyed her nervously. She was gorgeous with long, iron gray hair and huge dark brown eyes compliments of her Cuban heritage. Her full figure was more muscular than hourglass, and she carried a staff in one hand and an impressive shield on her back.

"Where's Greta? I want to show her this shield one of

the earth witches came up with. It absorbs the energy from any magic attack and transmits it straight to your weapon or spells so that you can conserve your own energy. Plus, it adds an earth punch attack." She slung the ornate shield off her back for Jessie to see.

"I understood maybe half of that," Cassie whispered to Jared.

"Witches use magic energy to fuel our attacks when we fight. It sounds like they found a way to make an earth energy shield that absorbs someone else's attack and reroutes the energy to you so that you don't have to use as much of your own energy. That's really badass," Jared explained with a note of admiration. He itched to look more closely at the shield.

"Greta left already. We didn't know you were the one coming by or she would have stuck around," Jessie told Riza.

Riza took a seat next to LaSalle, eyeing the never-ending goblet he stole from Mara's Court. Well, according to him, he was borrowing it for an indeterminate amount of time. Jessie pointed out that it was pretty much the same thing and was rewarded with more spilled beer for her efforts.

"Is that Scottish ale I smell?" Riza asked.

"Aye, you have a good nose," he belched. "Care for a nip?"

"Don't mind if I do." She gave him an appreciative nod as she took a healthy swig from the goblet.

"Wait, I thought alcohol dulled a witch's powers?" Cassie looked from Riza to Jessie, puzzled.

"No, it dulls mine and Greta's powers. Not all witches have the same reaction we do," Jessie explained.

"Thank the Goddess," Riza added with her own belch as

she passed the goblet back to LaSalle. She sobered as she looked at Jessie.

"I'll bring a group of guardsmen tomorrow night. I just want to get a feel for what's going on myself before they get here. I take it you're the Nain Rouge who is not officially helping and the Matagot who accompanies Madame Blanche."

"Indeed we are," Rupert sniffed, simultaneously grooming his front paws and whiskers.

"This is Jared. You're already familiar with his family," Jessie said with a nod in Jared's direction. He tried not to flinch under Riza's gaze, which seemed to go right through him and look into his soul.

"Hi, Jared. For what it's worth, I went to school with your mom. I never believed she had anything to do with your uncle. Too bad I wasn't where I am now, so I could prove that, although that is one of the many reasons why I fought so hard for my position," she said, with a pointed look in Jessie's direction.

It never sat well with her that Jessie and Greta had walked away from the Council instead of using their positions to gain the political strength necessary to help unfairly persecuted witches. Jessie refused to rise to the bait.

"Jared's uncle is why we're all here. Remember when we thought ogres were extinct?"

"Yeah, until one showed up at your bar, and you refused to tell anyone where he came from," Riza sat up straighter on her stool.

"Well, have we got a story for you! Jared, would you like to fill in the scary Witch Council Captain on how you broke my number one rule and found the ogres, or do you want me to do it?" Jessie asked with a malicious grin. She knew that when everything was said and done, he wouldn't be in serious trouble, but the more she could get him to understand the severity of his actions, the better.

"Wait, aren't you supposed to be his teacher?" Riza raised her eyebrow at Jessie.

"Yes, and I already yelled at him. You're just better at yelling than I am."

"And did you get involved in all of this?" Riza fixed Jared with the same piercing stare. He squirmed, shooting Jessie a pleading look.

"Uh uh," Jessie shook her head. "I told you there were consequences. Pissing off Riza is one of them."

He sighed and gave Riza the rundown on the last few weeks. When he was done, Riza stared at Jessie. LaSalle handed her the goblet without waiting for her to ask for it.

"Trust me, you need this. You probably need something a little stronger, too," he patted Riza on the back.

"Jessie, witches can't cast glamor over the fae like that," Riza finally said after drinking enough ale to drain a regular cup. She got up from the stool and started pacing around the bar.

"Is pacing a witch thing?" John asked Mikael.

"Yes," Mikael leaned back against the bar and crossed his arms, ignoring the annoyed glare Riza shot him.

"You know what this means, right?" Riza couldn't keep the alarm and urgency out of her voice.

"That the fae were part of the cabal? Yep, we figured that one out already," Jessie said, crossing to John and tucking herself back under his arm. It wasn't that she needed him to hug her all the time. It was just nice to physically feel the support.

"Where's the amulet now?" Riza asked.

"Robin took it to Oberon," Jared said. "Once Oberon held the amulet, the spell broke."

"Yeah, that's where we were earlier," Jessie said soberly, fighting back the tears when she thought about Dain lying still on the floor while Mara wept. "And where we discovered that this is worth killing over. While we were talking to Oberon, a redcap tried to assassinate Mara. Dain, as in the same Dain who went to that world with Jared and who also happened to be Mara's page, pushed her out of the way and took the poisoned dart meant for her. He didn't make it."

"Another fae is dead?" Riza's eyes widened.

"Yep. Oberon is pissed, he and Greta got into a yelling match, Mara is heartbroken, and we're trying to get the vulnerable fae out of her realm before she goes into mourning and leaves it unprotected. She loved Dain like a son and raised him as if he were her own."

Riza gave a low whistle.

"Man, you do not do anything by halves, do you, Jess?" She shook her head. "Okay, so we need to rescue the ogres before the new cabal can get to them. What else can you tell me?"

"Just that we need to plan to leave here around nine tomorrow night," Jessie said. "The way time moves differently there, we know the sun will have just set, and I want the vampires with us."

"Glad we serve some purpose," Nicky said wryly to his brother. Riza shot them a quick grin before turning back to Jessie.

"I'll have Isabel get here an hour early with the rest of the team. I'll give her the cliff notes version when I report back tonight. Since she's taken on the journeyman aspect of Jared's training, he'll have lots of time to tell her the whole story later. I can't wait to see what she does to him."

"Me either," Jessie smiled sweetly at Jared, who would be most grateful if Greta would come back so she could make the floor open up and swallow him.

"So, who's going?" LaSalle asked, hopping down from his stool. "I need to rally Matthias."

"Yes, you do. I know Robin's bringing some of Oberon's guard, but I would feel better if our friends were with us.

"Consider it done," LaSalle said with another belch. "Besides, he would never let me live it down if we went on a daring quest to rescue the ogrekin and left him behind."

"John, can you get the pack here around eight?" Jessie looked up at him.

"It shouldn't be a problem," he looked at his watch. "Seanan has to get her little ones to bed and make cupcakes for some school thing, and since she's my lieutenant and drives a mini-van that can comfortably seat ten, she's just bringing everyone with her."

"Werewolves have such normal lives. It is quite peculiar when compared to the rest of us," Rupert remarked.

"Yeah, really normal," John said with a wry smile.

"So that gives us our three fae, six members of the wolf pack, two vampires, three master witches, a journeyman witch, a Matagot, and an ogre on top of whatever backups the council and fae send," Jessie did a quick count in her head.

"We got this," Riza snatched the goblet from LaSalle and raised it in a toast.

"I like her. She doesn't spill beer everywhere," Jared said to no one in particular. Jessie laughed at LaSalle's scowl.

"Okay, I'll see you tomorrow night," Riza gave the goblet back to a disgruntled LaSalle and pushed off the barstool. She opened her portal to her Library and waved as she went through.

"We'll be back tomorrow," Nicky pulled on his coat, pointedly ignoring his brother's disapproving glare at the orange and brown striped monstrosity.

"Please wear something normal," Jessie hugged him.

"I make no promises," he sniffed as he followed Mikael out the door.

"I should go too. See you in the morning?" John pulled Jessie into a hug and gave her a kiss on top of the head.

"Make it afternoon," she stood on tip toe to get a proper kiss, grinning at the combined groans and coos from around the bar. He laughed and waved good night to the rest of the crowd.

Jessie turned back to her apprentices.

"Jared, get plenty of rest. Caroline, you and I need to have a very serious talk when we get back from the ogre world tomorrow night. I recommend that if the two of you have any more secrets then you start spilling them now. I clearly have failed to make you understand the seriousness of what we're up against, and I'm very disappointed in both of you."

She got up and walked to her office without looking back, but she heard LaSalle's whistle as she went down the hall.

"I'm glad I'm not either of you," he said, followed by a splash.

"Stop spilling the damn beer!" Jared yelled, and Jessie chuckled as she shut her office door behind her.

12

The next day Jessie let herself indulge in the luxury of sleeping in before heading to the bar to round up her charges. It was warm for late October, but she felt a chill in the air as she pulled her ancient Prelude into the parking lot at sunset. Jared and Tug waited for her on the porch.

"The ogres know we're coming," Jared said after she let them inside the bar and away from any prying eyes and ears lurking outside the building.

"Great. We should be ready to go on time," she nodded with satisfaction.

As the clear, starlit night settled over the bar, their friends drifted in one by one.

"I like our odds," Greta said as she perched on a barstool next to Mikael. Rupert waited patiently next to Tug, and LaSalle and Matthias had changed into sturdy leather armor. John texted Jessie to let her know that the wolf pack was en route.

"Good because we didn't have a lot of reinforcements we could send," a new voice joined them from the hall.

Isabel, head of the Witch Council, Jessie and Greta's oldest friend, and Jared's teacher in the arts of air magic, led a small cluster of witches. Ivan, the water witch who had helped purge Robin of an extreme case of iron poisoning, was with them. He had taken over Caroline's water magic training at Jessie's request. Riza brought up the rear and ducked out from behind the group to tackle Greta in a hug, at which point Jessie gave up trying to get their attention while they talked defense strategies, and Riza showed Greta her new shield.

"Hey, Isabel. What's going on? Is something wrong at the Council?" Jessie frowned, casting her eye over the small group. There were only about seven witches, two of whom wore their armor uneasily and handled their weapons with the apparent discomfort of people who were not used to combat.

"You could say that," Isabel's tone was grim as she kissed Jessie on the cheek and gave her a quick hug.

"We're just waiting for Robin to show up with some of Oberon's guards. John's lieutenant is on the way with their pack mates too. Otherwise, we're all set," Jessie told her.

"It's good that LaSalle and Matthias will be there. The Fir Darrig are fierce fighters and very sneaky. I'm glad he's on our side," Isabel replied with a note of satisfaction– and relief.

"Same here," Jessie agreed.

"You certainly have a knack for finding the most unlikely allies," Isabel grinned.

"Oh, she's always been like this? I thought we were just unlucky," Nicky examined his fingernails and then ducked, laughing, as Jessie threw a stack of coasters at his head.

"Jessica, focus," Isabel admonished.

"Fine," Jessie huffed a sigh.

Jessie and Isabel, who had been born months apart in the

same little Scottish village lost to time and memory, were so much alike that they could be sisters. Isabel so closely resembled a bird with her tiny frame and huge, bright brown eyes that seemed to see everything that it was no wonder her base element was air. Greta and Riza joined them.

"We still have an hour," Greta checked her watch. "Is there anything we need to go over?"

"Does everyone understand what we're up against?" Riza looked over the group, her tone serious. "If the cabal gets to the ogres before we do, it's all over. None of us can win that fight."

Jessie started to answer when her phone went off, startling her so much that she almost jumped. She went cold when she pulled it out and saw that it was a message from Jared– who stood right next to her.

Greg is here. The witch from the gaming store who asked about my world. He's at the back of this group. What do we do?

Jessie fought the urge to walk up to every witch in the room and put them under a binding truth spell. Instead, she forwarded the message to Greta, Mikael, and Nicky, and casually slid her phone back into her pocket.

"Suggestions?" Mikael asked quietly without moving his lips.

"The boys need to go now," Greta murmured without moving hers either. "Jess, follow my lead."

"Jared and Tug, come with me," she said in a normal voice. "Sorry, but we have to sideline you for this one. It's too risky."

She started toward the front door without waiting to see if they were behind her. Jared hesitated, glancing at Jessie for reassurance, much like Tug looked at him. She gave him an encouraging smile.

"It's okay. She's going to double back and take you to the Library," she whispered in his ear as she hugged him good-bye to sell the act. "Get to the ogres and try to warn them but come back immediately if it's too late."

"Okay," he whispered back before reluctantly letting go and following Greta out the door, Tug on his heels.

"Where are they going?" one of the members of the witch guard spoke up. Jessie could only assume it was Greg.

He was old enough that his hair had already turned gray. What Jessie had taken to be unease with his weapon and armor, she could now see was unease with his surroundings. He handled his sword with more skill than she had first thought.

"Greta's taking them to a safe house we have set up for things like this," Jessie said. She was proud of how casual she sounded. Her nerves were on edge, and she felt like she was about to burst out of her skin.

Isabel stood very still as she watched the exchange. She knew that Jessie and Greta would never have split Tug and Jared away from the group if they weren't in danger. Riza watched too with narrowed eyes, her dark gaze going between Jessie and the vampires. Jessie prayed to the Goddess that Riza wouldn't start questioning them until there was time to explain.

Luckily they were distracted by the arrival of John's pack. It took about another half an hour to get everyone up to speed and quell the arguments and protests– again– from the wolves getting left behind. By that point, Robin arrived with six elves from the Fae courts. The bar quickly became cramped.

Jessie never stopped watching Greg out of the corner of her eye, so she noticed his reaction when the elves arrived. His tension ramped up to eleven, and he dropped his sword. He may be skilled with a weapon, but Jessie would bet the bar that he had never actually been in a situation that required it.

He tried approaching two members of the fae contingent under the guise of introducing himself and was met with a sound rebuffing while the elves looked to see if Robin noticed the interaction. The uneasiness that made the hair stand up on the back of Jessie's neck grew. Picking up on her mood, John whispered something to his lieutenant and came to join Jessie at her side with Robin close behind.

"Is what I think's going on actually going on?" John asked in a low voice.

"Yep," she said. "Sorry Robin, but it looks like some of your troops might be on the wrong side."

"So I see. What are you going to do?"

"Take a page out of Greta's book and hope Nicky doesn't mutiny," she calmly replied, even though she felt anything but calm.

"Good luck," he grinned. He was pretty sure he knew what she had planned, and Nicky would almost definitely walk out if he had to clean up a disintegrated witch again.

Jessie sauntered over to Riza and pretended to be interested in the shield.

"We suspect one of the guards you brought is the one who tipped the cabal off to Jared's game world. I think it's time we see where everyone's loyalties really lie."

"I couldn't agree more," Riza said and slammed her staff against her shield, getting everyone's attention.

"Okay, it's getting crowded in here. Let's go ahead and move this to Jessie's Library," she called out.

"The Library?" Greg asked, startled. Was that fear in his voice? Of course, it was. All witches knew what happened to those who tried to cross the barrier to another witch's Library if they had ill intentions toward that witch.

"Um, yeah. Where did you think we were going?"

"But is the portal not at the apprentice's home?" he blurted out, realizing his mistake too late.

They had never told any of the guardsmen about the portal or mentioned Jared's apartment. Riza smiled, and her smile was the way Jessie envisioned a jaguar would smile when she cornered her prey.

"No, honey. It's in the Library. Now let's go."

Jessie knew immediately that Greg was done for. She slipped behind the fae contingency, John and Rupert by her side. The two elves Greg had tried to talk to exchanged panicked looks before they suddenly froze, caught in Robin's spell as he immobilized them and Greg before they could activate their own portals and flee.

"Going somewhere?" Robin asked in a deceptively mild tone.

"Um, no, milord. It's just that…" one started to say, his voice trailing off as he cast his eyes around wildly, looking for help.

"That witch made us nervous. We don't know his intentions, and we just thought maybe we should get assistance," the other chimed in. Jessie blinked before exchanging an incredulous glance with Robin.

"Please tell me the fae are better at lying in general," she said. "Because that was pathetic."

"I clearly have not done my duty as the lord of mischief," Robin sighed, shaking his head.

"Liars!" Greg shrieked, panicking as he realized that he had been hung out to dry. "It was their idea! They came to me! I didn't even know the ogres still lived!"

"What do you want us to do with these traitors, my lord?" an elf wearing armor inlaid with gold gestured to the rest of the group, who leveled their spears at the two frozen elves.

"Take them to Oberon and then come straight back," Robin said. "Tell him what happened here and let him decide their fate. He lost enough over this matter that I think he should have that pleasure."

"Understood, my lord," the elf nodded curtly as she herded the unfortunate captives through a portal. Jessie caught a glimpse of Oberon standing before his throne in regal splendor before the portal closed behind them.

"What about Greg?" Jessie asked Riza.

"I'll take him back to the council and have him put in a cell," Isabel spoke up. "Unless you want to try putting him through your Library barrier."

Everyone stared at her in horror.

"Absolutely not," Nicky was adamant.

"Okay, well, I guess you're taking him back then," Jessie managed to keep a straight face.

"I swear, it's like I work with children," Riza shook her head in exasperation. "Are there any other traitors in our midst? Because we're all going through the barrier, and believe me, you want to tell me now."

"Nope, we're all good," a plump, pretty witch spoke up. Jessie remembered that her name was Melissa.

"Great! If you'll all follow me," Jessie beckoned as she started down the hall, leading their unlikely team of adventurers while the rest of the bar watched them go.

"Should we have been so public with that? Yeah, we know most of the people in the bar, but there are always cryptids or humans we don't know so well," John asked, falling in step next to her, Seanan close on his heels. Jessie liked Seanan. She was a very no-nonsense woman who wore her long, dirty blonde hair in a ponytail and never failed as John's right hand in matters of the pack. She also liked poking fun at him almost as much as Jessie did.

"Maybe not, but we got our point across. Now they know that Greg and those two elves are compromised. Maybe the cabal will take care of them for us."

"Hopefully not before we get anything good out of them," Seanan added.

"When did I become surrounded by so many bloodthirsty women?" John shuddered.

"I can be a fragile, delicate flower if you want," Jessie smiled sweetly and fluttered her eyelashes. "You can be my big, bad protector."

John gave her a withering glare while Seanan made gagging noises. Jessie laughed, tucking her arm in John's as she led the way into her office just in time for LaSalle and Matthias to join them out of thin air.

Most of the fae opened portals and stepped through like

normal people. Others, like LaSalle, liked keeping everyone on their toes.

"Okay, guys. Here's the deal," Jessie turned to face the group. "A barrier protects the Library. You cannot pass through the barrier if you have ill intent toward us or are a traitor to our cause. Any attempt to do so will result in your immediate and, I assume, quite painful and very messy destruction. No, Nicky, you won't have to clean it up this time. I promise."

The wolves and elves exchanged uneasy glances, but no one backed down.

"Okay, then. Here we go," Jessie turned back to the wall, pressed the knothole, and led them through where the portal to the ogre world waited.

13

Everyone made it through without incident, and Jessie did not miss Nicky's sigh of relief. She really had meant it when she said he wouldn't have to clean it up. It wasn't her fault Greta made him do it the last time. Jessie had been too busy bleeding internally while passed out after dealing with the aftermath of a very vicious magic attack on the bar.

"Jared should be waiting for us," Greta told them from where she leaned against the back of the sofa while giving Ace tummy rubs. "If he's not there, then they're in trouble. Robin, do you have the amulet? We should have given it back to Tug while we were at the Hill, but I didn't think about it."

"It's right here," Robin held it up. The gem caught the light of the fire and briefly glowed red before he put it back in his vest pocket.

"Okay, then let's go," Greta turned toward the portal.

"Aren't you worried about something coming back through?" one of the elves asked.

"No, the same barrier protection spell is in place. Jared's dad is an earth witch too, and we put together a sort of portal tunnel that leads from the ogres' world to this one. Nothing that could break the covenant of the Library can make it through. And bonus, we won't have to clean up the mess!"

"Why has everyone fixated on that?" another elf wrinkled his nose in distaste.

"Because if you break the covenant of the Library, as Greta calls it, you immediately disintegrate into a fine mist of gore that sprays all over the place. It's very disgusting. There is barely enough of you left over to put in a small bag," Nicky snapped.

"Oh, my. I see," the elf blinked and moved closer to his companions.

"Don't worry, unless you suddenly have a complete and total change of heart, you're fine," Jessie reassured him.

"If you say so," he replied, his tone doubtful.

"Okay, here we go," Greta said, passing her hands over the portal and murmuring a spell. They filed through into the overgrown clearing on the other side.

"Of course, they're not here. That would make this an easy rescue mission. We can't have that now, can we?" Nicky muttered.

"I suppose it was too much to hope for," Rupert began grooming his front paws. Jessie and Greta looked at him and then at each other.

"You know what would be helpful?" Jessie asked.

"No, what?" Greta replied, all innocence.

"If one of our party could turn into a big, black bird and fly overhead to scout things out."

Rupert paused in his fastidious grooming to glare at the grinning witches.

"A bat would be more appropriate at night," he scowled.

"Yes, but bats can't see well enough, and they have to squeak to use echolocation. They would make terrible spies," Riza pointed out, coming to stand by Greta.

Rupert gave her a withering stare.

"Fine, if you insist on this madness," the large crow squawked at them from where a giant black cat had been a second before. He climbed into the sky and was gone.

"Okay, here's the plan," Riza turned to the rest of the group. Jessie and Greta took a step back and let their friend take over.

"Greta, you and Melissa are going to do your earth witch thing and shield us. Take a minute to familiarize yourself with my shield and see how well you can replicate its mechanisms to direct the energy from the enemy's attacks back to our weapons to give us an extra boost. If we get to the point where we have to spread out, everyone stay in one of two groups to make it easier for our earth witches over here. I don't want them to have to get overextended.

"Iona and Charlotte, you two work on air magic illusions for this. Let's start with invisibility as long as possible and then go to making us appear to be a larger group than we are. Jessie, you're with Victoria and me on fire attacks. Ivan and Annabelle will cover water attacks."

"How does a water witch attack?" LaSalle asked.

"Well, for starters, we can draw all of the liquid in your body into your lungs and drown you," Ivan shrugged.

"Never mind, forget I asked," LaSalle hurriedly backed away while Ivan grinned, tossing his shaggy gray hair out of his ocean-blue eyes.

"If it makes you feel better, we can make ice darts too," Annabelle shot Ivan a dirty look.

"What? Education is important," he was all innocence.

"Whatever. If you're done terrorizing our allies, can we please get on with it?" she snapped, tossing her long silver braid over her shoulder, clearly annoyed.

"Here comes Rupert," Jessie pointed at a large, black shape that blotted out the brilliant stars that blanketed the night sky.

The crow landed at their feet.

"It is not good," he cawed. "There is fighting all around. There are many more ogres than we thought. If I had to guess, I would say that Theodore brought the rest of the ogres he had hidden on this world."

"Where's Jared?" Jessie gasped as fear gripped her heart.

"I'm here," Jared stumbled up the hill. He bled from a cut on his head. He ran to Jessie, who clutched him in a desperate hug.

"What happened?" she demanded.

"Theodore showed up with that air witch from before, a bunch of elves, redcaps, and strange ogres, and they attacked us. Tug and his brothers are fighting, but we're outnumbered. We need the light from the amulet now!"

"Come on," Riza pushed past him and picked up speed as she charged for the path.

"Shit, get that shield up," Greta called to Melissa, running after Riza. The rest of the party fell in place behind them. John and his wolves shifted and brought up the rear.

"We're going on ahead," Mikael called. "We may be able to change the tide before you reach the battle."

"Go for it," Riza yelled back.

Jessie heard gasps and a muffled curse as the vampires turned. Most creatures never had the dubious honor of seeing a fully turned vampire. In their human shape, vampires looked as if they were still alive. Turning was another story. Their faces elongated, becoming leathery and batlike as their mouths filled with too many fangs. Wings grew from their shoulder blades, and their fingers became razor-sharp talons. The brothers took to the air and flew toward the fighting, Rupert leading the way.

Jessie felt the air flatten around her face as the earth witches cast their shield.

"I wish there had been more time for them to study my shield," Riza said as Jessie caught up to her.

"Greta can figure it out. Her brain's smart like that," Jessie tried to reassure her friend.

"I hope so," Riza glanced behind them.

She and Jessie led the charge with LaSalle, Matthias, and the elves behind them and the wolves and water witches at the back. The earth witches and Robin flanked them, Robin lending his magic to the shield to fortify it against fae attacks. Matthias carried a cudgel and had a battle axe strapped to his back. LaSalle carried an axe of his own.

"We'll see you on the other side," LaSalle called before he and Matthias dove into the underbrush and disappeared.

"Where are they going?" Riza was startled.

"There's no telling," Jessie couldn't keep the exasperation out of her voice.

"Well, wherever they're going, the wolves just joined

them," Riza pointed to the russet, black, and silver shadows that streaked past.

"Can no one stick to a plan?" Greta snapped.

"Apparently not. Just keep the shield up," Jessie yelled back.

The sounds of the battle ahead reached their ears as they came to the end of the path. It was all chaos and carnage laid out in front of them; towering rampaging ogres clashed against a line of witches and fae bolstered by spellbound ogres. Luckily for Jessie and her friends, Theodore's ogres couldn't reach their battle potential as long as they were under his spell. Jessie recognized some of Oberon's renegade elves, along with redcaps, boggarts, and goblins. Theodore was there alright, along with a witch she didn't recognize whose hands moved in an intricate pattern. He must be the air witch Jared told them about.

"Do you recognize any of the witches with Theodore?" she yelled over the noise.

"I recognize all of them, but they're supposed to be dead or imprisoned," Riza yelled back. "We'll deal with that later, though. What's going on with the ogres?"

"The ones Jared freed are rampaging," Jessie explained. "They grow in size and strength, and their skin gets diamond-hard. That's also why they're almost impossible to defeat. But Theodore's spell suppressed that ability, so his ogres can't do it. It gives us an advantage as long as we can make sure that the free ogres don't decide that all witches should die."

"Yes, that would be unfortunate. Look, the wolves are behind the enemy lines. Shall we join them?" Riza grinned from ear to ear. Jessie forgot how much someone who was so by the book and disciplined loved the thrill of a good battle.

"After you," she grinned back.

"We're splitting off and flanking them from the other side," Robin called to them. He and the rest of his elves moved out from the center of their column and disappeared from view as their magic warped the air around them to cast an invisibility spell. Meanwhile, Iona and Charlotte worked their own invisibility spell on the witches, and Riza led them down the embankment and behind the enemy line.

"Once we attack, the invisibility spell will stop working, so everyone be ready," Riza warned them.

"Go for it," Jessie said.

"Everyone ready... attack!"

The enemy line was unprepared for attacks on all sides, but they were not the green apprentices Jessie and her friends had faced a few weeks before. The wolves focused more on the ogres, ripping at their hamstrings, knees, and ankles from behind and adroitly dodging the counterattacks. They still weren't fast enough. Jessie felt fear grip her heart as she heard a meaty thump followed by a high shriek of a yelp and howls of loss.

"Jessie, focus!" Riza snapped.

"But John," Jessie looked at Riza and Greta, panicked.

"He's fine," Greta pointed at the russet blur moving almost faster than the eye could see behind the ogres. "Come on. We only have one shot at this."

Jessie and Riza shot wave after wave of fire darts, arrows, and ropes at the witches and fae who faced them while Greta deflected attacks with her shield and opened the ground beneath the enemy, trapping them in the earth. Jessie was right– it didn't take Greta long to figure out how to deflect the energy from the enemy's attacks to her friends and boost the power of their attacks. Jessie felt her adrenaline surge in the battle, her power driving her attacks with razor precision and depth. She kept the enemy's earth witches busy trying to defend their line; still, it wasn't long before Greta found herself trying to rescue their compatriots from the earth when the enemy used her strategy against them.

Robin and his elves did their best to engage the fae who fought with the cabalists, but they were outnumbered two to one and hampered by the nobility of Robin's elves, who insisted on fighting with honor. Luckily for Robin, LaSalle and Matthias didn't have the same hang-ups. The two of them ripped through the enemy lines swinging their weapons in low blows from behind, LaSalle popping in and out of sight at will.

Mikael, Nicky, and Rupert had taken out the weaker fae and witches on the edges of the line, but they found themselves up against Theodore's ogres, who rallied around their master and formed a protective ring around the last of the cabalists.

"Now would be a good time to get that amulet to Tug and his brothers," Riza shouted to Jessie.

"Where's Robin?" Jessie called back.

"I don't know. I can't see him."

"Rupert! I need you!" Jessie hoped Rupert could hear her over the battle. He appeared by her side.

"Go find Robin. We need to get that amulet to Tug and his brothers," she yelled, shooting a fire arrow at a cabalist, who batted it aside and sent one back. In a split second, she reached into the heart of the arrow and pulled control of its fire away from its owner. She sent it back at her attacker, and he stared down at it protruding from his chest in surprise before sliding to the ground. Rupert spared a glance for the cabalist before launching himself off the ground, becoming a crow in mid-leap.

"Jessica!" a familiar bellow came from the other side of the battle. She looked up as Tug barreled toward them, followed by two ogres who were even bigger than he was and who she could only assume were his brothers.

"Tug! We need backup!" Jessie called to him. The cabalists used their ogres as shields and attacked Jessie's party, who was still out in the open. Ivan pulled all of the moisture from one cabalists' body, immediately mummifying him. Annabelle turned the moisture Ivan took into razor sharp knives that she flung back at the cabalists, taking out two redcaps and an elf. Melissa shielded them, but Jessie could tell that the earth witch was tiring fast. Iona was a crumpled heap on the ground, a victim of a fire attack. Victoria fired flame darts as fast as she could, aiming between the ogres and their legs to take out the cabalists huddled in the middle of the group, while Charlotte fanned the flames with her air magic from behind Greta's shield.

"Brothers, to me!" the biggest of Tug's brothers bellowed.

Jessie thought she knew what an ogre bellow was. She had no idea. She was pretty sure her bones would never stop vibrating. As one, the village ogres turned toward the sound of Melodium's voice and charged across the line, trampling a few unfortunate and unprotected enemy fae as they went.

"These are the ones who have come to help us," Melodium

thundered. "And now we must protect them so they can destroy our enemies with their magic!"

"These puny ones are the only aid offered to us?" an ogre spoke up from the back.

"That stings," Riza objected.

"I mean, he kind of has a point," Greta admitted.

"Yeah, compared to an ogre maybe," Riza scowled.

"One of our own has the amulet," Jessie called, gambling on Rupert and Robin. If they didn't come through, it wouldn't matter. The ogres had been abused by witches for too long. She and her friends wouldn't live if they couldn't help. "We brought it so you can free your brethren."

"Where is the amulet then?" the ogre challenged before he was interrupted by a crow's caw overhead.

"There!" Jessie pointed. Rupert dove for her, but a line of fire darts was right on his tail.

"Greta!" Jessie yelled. Greta threw an earth magic shield in the air, barely missing Rupert in the process, just as a wave of water cascaded from the other side, dousing the flames. Ivan gave them a cheeky grin and turned the sheet of water into a jagged wall of ice which he drove at the ogres.

"Don't hurt them. It's not their fault," Annabelle snapped, pushing her bangs out of her green eyes and tossing her long braid over her shoulder again. "We're trying to save them, remember?"

"Yes, but I'm not a fan of dying in the process," Ivan snapped back.

"Take the amulet," Rupert gasped, collapsing in front of Jessie.

"Rupert! You're hurt!" Jessie cried, falling to his side. An arrow protruded from the membrane in his wing.

"Worry about that later. Use the amulet, Jessica! It is our only hope."

"Melodium, take it," Jessie thrust Oberon's amulet at the ogre. The second it touched his skin, brilliant red light exploded like a sun. Oberon's touch was all the amulet had needed to unlock its true potential, and Melodium was the key that opened the door. Jessie gasped, stumbling backward, blinded. The world was a red blur.

"Brothers, I free you from the spell these accursed mages have placed on our kind! See the light shine forth and know the name of Oberon, for he is the one we serve!"

The collective roar was staggering, and Jessie tripped and fell to the ground, still blind and now deafened. She was vaguely aware of Rupert's screaming caw of pain as he tumbled from her arms. She was completely disoriented.

"Jessie, where are you?"

Greta's voice sounded like it came through a warped tunnel, but the new, snarling voice by her head was very real and very close.

"Bitch! I should have killed you centuries ago, you and your meddling friends," Theodore's voice, thick with hate, spat in her ear. He grabbed her hair and roughly jerked her head back before she knew what was happening. She felt something wrench in her neck, and she knew it was bad. She struggled to get her feet under her and gathered her magic.

"Are you a Scooby Doo villain now?" she gasped.

Jessie grabbed Theodore's wrist, forcing the fire out of her fingertips and into his skin until it blistered. The sickening smell of burning flesh filled her nostrils. He screamed in rage and pain, stumbling backward. She pressed the advantage, forming arrows out of her fire darts and blasting them into his chest, but he was able to hastily throw an earth shield between them. It was much stronger than she remembered his magic ever being, and she couldn't penetrate it.

Theodore bulldozed toward Jessie, his earth magic already healing his skin, and grabbed her arms. He gritted his teeth as her fire finally cracked his shield and his hands blistered again. He threw her down and pinned her to the ground. She looked up, her vision finally beginning to clear, and saw him lift the dagger. He had pinned her arms under his knees, and she felt the bones in her wrists move as they fractured under his weight.

"*Jessie,*" Greta screamed. She heard the howl of a wolf, but it was so distant. The dagger started to fall toward her chest, hate glittering in his eyes that were so much like Jared's, teeth bared in a face that was so much like Jared's, it all happened so fast, she knew they would never reach her in time.

And then he stopped, stunned, staring down at the sword that burst through his chest as the dagger dropped out of his nerveless fingers to dance harmlessly off her face. He looked at her, bewildered. The life drained from his eyes before he fell to the side, leaving her to look up at Jared. Her apprentice, who couldn't even kill a goblin, who couldn't bear to look at death in any form, had killed his uncle to save her life.

All around them, the ogres bellowed. With Theodore's death, the remnants of the spell that kept them trapped was gone. Jessie struggled to sit up, her broken arms dangling uselessly by her side. She couldn't lift her head. Greta and John reached her first.

"Jessie! Stop moving!" Greta cried, casting her magic along Jessie's neck and finding the places where the sinew had torn. Then Greta started to knit the bones back together in Jessie's wrists while John wrapped his arms around Jessie and buried his face in her hair.

Jared was frozen, a stricken look on his face. He looked at Jessie, and a world of shattered innocence, grief, and self-loathing filled his eyes. Riza came to him and gently took the sword out of his hand.

"Come on, little warrior. Let's get you home," she said as she wrapped an arm around his shoulder and turned him away from his uncle's body.

All around them, the ogres rejoiced with abandon, reuniting with lost loved ones after centuries of living in a stupor. Some ran to each other, arms outstretched. Others sat down on the ground and openly wept. Their joyous roars deafened the witches and fae who watched the celebration nervously.

"We need to get to safety before we get trampled," Ivan joined Jessie and Greta, helping Jessie to her feet.

"We have to get the ogres back to Oberon," Jessie stumbled. She felt like her world was spinning in a sick circle, and her head still ached where Theodore had jerked it around like a toy. Greta and Ivan exchanged glances and then stood on either side of her.

"John, I know this sucks, but I need to ask you to move for a second so we can finish healing her the right way. She can't get back up the hill like this," Greta gently moved the werewolf away from Jessie. She nodded to Ivan, and they closed their eyes, concentrating. While Ivan restored Jessie's equilibrium, Greta found the rest of the stretched and sore tendons.

"Oh, that is so much better. I love having healers at my disposal," Jessie sighed in relief. "Where's Jared? And has anyone seen Rupert? He was shot, and I dropped him."

"Riza is waiting at the portal with Jared so she can take him back. I had to heal you before letting them through into the Library. He's in shock. Come on, he's going to need you," Greta pointed at the path to the portal.

"Mikael and Nicky grabbed Rupert. I'll be along in a minute. I have to get the body of my fallen to take back for the funeral rites," John kissed Jessie gently before reluctantly letting her go.

"I have him," Seanan said sadly from behind them. She carried a wolf Jessie didn't know in a fireman's carry across her shoulders.

"What about the fallen witches?" Jessie asked, looking at Iona on the ground. Annabelle hadn't made it either. She lay not far from Iona, an ugly spear protruding from her back from a redcap who had snuck up behind her. Melissa lay further beyond where an ogre's club had flung her like a rag doll to land in a lifeless tangle of limbs. Jessie felt a pang as she realized that she wouldn't hear the bright-eyed witch's merry laugh ever again.

"We shall carry your comrades for you. You have freed us from our imprisonment and brought us forth into the light. It is the least we can do," Melodium said with a deep bow.

Together, the ogres, remaining witches, and fae formed a

train heading out of the village and back toward the portal where Riza and Jared waited.

"Oh, shit. I forgot to warn them about the Library!" Greta yelled and ran as fast as she could for the head of the column with Jessie right behind her.

"Wait! Don't go through yet," Greta gasped, holding her side. She really hated running.

"Before you do, this leads to our Library. If any who harbor ill will toward us try to pass through, they will be obliterated."

The ogres looked at each other uneasily. Jessie could hear angry muttering from behind Tug and his brothers and saw more than one baleful glare cast in the witches' direction.

"While we are grateful for your assistance in our liberation, I cannot promise that none of my brethren harbor ill will toward you. After all, it was a witch who imprisoned us," Melodium pointed out.

"We can move the portal to Oberon's castle," Jessie suggested.

"Time moves differently here, though," Greta reminded her. "It could take days or weeks."

"If Robin goes through right now and uses the fairy paths to move the portal to Oberon's castle, then perhaps an hour will pass here," Tug said.

"Is that acceptable?" Jessie asked Melodium.

"It will have to be as we must leave our imprisonment behind and step forth into the world that was always meant to be ours," Melodium replied. "I will make my brethren aware of the necessity for this delay."

"Come on, Robin, let's go move a portal," Greta said.

"Wait, I need to take my fallen pack mate back to his mate," John said, gently taking the wolf's body from Seanan.

"I need to go with you," she said.

"Anyone else?" Greta asked with raised eyebrows. "Anyone who's wounded and needs immediate help? Come now because you're going to be stuck here for a little while longer."

"Jared and I are going through. I need to get back to Isabel and let her know what happened, and I think he doesn't need to be here right now," Riza said.

Two elves carried a third on a makeshift stretcher, and Mikael gently handed Rupert, still in crow form, to Greta. Jessie winced when she looked at the arrow protruding from his wing. Matthias and LaSalle joined her with a gore-covered Nicky close behind. It was amazing that such a fastidious vampire could get so disgustingly gross in a fight.

"We'll wait with you and Tug," LaSalle said in no uncertain terms.

"I think we should start calling him Elisian," Jessie realized that with the breaking of the spell, there was no reason to hide Tug's identity anymore.

"Elisian then," LaSalle said, a grin spreading across his beak-nosed face.

The ogres huddled in groups reuniting with each other for the first time in centuries. Melodium went from group to group and offered words of comfort and reassurance while Jessie and the remaining witches stayed off to one side and tried to look as non-threatening as possible. Barely an hour passed before Robin stepped through the portal, beaming from ear to ear.

"My dear ogres, please follow me. Your home awaits," he

said with a grandiose bow as he ushered the ogres through the portal. Most hung back with uncertainty, but Melodium stepped through with a confidence that was hard to resist. Soon the witches, Jessie's companions, and Robin were the only ones left in the clearing.

"What are we going to do with the portal?" Jessie asked as she looked at the disc on the ground. "Is there a way we can destroy this gate without someone having to stay on this world? I know we can destroy the gate on our world, but we don't know for sure if Theo was the only one who could get between the two worlds. Once Jared reopened the portal and Theo escaped, the cabal members could have figured out how to make another portal that linked to this one. It doesn't seem like they would only want one way to a world that offers so many resources."

They all looked soberly at the black disc.

"You're right," Robin admitted. "We need to destroy or bind this gate, but I do not know a way unless someone stays behind."

"We'll do it," Charlotte stepped forward, tugging nervously on a silver curl of hair that had escaped her bun. Jessie looked at the air witch in surprise.

"What do you mean, 'we'll do it'?" she demanded. "You're not getting stuck on this world! We need you in our own world to help fight what's happening!"

"Jessie," Victoria stepped forward by Charlotte's side, her brown eyes shining in determination. "This needs to be destroyed, and we need to make sure the cabal doesn't have another way back here. The resources here are too valuable to let the cabal have unlimited access to this world, and you know it. We'll be fine. When this is all over, send a rescue party."

"You're right, but I don't like it. Riza's going to kill me. I hope you realize that. You won't even be able to come to my funeral," Jessie hugged them both.

"It's okay," Victoria's dimples flashed across her smooth, mocha-colored skin. "We'll just resurrect you so she can kill you again and we can bury you properly."

"You are *horrible* friends," Jessie accused her.

"Guilty as charged," Charlotte laughed. "Come on, Vic. Let's see what we're working with here."

They waved before heading back down the path toward the village. Jessie watched them go with a worried look on her face.

"This world is so much purer than ours that they'll be stronger than any of the cabal idiots in a matter of days," Nicky comforted her. "They'll be fine until you can get them home."

"Please don't hug me. You are so gross," Jessie wrinkled her nose and took a step back.

"Well, come on. We haven't got all day. I'll make sure to send each of you back to your own homes as soon as we reach our world," Robin shooed them impatiently, and Jessie grinned despite herself as she stepped through.

Fae portals were very different from her own. Before she was back on solid ground, she had a glimpse of supernovas and billions of stars, hearths and workshops, forests and ponds. She barely had time to look around before Robin whisked her through another portal into the comfort of her familiar bar. She sagged against the wall regaining her equilibrium; fae portals were not kind to witches.

She felt the tension go out of her shoulders as she took in the fire-cured wood of the walls and bar, the ivy Greta grew in window beds under the cut glass windows on one side of the bar and stained glass windows behind the bar itself, the antique mirror, her friends on their stools. It felt good to be home– right up until she turned around and came face to face with Sharon's tearstained face and accusing eyes.

14

Sharon's arms were wrapped around her torso, her hands clenched into fists. She stood as rigid as a board and looked completely and utterly alone, even with her husband by her side.

"You said you would protect my boy, Jessie. You *promised*! He had to kill a man! His uncle! Do you have any idea what I felt when I looked into my son's eyes and saw what he had to do? What he suffered? How much he's suffering now?"

"Sharon, Theodore was about to kill me. He had me pinned down. I didn't know Jared was about to kill him, or I would have stopped him. I never wanted Jared to go through that, especially with his uncle," Jessie tried to explain.

"I will *never* forgive this, Jessica. I will never forgive you, the Council, all of you can go to hell! Everything my family has gone through since Theodore, all of the hiding, the accusations, being shunned, I worked so hard to protect Jared from it, and you were supposed to keep him safe. You were supposed to make sure that he was protected too!"

"Honey, stop," Fred moved between his wife and Jessie. "You know damn well that Jared was going to get in trouble one day because he could never leave something alone until he figured out how it worked. Jessie didn't make that portal and send him through it. She didn't make him find Theo again. She tried to protect him from ever having to go through what you did, and this is not her fault. I know you don't want to hear this right now, but sweetheart, it's only one person's fault, and that's Jared's. He's her apprentice, not her ward."

"That's right, Mom. I'm sorry. I know you're mad, but I did this to myself. Jessie didn't do it," Jessie turned to see Jared standing behind them, still wearing the blood-stained armor. He began pulling pieces of it off as he walked toward them. Caroline came to his side and helped pull it over his head.

"I know you're yelling at Jessie because you want to be mad at someone, but you need to be mad at me. Not her," he continued moving forward until he was in front of his mother. Sharon flung herself into her son's arms and held him, sobbing as if her heart were breaking. Which, Jessie reminded herself, it probably was.

"What's going on?" Greta whispered from behind them as she came through the portal and stopped, confused. Jessie glanced over her shoulder at her best friend. Mikael and Nicky had joined them and were considerably cleaner.

"Where's Rupert?" Jessie frowned.

"With Madame Blanche. There's a healer in France who specializes in cryptids like him who's fixing his wing. He can't turn again until it's healed, and he's a lot more vulnerable as a bird than a cat. Wait, why's Sharon– oh," Greta finally put two and two together.

"Yeah."

They stood awkwardly, uncertain of anything they could

say or do to make things better. Riza finally stepped forward and cleared her throat.

"Jared fought with honor. No one in the Council believes that he had anything to do with his uncle's reappearance."

Sharon whirled on the other witch, teeth bared in a snarl.

"He should *never* have been in the position to defend his family's honor, and if your precious *fucking council* hadn't made it their personal mission to destroy the lives of innocents, then he wouldn't have had to do what he did."

"Mom, yes, I would. No one else could reach him in time. He was getting ready to kill Jessie. He had hurt her really badly, and he had her on the ground. He pinned her. She couldn't defend herself, and no one else was going to get to her in time. They all tried, Mom. Everyone tried, but I was the only one close enough. I didn't do it because I needed to defend our honor. You would have done the exact same thing that I did if you had been in my position. She's my teacher, and she's my friend, and she's your friend too. You taught me better than to stand by and let someone suffer if they can't defend themselves. You didn't see what Theo did to her. It took Greta and Ivan both to heal her. You didn't see what kind of shape she was in, so you need to back off of her. Please. For me."

"Theo had years of exile on that world to get stronger than any of us realized," Riza said. "That world has no pollution, so the elemental ties and resources are much stronger than they are here. He may have been a shitty second-rate magician on our world, but he was able to take Jessie down fighting. You know how hard that is to do. I know you don't want to hear this, but your son did what no one else could do, and he saved Jessie's life."

Jessie bristled at the implication that she was too weak to defend herself, but she held her tongue. Theo *had* been much stronger, and she would have died if Jared hadn't saved her. The thought made the guilt curdling in the pit of her stomach tighten into a knot.

"Come on, let's all go home and talk about it and just take a step back," Fred said, wrapping his arms around his wife and son in a comforting embrace and gently guiding them to the door.

"Yeah, okay. I want to get away from the stench of this place anyway," Sharon's voice was ice cold. Jessie flinched but held the other woman's angry gaze before Sharon broke eye contact and stormed out the door. Jared hesitated, looking back at Jessie.

"It's okay. She needs you right now, and you need a break from everything for at least a night, if not more," Jessie faked a smile.

"Okay, I'm sorry I got you in trouble," he winced.

"Doofus, stop apologizing! Thank you for saving my life. That would have sucked," her smile was more genuine this time. "Oh, before you go, I need to ask you something."

"What's up?" he asked as she followed him and Fred out the door.

"I need to know more about Caroline's brother. He helped you make that thing, and we almost lost each other because of it. This is getting very serious, especially now that we know the fae are involved with the cabal," she lowered her voice, ignoring Fred's gasp of surprise.

"I'm sorry, but I don't know much," Jared gave her an apologetic grin and a shrug. "He lives in a kind of bad part of Atlanta, somewhere close to the western part of I-20. He has this weird human friend who's always around, but that's about all I know. He's really good with his hands, with mechanics and stuff. He checks in on Care sometimes, and that's how I got to know him. I think she's been wanting to tell you for a while now."

"Okay, go home and get some rest," she hugged him again, trying to ignore the fact that Sharon was trying to set her on fire with a death glare through the car's windshield. She was very glad Sharon's element was water.

Then again, water witches could do some pretty nasty stuff to a person's body. She quickened her pace and felt much better once the door shut behind her.

"I have to head back and fill Isabel in on everything that happened. Are *you* okay?" Riza fixed Jessie with a piercing stare while giving Greta a farewell hug.

"I'll be fine. What are you going to tell her about Jared?" Jessie couldn't keep the worried note out of her voice.

"Exactly what I just told Sharon," Riza said with a quick, reassuring smile. "We have to log his undocumented use of the portal since he's still an apprentice, but that doesn't mean it has to be associated with his uncle. He's a good kid. They're a good family. They should never have suffered that much because of that fucking prick."

"This really, really sucks. It's hard enough being Black in this world, especially at the time of the first uprising. Add family stigma to it, and I don't blame Sharon for being upset," Jessie sighed.

"Me either," Riza agreed.

"Maybe Isabel can help explain some of what happened to him on the ogre's world, like how he was able to work with the air to save the ogres so easily. I bet it had to do with air being his element and that an earth witch tried to force the air to do his bidding," Greta added.

"I think so too," Jessie nodded.

"Come on, you can use the Library to get back," Greta waved Riza down the hall.

"*Wait for me in the Library,*" Jessie sent the thought to her friend, who glanced over her shoulder with a little nod.

Jessie watched them go before turning back to the bar where Caroline, Cassie, Charlie, and Mary Jo watched her with some trepidation, Caroline more than the others. Jessie crossed her arms and looked at her apprentice in silence. Caroline held the gaze for a minute before she looked down at the bar.

"What's going on?" Cassie, who missed nothing, looked from one to the other.

"Caroline, we need to talk," Jessie said in the gentlest voice she could muster. "Nicky, you're on the bar."

"Alright, now we're talking!" Nicky bounced excitedly behind the bar and did a three-hundred-sixty-degree turn of his new domain. Jessie and Caroline looked at each other and sighed.

"This one's on you," Caroline reminded Jessie as they walked toward the Library together, where Greta waited. Jessie had already decided that Greta was sitting in on this talk.

"Yeah, don't remind me. Let's just hope there's any liquor left when we get back," Jessie pushed open the knothole, ushering Caroline through the portal, and nodding toward the sofa for her apprentice to take a seat.

This time Lemur was the one who decided to be cuddly while Ace flopped on his back for tummy rubs within Caroline's reach. With Lucy in her lap, Greta curled up in her favorite chair. Jessie sat in the other chair flanking the massive stone fireplace and scooped up Aleister.

"I'm not going to beat around the bush on this, Caroline," Jessie began.

"You need to know about my brother. Christopher," Caroline looked up from the cats, her voice surprisingly calm despite the bright red spots on her cheeks.

"Um, yes," Jessie and Greta exchanged a startled glance.

"Yeah, I figured this was coming sooner rather than later after he helped Jared with the damn portal. Just so we're clear, I don't blame Jared. Chris just can't expect me to keep his existence a secret and then pal around with my friends on secret projects that are going to blow up in everyone's faces," her voice sounded angrier as she spoke. Lemur jumped out of her lap with a protesting squawk as she stroked him harder.

"I'm sorry, that was uncalled for. I'll do better, okay?" she coaxed the gray tabby back into her lap. He sniffed before finally giving in.

"I have so many questions," Greta murmured, shifting in her chair. Lucy stretched, yawned, and went back to sleep unperturbed.

"Oh, yeah. Me too," Jessie took up Greta's practice of pacing in front of the fire, much to the extreme disgust of the cats.

Spot stole the warm spot on Jessie's chair before Aleister

could get to it. Sunny chose to ignore Caroline and come out of hiding in light of the more pressing and vital problem of the cats hadn't eaten dinner yet. After tripping over him for the fourth time, Jessie gave in and pulled out their food bowls. All of the cats came running; Greta yelped as Lucy used her lap as a launch pad.

"How are we just now hearing about him?" Jessie demanded, looking up from the cans of cat food and trying not to fall as Sunny, Spot, and Ace wound around her ankles. "You know that any young witch is in danger if they don't have a teacher. I'm assuming he's young, right?"

"You could say that. He's my twin," Caroline met her teacher's eyes with a defiant lift of her chin, ignoring Greta's gasp.

Twins were a once-a-century phenomenon among witches. Like many twins throughout mythology, witch twins were dualistic by nature. They were polar opposites in strengths, elemental magic, and even aspects of their appearance. Their magic was also far stronger, which explained why Caroline's magic was so powerful at such a young age. When she was fully grown and trained, very few would be able to stand up to her, and if the cabal got their hands on her or Christopher... Jessie didn't want to think about what the cabal would do to them.

There were rumors that Gertrud, the *völva* whose daughter had orchestrated the attack on Jessie's bar and who was one of the most powerful witches to ever live, had a twin. Gertrud was only a few hundred years older than Jessie and Greta, but her powers were vast in comparison to theirs. If it were true, Jessie had never seen any proof during the brief time she studied the arts of Seidr under Gertrud's tutelage before the first cabal's uprising.

"He was bullied a lot when we were younger, and he didn't do as well as I did in school," Caroline continued with a brief smile at the cats. "He's really smart, but he struggled with learning in a classroom. I think he probably has some kind of learning disability. So that combined with the bullies… he finally dropped out. He's always been a loner. He still doesn't have many friends now. He hangs around the hedge and hood witches in Atlanta, but I've never been to his place. I don't even know if he has one. I try to give him money and stuff when I see him, but he's too proud to take it. He's afraid that people will say he's not good enough and his sister has to bail him out."

Jessie looked at Caroline and waited, sensing there was more.

"It's not his fault that he's like this," a defensive note crept into Caroline's voice. "He's my twin. He's my opposite. Where I'm blonde and always looked tan and, well, normal, his skin is so white that it looks like paper, and he's so skinny, and his hair and eyes are black, like coal. He scares people. I tried to get him to talk to you. I told him you wouldn't care, but he sees the people who come here, and he thinks he would scare them into leaving, and then you wouldn't want him around here anymore."

"Well, that's bullshit. You know I would never kick a witch who needs help to the curb," Jessie snorted in indignation.

"Yes, Jessie, I know. But he doesn't," Caroline sighed. "And I can't convince him otherwise."

Jessie and Greta exchanged another glance.

"If your element is water, then I'm guessing his is fire?" Greta asked from her chair where she crisscrossed her legs.

"Yeah."

"There's your in, Jess," Greta shrugged at her best friend. "We can reach out to Emma. I think she's still running things out there."

Just west of the downtown area was a cluster of warehouses and shipyards along the I-20 corridor that was the source of business for several hedge witches. Jessie and Greta treated the hedge witches and the often accompanying hood and hearth witches with a great deal of respect. Plus, their weekend Night Markets were always a source of entertainment and rare finds. Their hedge witch friend Emma was the de-facto representative for the group, often speaking on their behalf when they had to reluctantly emerge from seclusion to deal with the outside world.

"She is," Jessie said. "I'll call her when we finish up here."

"She can't go with us," Greta nodded at Caroline, who started to protest.

"No, she's right," Jessie cut Caroline off. "You look too wholesome. No one would give us the time of day, and if they found out that he's responsible for you being there, then it could be bad for him. Does he have any friends you know about? What about the human kid Jared mentioned?"

"Zach," Caroline said, wrinkling her nose in distaste. "He's some really rich human who's obsessed with witches and the fae. He's a dick. I think he threatened Chris somehow, but Chris won't admit it. Ever since they started hanging out, Chris stopped doing magic, or at least he stopped when he knows Zach is watching. And Zach *always* watches. He wouldn't come in the bar the one time Chris brought him here, though."

"Chris brought him to the bar?" Greta leaned forward.

"Yeah. Chris meets me here sometimes when he wants to check in with me. He doesn't want to go to my apartment. He said he's afraid he might attract bad elements to it, but he knows that nothing will try to fuck with you."

Greta and Jessie exchanged a long, speculative look.

"Okay, I'll call Emma and reestablish our invitation," Jessie dug her phone out of her pocket. "Caroline, do not, under any circumstances, let Chris know I know about him or that we want to try to go to the Night Market. If he gets spooked and runs, there's no telling what will happen to him. And if *you* don't like his friend, then it's a good bet the guy's not someone nice."

"True. Okay, you win," Caroline reluctantly admitted defeat as she stood up and let Lemur take the warm spot on the sofa. The cats had inhaled their food and were ready for naps. Caroline stepped through the portal to the office while Greta held it open.

"I'll be up in a second," Jessie said. "Please get Nicky off the bar as soon as possible."

"Yeah, what were you thinking?" Caroline grinned.

"It was him or Mikael. Would you rather have the fun vampire or the one who judges everyone's drink choices?"

"Good point," Caroline was already out the door. Greta hung back, watching Jessie anxiously while she pulled up Emma's number.

"Hey, Emma, it's Jessie," Jessie tried to hide her nervousness.

"Hey! I know, silly. There's this thing called Caller ID.

What's up?" Emma's perky voice came through the other end. Was it Jessie's imagination, or did Emma sound a little *too* perky?

For someone who was barely four foot eleven, Emma's personality filled up the world. She moved through it with all the ferocity of a lioness, and she had a voice to match. Jessie didn't need to put the call on speakerphone. Greta could hear everything.

"Greta and I need to come to the Night Market. I know you said our invitation was open-ended, but I wanted to let you know before we just show up."

There was a long pause. As former representatives of the Council, even though Jessie was retired, Jessie and Greta were not exactly welcomed with open arms by certain tribes within the witch world.

Hedge witches flew solo, and each one had their own code of ethics. They did not answer to any power or ruling body, and they frequently gave refuge to those in trouble with the Council. Jessie and Greta had earned Emma's gratitude by helping her husband, a hearth witch named Frank who owned and ran a five-star restaurant in Midtown. They proved his innocence when he was framed for poisoning a delegate to the Council, and that gave them a little more respectability in the eyes of the hedges. It wasn't always enough.

Hedge witches worked side-by-side with the hood witches, Black women known for their work with crystals and healing and who maintained peace in their communities. And Sharon was a hood witch.

"Um... yeah. I see," Emma's voice climbed an octave. Jessie

could picture her in her warm, cheery kitchen, looking wildly around for any way out.

Emma was plump, her pleasant face and merry blue eyes framed with short, ash-gray ringlets. She looked like someone's favorite aunt, which made her foul mouth, shrewd business mind, and love of pipe smoking all the more delightfully anachronistic. Jessie took a deep breath and decided to just go for it.

"Look, I'm not trying to put you on the spot. Just hear me out. We're looking for someone. It's personal, not Council business. You know, Jared? Sharon's kid and my apprentice? Well, the witch we're looking for helped him build a portal to another world behind our backs. It turns out his twin sister is my other apprentice. He's in danger, Emma. The witches, oh, and the fae, who were involved in the original cabal, will know that he's out there soon if they don't already. Someone's going to come looking for him, and they're not going to care who gets in their way."

Jessie heard a faint thud on the other end and guessed that Emma had fallen into a chair.

"Jesus fuck, Jess. You don't dick around anymore, do you? Look, I want to help you. I still owe you for helping Frank. Hell, I'll always owe you for that. But Sharon's already reached out to me. She's really upset that Jared was the one who had to kill his uncle like that. This is her safe space, you know? I don't think you should come around. Did that really happen?"

"Yeah, and I'll tell you everything later, but it was really bad, and it was really hard, and I just don't want to talk about it right now," Jessie rubbed her face and tried not to think about Jared's sword coming through Theo's chest and the shattered look in her apprentice's eyes. She wasn't surprised that Emma already knew what happened.

"Okay, you don't have to talk about it. I'm sorry, honey. I wasn't trying to put you on the spot either. But yeah, I don't think I can let you in the Market right now. Like, Sharon knows that it wasn't really your fault. She's just hurting. The other hood witches want to get her to a safe mental place where she can accept what happened and heal. I think she just needs space. You know I have to make her a priority for that."

"Yeah, I kind of figured that was the case. Can you help us at all? We'll sneak in, or maybe you can bring him to us if we wait outside."

"Who is this witch?"

"His name is Christopher?" Jessie looked at Greta, trying to remember what Caroline had said. Greta nodded. "Yeah, Christopher. He hangs out with some witch groupie named Zach."

"Ugh. Yeah. I know them. Chris is a sweet kid. He really is. Zach though... We had to ban him from the Market. Chris hasn't been back since."

"What do you know about either of them that you can tell me?"

Jessie had to be very careful here. Once a hedge witch decided that a topic was off the table, no power on earth or in the universe could get her to open up again. Jessie bordered dangerously on asking Emma to be a snitch, and they both knew it. Emma sighed, answering slowly after a weighted pause.

"I'm only telling you this because you teach Chris' sister, and something weird is going on with him. Like I said, Chris is a really sweet kid. He's loaded with street smarts, but from what I understand, he didn't do so well in school."

"Yeah, his sister said the same thing. She thinks that it was because other kids bullied and shunned him, not that he lacked intelligence."

"He's neurodivergent too," Emma said. "I did a stint as a therapist way back before we could be in the open, and I know all the signs. He's ADHD and dyslexic. I would bet my garden on it."

That was saying something. Their garden was a hedge witch's gold mine and lifeline.

"Okay, so we have a kid who doesn't look like he fits in," Jessie began.

"Only because he does it to himself," Emma interrupted. "If he had more self-confidence, he could do a lot with his appearance."

"Right, but he still lacks confidence. He struggled in school, and I'm guessing he can't keep a job. Where does Zach come in?"

"Chris hasn't been the same since Zach showed up in his life. Zach is some rich brat who came out of nowhere as far as I can tell. Chris wouldn't talk about how they met," Emma snorted in disgust. "Zach's obsessed with the fae and witches, and he's somehow convinced that he can 'learn' magic. He follows Christopher everywhere, trying to talk Chris into doing magic for him."

"Does Chris do it?" Jessie cut in.

"He said that Zach saw him do magic once, and Zach's reaction scared him. Apparently, this kid started talking about harnessing magic. Chris made excuses not to do magic in front of Zach ever since. Zach keeps trying to give Chris food and clothes, but Chris won't take any of it. I think he's afraid that it's a trap."

"Yeah, are Zach's actions motivated by altruism or is he trying to make Chris owe a favor somewhere down the line?" Greta asked. Jessie relayed the question.

"I don't know, babe. Your guess is as good as mine, but I'm pretty sure we're thinking the same thing. To be completely honest with you, I don't trust him one bit."

"We need to figure out how to get Chris away from Zach. Caroline said Zach wouldn't step foot in my bar when Chris came by to see her. I wonder why."

Emma's laugh, one of the best laughs in the whole world, came from her gut, rolled out of the phone, and filled the Library.

"Seriously? Babe. Jessie," Emma tried to get out around giggles. "You're the oldest witch around, and you told the council to fuck off and probably some other things worse than that and walked away to open *a bar*. You're the most talented and powerful witch on this continent, and you opened *a bar*. If that doesn't scream total badass, I don't know what does. Witches like Chris admire the hell out of you. They look up to you. I don't know why he hasn't come to you for help yet. He's been trying to get up the nerve for a while, but he begged me to stay out of it and let him do it in his own time, or I would have had your ass down here years ago when he first showed up. But he has to try to do it, or he will always feel like a failure who gets bailed out. But Zach, he knows who you are too. He knows that if he gives you even the slightest reason to suspect that he has bad intentions, if he so much as looks at you the wrong way, then no one will even remember he existed."

"I am not that bad!" Jessie protested while Greta snickered. "Greta's the bloodthirsty one!"

"Yes, but she still sort of works for the Council. You don't. You made your own way. Sorry, Greta, I know you can hear my loud ass, but it's true. No one thinks Greta's weaker. They're just more impressed that you left completely. You left it all behind because of your principles."

"Yeah, well, maybe I should have stuck around. Maybe what happened with Jared and the portal and Theo and Sharon wouldn't have happened."

"And maybe pigs will fly. If you hadn't been there to be Jared's teacher, he would have stumbled on that portal sooner, and you would have a bigger mess on your hands."

"Not quite," Jessie sobered. "The portal was in the Council vault this whole time along with everything else that was confiscated when the cabal was razed."

"Wait, what? What are you saying?" Emma stopped laughing.

"Someone set Jared up," Jessie told her. "Someone in the Council took the portal out of the vault and hid it in Sharon's and Fred's garage. I don't even know if they meant for Jared to find it. I mean, he moved into his own apartment a few years ago. They could have been setting up Sharon and Fred."

Emma was quiet for a moment. Jessie could almost hear the wheels turn and silently prayed to the Goddess that Emma would decide to help them instead of closing ranks and shutting down the Night Market. She wouldn't blame Emma for the latter. The witching underworld was the first to feel the Council's heavy hand when the cabal formed hundreds of years ago.

"Okay, I'll bring him to you," Emma said with a note of finality. "But Frank and the dogs are coming too."

"That's fine," Jessie grinned. "The dogs are more than welcome. You know that."

"Well, they're assholes. Cute assholes, but assholes nonetheless. Let's see how much they bark at everyone and then you tell me if they're welcome."

"Whatever. You know we love them. Thanks, Emma. When do you think you can bring him?" Jessie didn't bother to say she owed Emma one. Emma would just get insulted at the idea. She decided that Jessie owed her nothing until she was good and ready to feel that she and Frank had repaid Jessie and Greta for their help.

"The earliest we can get there is tomorrow night. Frank's got an event at the restaurant he can't miss. I'll try to leave Zach at home, but I can't make any promises," Emma sighed in disgust.

"No, bring him if you can. I want to take a look at him myself," Jessie decided, meeting Greta's eyes. Greta nodded fervently.

"Okay, I mean, if that's what you want," Emma sounded downright disgusted at the idea of being stuck in a car with this guy for almost an hour. There was no way she was going to bring him into her Library and through her portal though.

"Yes," Jessie was firm. "Thanks, Emma. We'll see you soon."

"Okay, and stock up on rum. I'm going to need it if I have to deal with Zach all night."

"You got it," Jessie laughed before hanging up and looking

at Greta. "Well, I guess we're going to have company. We also need to figure out how to get back to the ogre world too. We can't leave Charlotte and Victoria alone there forever."

"We need to check on the ogres too and make sure they're settled in," Greta reminded her. "Don't forget to add that to our to-do list."

"Yeah, I'll see if Robin can get Jared involved in that. It might make him feel better about the whole killing-his-uncle-to-save-his-teacher thing," Jessie grimaced.

"Hey, I have a question. Remember when you told me about that crone who showed up when you talked to Jared, Caroline, and Cassie after we rescued Charlie? Did you ever go after her?"

"No, not yet. I have it narrowed down to two possibilities. Trust me, you'll be the first to know when that happens because you're going with me. I just wish we knew how many people were involved and how bad this whole new cabal could be."

"Remember when a crazy night meant you had to throw some drunk guy out of the bar? I miss those days," Greta gave a spectacularly despondent sigh. Jessie rolled her eyes.

"Come on, winner of the most dramatic witch of the year. Let's go tell Caroline what's going on."

"Do I get a trophy?" Greta asked, following Jessie out of the room.

"No."

15

Jessie tossed her keys on the bar, squinting in the early-afternoon autumn sunlight streaming through the stained glass windows. Her head felt like it was full of sand. She had tossed and turned more than she had actually slept.

She gave a gaping yawn and paused, looking around. It looked like Annie had already come to clean the bar like she did several times a week. Being friends with a brownie cleaning service had its perks, but Jessie felt uneasy. If Annie had come by, then that meant Mara hadn't started the funeral rites for Dain.

The fae were meant to be immortal. Losing one of their own was exceedingly rare, and it was devastating. Now they had lost two in a month between Brigitte and Dain, and, despite herself, Jessie had to admit some of Oberon's finger-pointing at the witches was justified.

To not begin the rites went against the natural order of the fae's world and only happened in extenuating circumstances, like war. But if the fae had declared war, then Annie would be at the Hill, helping her liege plan for battle– not cleaning up a bar. So why were they going about their everyday lives instead of preparing Dain for his journey to Fiddler's Green? Jessie mentally added checking on Mara and her Court to the day's already exhausting to-do list.

Despite Greta's and Ivan's healing, Jessie still felt sore and exhausted from the night before. She hadn't been able to get the image of Jared's stricken face as Theodore's body slid down Jared's sword out of her mind either. It bothered her much more than she wanted to admit– that he had been put in the position where he had to make that impossible decision and that she had been unable to defend herself.

Plus, while the battle had raged for hours, only a few minutes had passed in their world. It was disconcerting, like living two nights in one. She wondered how Jared had managed it every night for months before concluding that he probably took naps on the ogres' world where time moved more slowly.

"That's what I would do," she muttered to herself, moving deeper into the bar.

"What's what you would do?" Charlie popped out from behind the bar, making her shriek.

"Damn it, Charlie, you almost gave me a heart attack! No offense."

"None taken," he drifted through the bar and sort of perched on top of a stool. The bar staff and patrons tried to respect Charlie's change in life status, but there were a lot of idioms that revolved around death and dying. It was a hard habit to break.

"Hey, did Annie say anything when she came by earlier?" Jessie asked.

"Yeah, she wanted to know when you would be in. Said she needed to talk to you about Mara. Is everything okay?"

"No. The fae should have started the mourning rites for Dain by now. We shouldn't have seen Annie for another three days. I'm worried about them."

"Well, I told Annie you'd give her a call when you get here," Charlie absently rubbed at the neat, short beard on his chin. Not that he actually felt the hair anymore, but, even in death, old habits were hard to break.

"I will in a second. There's something I need to take care of first," Jessie said.

She walked behind the bar, grabbed his spirit mug, and poured him a beer. It was a neat little piece of spellwork. While his spirit was anchored in her bar by virtue of being a ghost, he existed in a fuller form on the spiritual plane. Her mug transported whatever he wanted to that plane where he could enjoy it. That was usually beer. She had done something similar for the spirits in the garden as a thank you for their help when she and Greta had to traverse the spirit plane with the help of their shaman friend Caliste to save Charlie's soul.

"Thanks," he said with some surprise. Usually, she waited until the bar was at least open. He took a hearty swig before he paused, eyeing her suspiciously as he turned a faint shade of burnt ochre.

Learning that he could change colors to match emotions was just the tip of the iceberg when Charlie and Jessie discovered that ghosts have powers of their own. He was considerably less pleased when Jared brought in the biggest box of Crayola crayons he could find and started playing "match the color to the emotion." Most of Charlie's colors stayed red and salmon pink that day– his go-to when he was annoyed and pissed off.

"Jessica," he frowned. "What do you want?"

"Why would you think I want something?" Jessie was all big blue eyes and innocence and sweetness.

"Because you do. Out with it."

"Okay," she gave in. "I need information."

"Will you finally get the NFL Sunday Ticket?"

"Fine! Even though it's going to cost me an arm and a leg, and the Falcons are probably going to–"

"Don't you dare say it, young lady!" Charlie warned her before taking another swig from the mug. She grinned.

"How much do you know about Caroline's brother?" she asked carefully.

Charlie became very engrossed in his mug, which told her everything she needed to know. She gave an exasperated huff.

"Right, well, since all of you decided that hiding secrets from me was more important than keeping you, me, this bar, our friends, and the world safe, I'm now left with a huge mess since this kid is the one who helped Jared reconstruct the portal. Now we have two stranded witches, we're blackballed from the Night Market and all of the information and resources it can give us, and we have an even bigger target on our backs."

"It wasn't my secret to tell," Charlie protested.

"I'm really tired of those words," Jessie snapped. "This isn't a game or a joke or elementary school recess where all of you can stand around whispering behind your hands. Your decisions to keep information from me are literally costing lives and putting all of us in extreme danger. I'm sadly not surprised that the kids are doing it, but I expected better from you, Charlie."

Charlie flushed an ugly pink. Jessie was right, and he knew it. That didn't mean he had to like it.

"I'm sorry, Jess. You're right. I don't know a whole lot, honest. He seems like this really sweet kid who's a genius at figuring out how mechanical stuff works. He loves working with clockwork mechanisms and gears and figuring out how to take something apart and put it back together. If the whole witching thing doesn't work out for him, he could become a master clock or toymaker as long as he stays away from the electrical stuff. He just looks like he's a little down on his luck, you know? I know Caroline wants him to come to talk to you about maybe working here if he can ever get rid of that Zach kid. I hope he does. Zach gave me the creeps, and that's impressive for a ghost."

"I thought Zach didn't come into the bar."

"He didn't," Charlie took another drink. "I watched him through the window. That was close enough for me, thanks. He sat there in the parking lot leaning on some fancy car and smirking with his nose in the air like he was too good for this place. But I tell you something, he has his eye on Christopher for a reason. He looked at Chris the whole time like Chris was some kind of trophy for the taking. Whatever he's got planned, it ain't good."

"Yeah, from what everyone's saying, I'm going to have to deal with that kid soon. Just add that to the list along with everything else," Jessie sighed.

"Any word on Rupert yet?" Charlie turned pale yellow, matching his concern.

"No, not yet. Madame Blanche has him with a healer who specializes in cryptids, especially ones like him who are more spirit based and have difficulty becoming humanoid."

"Poor little guy," Charlie shook his head. Never mind that Rupert was roughly the size of a wolfhound or sometimes a small pony in his feline form.

"Don't worry, he'll be fine," Jessie used her most reassuring voice, stopping herself just in time from patting him on the shoulder.

Physical contact with a ghost was very uncomfortable for everyone involved. It was sort of like getting stuck in a slightly musty, foggy swamp, and Jessie really did not want to go through that again. Neither did Charlie. Only Mary Jo's ties to the demon world as a succubus allowed her to achieve a slightly incorporeal form that let her and Charlie... Jessie didn't want to think about what they got up to when she wasn't around. Or where, for that matter.

"Want to call Madame Blanche with me?" Jessie pulled out her phone, thankful for the millionth time that Cassie was on her payroll and made a device Jessie could actually use.

"Sure," Charlie brightened.

Jessie smiled as the phone rang. It was fleeting, but Charlie was glad to see it.

"*Bonjour, mon amie*," Madame Blanche's cultured, Parisian voice sang through the speaker. It was easy to picture the tall, ethereally beautiful, and extremely pale woman on the other end.

In life, she had been Charlotte de Valois, the illegitimate daughter of Charles VII who was killed by her jealous husband in the late fifteenth century. She was considered the first of the *Dames Blanche* or White Women in France– an honor that gave her the status she needed to become the cryptid emissary for the Fae, Cryptid, Witch, and Human Alliance.

It also made her a target for the cabal as Jessie and her friends discovered when Madame Blanche was kidnapped a few weeks before and held prisoner. She had saved Charlie's afterlife by linking herself to the spirit trap that held his soul and feeding her essence into it until Jessie could rescue them both.

"Hello, it's Jessie and Charlie here. We wanted to check on both of you. We're worried about Rupert. Is he going to be okay?"

"We are, how do you say it, playing the waiting game. The compound on the arrow that penetrated his wing..." her voice trailed off.

Jessie and Charlie exchanged an uneasy glance. A Matagot's coat was almost impenetrable. Almost. Matagot pelts were priceless on the supernatural black market, and the original cabal had gotten their hands on something that could actually kill a Matagot and almost drove the species to the point of extinction.

"Well, it's a pretty good bet that we're dealing with some members of the original cabal. It makes sense that they would know what was used to kill Matagots to begin with," Jessie said, thinking about the crone and Theo.

"*Oui*, and I wish I could share that information with you. This compound is the only known substance that can penetrate a Matagot's protective coat. I believe it would help if you could track down the elements of this vile poison and find the agents of its creation. But Rupert needs to give his permission as his life and the lives of his family are on the line if that information becomes known."

"It's already known. Someone almost killed him because they had that information," Charlie pointed out. "For all we know, this group is hunting his friends and family even as we speak."

Jessie's eyes widened. That had not occurred to her. From the startled oath on the other end of the line, it apparently hadn't occurred to Madame Blanche either.

"Okay, we need to get someone on that right now. Madame Blanche, start tracking down the remaining Matagot. See if you can get a census for anyone left. I'll bring it up to Isabel too. We need to be on top of it. And I don't care what Rupert says, we need to know what's in that compound."

"It shall be done. I wish I had not destroyed the arrow, but I did so thinking it was in his best interest."

"Yeah, I don't blame you. I probably would have done the same," Jessie admitted.

"Farewell, my friends. I will give Rupert your warm wishes for his continued recovery and share our conversation with him."

Charlie and Jessie stared at each other as the line went dead.

"Well, that just made me feel a lot worse about everything going on," Charlie said.

"Same here. I feel so stupid. I should have thought about Rupert's clan."

"You're not a hunter. I am. Or I was, anyway. Don't beat yourself up about it. Let's just do what you said and make sure everyone is safe," Charlie comforted her.

They both turned toward the sound of the door opening. Jessie's shoulders tensed as Jared slowly walked into the bar.

"Hey," he gave her a small wave. His usual charming smile and bounce were gone, and Jessie could see the weight of what he had been forced to see and do like a bruise behind his eyes. His shirt was wrinkled as if he had slept in it– a far cry from his painstaking efforts to look trendy and put together. Her heart wrenched in her chest.

"Hey, honey," she crossed the room and grabbed him in a fierce hug. "You don't have to be here today. You can have some more time if you need it."

"No, I want to be here," he hugged her back.

He reluctantly let go and looked around the bar, eyes finally settling on Tug's usual spot at the door. If it was possible, his face fell even more.

"My mom just wants to baby me and yell about the Witch Council. At least she doesn't blame you anymore. I keep thinking that if I hadn't built that portal then Dain would still be alive and none of this would have happened. And now I don't even have the ogres to help. Every time I try to sleep, I see... I just don't want to be at home."

"If you hadn't built that portal then the ogres would still be prisoners forced to fight for the cabal," Jessie reminded him. He paused, considering.

"Yeah, that's true. I didn't think about that."

"Well, if you need something to do, you can clean out the dry storage and the walk-in," Jessie suggested with a gentle nudge toward the back of the bar. She recognized the signs of a lost soul in need of direction.

"Yeah, okay, I guess," he wandered into the storage room behind the bar.

"Poor kid," Charlie murmured with another sip of beer.

"I know. Greta and I talked last night about getting Jared involved in the ogres' transition from that world to their rightful place. I wonder if Robin can help," Jessie mused, pulling out her phone and dialing. "Hey, LaSalle. Can you get in touch with Robin for me? I need to ask him a favor— okay, never mind."

She hung up as Robin and Annie dusted themselves off, Annie scowling, her little face like a thundercloud. Robin's normally impeccable bright red and green waistcoat and trousers and Annie's neat little blue and white checkered dress were filthy. The two fae were covered in grime and cobwebs.

"Did you have to drag us through all that mess just to get us here?" Annie snapped with her little fists on her hips.

"It's the fastest way from the ogre district! It's not my fault that the tunnel fell into such a bad state of disrepair," Robin protested before turning to Jessie with a sigh. "I remember the days when I was someone who was respected and feared."

Jessie snorted.

"Yeah, that doesn't last long around here. I'm glad you came, though. I need to ask for your help with something. We need to know if there's any way you can track down the compound used to wound Rupert. We believe the rest of the Matagot might be in danger."

"I certainly can look into it," the Puck nodded. "Our court healer keeps excellent records of all poisons, potions, healing aids, and elixirs. Give me a day. What is being done to find his family?"

"Madame Blanche is reaching out to do a census, and I plan to discuss it with Isabel as soon as I can. But why are you here? Not that I don't want to see you, I just thought you would be busy between the ogres and the funeral rites."

"We need your help on both counts," Robin's gesture included Annie. "I hoped you perhaps knew Jared's whereabouts. I believe that his assistance would be invaluable with the ogres right now. Oberon's magic did much to restore their home, but they seem... lost and uncertain. He is a familiar friend to many of them. Do you think he would help?"

"Ironically, I was going to ask you the same thing. He seems a little lost himself," Jessie said with a little laugh before calling for her apprentice. "Hey, Jared, can you come here for a sec?"

He poked his head out of the storage room.

"What's up? Oh, hey, Robin. Hi, Annie."

"Jared, my friend! I am so relieved to see you. If it's not too much of a bother, the ogres wish to see you. It seems they need guidance from one they trust and look to as a friend. Will you come?" Robin anxiously clasped his hands together.

"Really? They need me? Sure, man, let me grab my things! I mean, unless you want me to finish up here, Jess," Jared's face showed a faint glimmer of his old self. There was no way Jessie was going to tell him no.

"Go ahead, I'll take care of things here," she smiled.

"Thank you!" He grabbed his book bag and almost ran to Robin's side.

The two of them popped out of sight, leaving a cloud of

dust behind. Annie watched a single cobweb drift through the air in resignation as Jessie turned to the brownie.

"Did you need something too, Annie? I mean, of course, you're always welcome here. Do you want some tea?"

"No, it's kind of you to offer though. I need you to come to see Mara. Please, Jessie. In the name of our friendship, please come!" Annie grabbed Jessie's hands.

"Of course, I will! I planned to check on her today anyway. What's wrong? What do you need me to do?"

"She's going into deep mourning," Annie said, opening a portal to the cathedral's parking lot and urgently dragging Jessie toward it. "If we can't get her to snap out of it, the Hill will go into mourning with her, and she and her subjects will be defenseless. We got as many of the vulnerable ones to Oberon's kingdom as we could, but there are so many we haven't been able to reach."

"Okay, but let's go through the Library so I can get my portal ring."

"I'm sorry to hear that," Charlie shook his head. "Annie, tell Mara that Mary Jo and I are thinking about her, you hear?"

"Of course, Charlie," Annie paused long enough to smile back at the ghost before disappearing down the hall with Jessie in tow.

They passed into the Library without incident, grabbed Jessie's portal key, and were in front of the abandoned cathedral in minutes. Jessie couldn't hide a gasp of dismay.

"Oh, Annie. Why didn't you get me sooner?" she asked, dropping Annie's hand and running for the entrance.

The once stone and brick building was pitch black, the edges of the stone deteriorating faster than she would have thought possible in just a few days (*had it only been that long?* she thought as she ran). The oaks and sycamores were bare, their fall foliage lying dead and brown on the ground.

"This way, Jessie!" Annie snatched Jessie's wrist and dragged her down a side path.

They rounded a curve and came to a stop at the entrance of a rose-filled bower. The once beautiful rose bushes were dying, leaves turning brown, flowers withered and rotting on the stems. The trees around the courtyard dropped brown leaves like discarded paper. No beautiful orange, scarlet, and radiant yellow transitions into winter's sleep here– this was only a place of death.

"Mara," Jessie breathed when she finally made out her friend in the gloom. Mara was on the ground, dressed in black, her hair in a wild fall spilling down her shoulders and arms. On a bier above her was Dain, laid in state. He looked like he simply slept.

Jessie ran to Mara and fell to her knees, gathering Mara into her arms. The Duchess clung to Jessie as tightly as she could and cried deep, wrenching, heartbroken sobs from the depths of her soul. Jessie held Mara, gently rocking back and forth without saying a word, while Annie stood by, watching helplessly.

Finally, Mara's tears seemed to dry themselves out, and she reluctantly let go.

"Hey, talk to me," Jessie gently tucked a wayward lock of Mara's hair behind her ear. "What can I do to help you?"

"Oh, Jessie. Please excuse me. I know you don't need this right now," Mara's bottom lip started to quiver again.

"Oh, no. Stop that! This happened because of something

that involves all of us, and don't you dare apologize or even remotely imply that you're a burden to me!" Jessie snapped, probably more harshly than she should in order to get her point across. "You are my ally and my supporter, but most importantly, you are my *friend*, and you do *not* get to deal with this level of heartbreak alone! Dain was important to all of us, but he obviously meant something even more to you, and you are going to get through this with our help because that's what friends *do*. That's what you have given me every time I needed help and support."

"I know, you're right," Mara sniffled. Even the most beautiful and elegant fae weren't immune to runny noses from crying. Jessie pulled a handful of leaves toward them, whispered a spell, and handed the resulting tissue to Mara.

"That's handy," Mara observed with a hint of her usual dry humor in her voice.

"Yes, well, why be friends with a witch if she can't make Kleenex magically appear out of some leaves?" Jessie's tone was airy to hide her relief. "Do you want to talk about it?"

"Did you know I used to have a child?" Mara asked, her voice small and forlorn. "It was long before I ever met you. I lost him to a stray arrow, right before the ogres vanished. Dain was... I don't know. I know he wasn't my child, but he was orphaned, and somehow he became like my son. He was going to be granted a demesne to the North once he came of age. I love– loved– him so much, you see."

"Oh, Mara. I had no idea."

"I know. Most people don't. Back then, after my son died, my uncle cared for my Hill until I could stand on my own again, for he did not wish for me to share my loss with my subjects or the rest of the Fae— not because he thought it was wrong. He grieved almost as much as I did. He felt, and I agree, that my grief could be perceived as a weakness and exploited. This time though, he has no one to send. The ogres' return is a blessing, but the realization that fae are involved and possibly were the whole time is too much for him to try to take care of me too."

"Mara," Jessie said as a glimmer of an idea wormed its way into her mind. "Whatever you need from us, you know we'll give it. Your Hill cannot fall. I mean that as your friend, not as someone looking at it as a strategic advantage in battle. It is part of you, you love it, and you have made it a sanctuary to hundreds if not thousands of fae over the years. But you're in mourning right now, and your resources are not what they could be."

"That's a very pretty way to call me weak and possibly incapacitated," Mara objected with a reproachful look.

"Am I wrong?" Jessie returned the gaze. Mara sighed and looked away.

"No, you're not. I take it you have a plan."

"Yes. First things first, though. I want you to seal Dain in here and come with me," Jessie came to her feet and lifted Mara up by the hands in the same gesture.

It was not easy. Jessie was tiny, and Mara was, of course, tall and willowy and considerably heavier. With Annie's help, Jessie finally got Mara to her feet, and she followed Jessie to the entrance of the little bower. Mara turned and looked at Dain one last time before she made a complicated knot with her hands, pulling the roses together to form a thorny wall. The thorns were several inches long; Jessie prudently took a step backward.

Tears streaming down her face, Mara turned and walked toward the cathedral with Jessie and Annie trailing behind. When they reached the entrance, Mara turned to Jessie again.

"I did what you asked. What's the second thing?"

"I want you to meet a witch named Christopher tonight."

Mara looked at her, brows knitted in puzzlement.

"Why?"

"Because I think you can help each other," Jessie explained. "He's Caroline's twin, and he doesn't have a safe place to go. Witch twins are more powerful than anyone can imagine, and we can't risk the cabal finding out about him or trying to track him down. He's also the one who helped Jared open the portal. We wouldn't have the ogres back without him. And I know this wouldn't have escalated to the point where we lost Dain if Jared hadn't found the ogres, but we all know that it was a matter of time before someone found a way back to that world. I suspect that the fae were already in communication with Theo. Please. Just meet Christopher. If the cabal gets hold of him and his wild magic, we'll all be in serious trouble."

"And you want me to do what exactly?" Mara asked, staring incredulously at Jessie.

"Just talk to him. Help me make him feel safe. He has this weird human friend who keeps talking about harnessing fairy and witch magic, and I don't know Mara. Christopher needs help. He needs a safe place to go, and we can convert one of your properties into safe house. He needs protection."

Mara stared at Jessie for a long second. Jessie knew what

she was asking. It was a lot to expect her friend to put aside her loss to care for another foundling, but Mara had property scattered throughout the town as part of her investment in the place she chose to call home. Chris– and Caroline and Jared too– could be safe there.

"I will consider it," Mara finally spoke, a hint of coldness in her voice that had never been there. "Bring him to me tonight and bring his sister. I want to see what we're dealing with. This is a lot to ask of me right now, Jessica. I hope you understand that."

Jessie winced before she could stop herself.

"I know, and I'm sorry. But if you and I work together, maybe we can keep everyone else safe. Or as safe as we can, anyway."

"You're right, of course," Mara sighed, the coldness in her voice thawing. "I have a house close to the Hill where he will be safe. If I may make a suggestion, Jared should move into it with him. Keep Caroline in the apartment over your bar. That way they will all be under our watch. I'll have Annie start work on the house tonight."

"Thank you, Mara," Jessie said, ignoring Annie's startled glance. Thanking the fae was dangerous. It implied that you owed them a favor, and when they cashed in on it, you had no choice but to go along.

"I'd also like you or Robin to look at Rupert's injury," she continued. "The attackers put something on an arrow that allowed it to penetrate his wing. Madame Blanche destroyed the arrow, but she said the compound is the only thing that can kill a Matagot. We need to know what it is, trace it if we can, and stop them before they slaughter any more fae or cryptids. Robin is going to Oberon's healer for advice, but we need to get eyes on all fae and cryptids who could be targeted this way."

Mara thought for a moment.

"I'll reach out to the Puck and have him go see Madame Blanche personally. Since he is her colleague and fellow ambassador, I think she would be more receptive to a visit from him than to one from me. I also believe it would be advantageous to reenter the ogres' world. I would like to make sure the enemy did not leave behind a base of operations that can be used against us."

"I'd like to get our witches out of there too, if we can manage that," Jessie agreed.

"Then tomorrow night we shall attempt to go back. I need to get my own house in order before we do. I can't leave it undefended. Annie, will you help me restore the Hill? We must get our subjects back from Oberon and make them feel safe once more. Soon we will begin the funeral rites for our beloved Dain, but first we need to make this place the way he loved it," her voice broke, but she stood tall as she held her hand out to the brownie, who beamed in relief.

"It would be my honor, Your Grace," Annie took the offered hand and followed Mara up the steps.

"Tonight after sunset," Mara called over her shoulder. "Don't be late. And Jessica— thank you."

"Could you give me a better time frame than about eleven hours of darkness?" Jessie called back, but they were already gone.

16

"How did it go?" Greta joined Jessie on the front porch of the bar where she sat with a sweet tea and stared moodily at the parking lot.

The blue sky to the west began to shift into streaks of peach and golden orange. Jared had returned from the ogre village half an hour before. He looked better– almost like his old self. Spending time with the ogres and helping them adapt gave him a new sense of purpose.

The witches glanced at Tug and Rupert's usual spots and sighed in unison.

"Okay, I guess," Jessie said.

She filled Greta in on her visit with Mara, making sure to play up how desolate the Hill looked and how badly its infrastructure fell apart while leaving out important parts of the conversation– like Christopher and the plan to revisit the ogres' world. If an eavesdropper lurked nearby, and that was a pretty safe bet, then it wouldn't hurt to let the bad guys think they were winning.

"I got Mara to agree to meet Chris. She is willing to move him into a safe house and help him. Then she wants to go back to the

ogres' world and make sure the fae and Theo didn't leave behind any surprises," Jessie projected into Greta's mind.

"Poor thing," Greta sat down on the porch and leaned against a post without giving any indication that Jessie had just clued her in on a new plan. She hugged her knees to her chest.

"I know," Jessie unwound herself from the chair and sat down next to Greta where she leaned her head on her best friend's shoulder. They stayed that way for a minute before they were interrupted.

"Hey, I'm just checking on you," Caroline opened the door and joined them on the porch. "The bar's pretty much set up for the night, but everyone's in kind of a mood. If Nicky pouts about one more thing, I might throw a glass at his head."

"I don't blame them," Jessie sighed. "Have you talked to your brother recently?"

"Yeah, he told me that a witch named Emma was bringing him here. I'm glad. I mean it. Look, I just want to talk to you about him for a minute. He's my brother, and I love him. I just want to make sure he doesn't get roped into anything that will get him hurt, killed, or used."

"I know, and I promise that whatever happens, you will be involved in every decision," Jessie said in her most reassuring tone. "In fact, we're all going to the Hill tonight. Mara wants to see you. You can bring Cassie if you want."

"Why?"

"I'll tell you when we get there," Jessie laughed at the look on her apprentice's face.

"Can't you tell me now?" Caroline made an unhappy moue with her lips.

"Nope, sorry, kiddo. You gotta wait," Jessie grinned.

"I hate waiting," Caroline scowled.

"You and me both," Greta agreed.

"I love that the two of you, who are gifted with the slowest of the elements and whose magic requires the most patience and thought, hate waiting," Jessie remarked, ignoring their glares.

"Oh, and Zach is coming too," Greta said with a grimace.

"Ugh. Do you think that's a good idea? He's really obsessed with magic," Caroline wrinkled her nose in disgust at the thought of being forced to go anywhere with Zach.

"Mara wants me to bring him, and I want to meet him anyway. So yeah, we're stuck with him. Sorry," Jessie said. "Did Jared say anything about the ogre district?"

"Yeah, apparently, after the ogres disappeared, Oberon just let the district fall into ruin. He did a lot to get it fixed up, but there's still a long way to go. Jared's looking forward to helping them get it straightened out. I think helping the ogres will help him too."

"I agree," Jessie smiled.

"Jessie! Greta! Caroline! Just the witches we want to see!" LaSalle popped in from out of nowhere with his goblet and Matthias and Tam at his side. By the looks of it, the three of them had been going at the never-ending goblet for a while now. Tam, the leprechaun who had shown Jessie and Greta how to find Matthias and aided their efforts to rescue Charlie, loved appearing in the bar at random times– mostly when the goblet was involved.

"We would like to report for security duty," LaSalle gave a deep bow, splashing Caroline in the process.

"Okay, for one thing, you can't be on security when you're drunk, and two, how did you not see that the goblet was going to spill?" Jessie tried not to laugh.

Caroline stormed inside, yelling about the lack of consideration of certain faeries. LaSalle snorted.

"She's a water witch. She can clean it right out of her jeans. Shame about the steps, though," he peered blearily at the ground.

"Yeah, we're good on security. But you can clean up all the beer you just spilled before someone slips and hurts themselves," Jessie gave him a pointed stare.

"Oh, yeah, we just wanted to do security. But I'll tell Jared! He'll be happy to take care of that. Hey, Jared!" LaSalle stumbled through the door, Matthias and Tam on his heels. Jessie was not surprised when he was pushed back out with a mop in place of the goblet.

"You get this back when you clean all of that up," Jared snapped, waving the goblet in the air before he slammed the door in LaSalle's face.

Jessie and Greta managed to keep from laughing right up until LaSalle tried to port back inside the bar and wound up bouncing off the door, landing flat on his ass. Jared flung the door open long enough to shove Matthias and Tam out too and paused to glare scathingly at his teacher, who howled with mirth, tears streaming down her cheeks, before he slammed the door shut again.

"Well, this is an outrage!" LaSalle yelled. "I'll show him who's going to mop around here!"

He tried to break the mop over his knee, but he didn't see Greta's little wave that reinforced the mop handle.

"Or you could clean it up since you made the mess," Jessie pointed out, wiping the tears off her face and trying to catch her breath. Her cheeks hurt. It felt good to laugh like that.

"Yeah, Jared's had a rough couple of days. How about you stop making things harder for him?" Greta admonished him after she got her own laughter under control.

LaSalle looked crestfallen.

"Yeah, I forgot. Okay, I'll clean it up."

"See how easy that was?" Jessie beamed as the door clicked open. The three fae pelted back through the door, yelling for Jared to come to see their work.

"Thank you for taking care of that. It looks very nice," he patted them on the shoulders. They cheered and ran back inside. He looked at Jessie and Greta.

"Did you make it so they couldn't get back in?"

"I figured you could do with a break, and I'm tired of finding beer all over the place," Jessie shrugged.

"Well, thanks," he awkwardly scuffed the toe of his shoe on the porch.

"How are you doing?" Jessie asked.

"I'm okay. Seeing the ogres helped. Caroline said you asked her about Christopher."

"I did. I'm still really pissed that you all kept him a secret. In fact, all of the secrets stop now. If I find out that you withheld anything else from me, you will no longer be my apprentice."

Jared looked at her in shock, but she ignored it.

"At some point, you have to understand how dangerous it is to keep information from Isabel, Greta, and me. Yeah, I probably should have pushed harder to find out where Tug came from, but it can't ever happen again. I don't care who you made what promise to. All of this would have gone down so differently if I had known about it, and now Chris is in a lot of danger too. I mean it, Jared. No more."

"Yes ma'am," he hung his head, looking utterly dejected. She felt terrible for kicking him while he was down, but he hadn't given her much choice.

She pushed herself off of the swing and walked past him inside the bar, Greta following behind.

"Come to the Library for a minute. I want to check you out and make sure that your wounds are healing."

He followed, still looking like a lost puppy, but she refused to budge. Once they were in the Library, Greta gently checked his arm and head while Jessie poured a cup of tea and filled them in on Mara's decision to go back to the ogre world.

"We need the spell book that had Theo's portal spell, and we need anything else he used. It might have clues to what he and his buddies have planned."

"Okay, but the book with the spell is at my apartment. Can we go get it?" he asked.

"Yeah, let's go," Greta opened a portal to Jared's apartment.

"What the fuck?" Jared froze on the portal's threshold. His apartment was ransacked. He looked at the overturned furniture, broken dishes, strewn clothing, slashed cushions, and all of his shattered collectibles, and sheer anger flashed through his dark eyes.

Jessie swallowed her own anger. They should have gotten that book out of there before now, and it was probably gone. Even the refrigerator and oven stood open. Whoever broke in left nothing unturned or unsearched.

"Let's get out of here. Whoever came looking might still be around or left a booby trap," Greta gently pulled Jared back away from the apartment.

"Wait, I see it," Jared slipped out of her grasp and darted forward, grabbing something off the floor.

He held it up, and Jessie blinked in surprise. What she thought was a copy of the swimsuit issue of Sports Illustrated shimmered in his hands and became a much larger red tome.

"Good job," she said, although she was surprised that whoever was responsible for ransacking Jared's apartment was fooled by a simple illusion spell.

He glanced back over his shoulder at the mess before he started to follow them back through the portal– and was thrown backwards when the book exploded in his hands.

"*Jared!*" Jessie screamed.

She leapt through the portal and grabbed her apprentice, who lay dazed on his living room floor, pulling him into the safety of the library just as a redcap vaulted over the upturned sofa. Jessie thrust Jared behind her and stopped at the portal's entrance to stare down the redcap.

"If you think you're so brave, come out and face me," his red eyes glowed with venomous hate.

"Sorry, I have more important things to do. Say hi to your owner for me though! Let her know I'll be along real soon for a nice chat."

He snarled in rage and lunged forward, hands outstretched and ending in vicious claws, stopping himself just in time before he made the fatal mistake of crossing the Library portal. Jessie gave him an ice-cold smile before she cut the portal connection with a decisive snap of her fingers.

"Jess, stop antagonizing the redcaps. And yes, I can't believe I'm the one telling you to stop. You're just going to make them madder, and we don't need them to start attacking our friends. Jared, they probably did something to the book. My guess is a tracking spell or some kind of attack spell. Either would make the book explode as soon as you tried to bring it into the Library," Greta patted Jared on the shoulder. "It was a good illusion, but the fae are masters of glamour. So don't feel bad."

"Here, write down everything you remember about Theo's spell," Jessie crossed to the old desk in the corner and dug out paper and a fountain pen that had seen better days. She had trained her apprentices to memorize as much as possible, a trick that served all witches well.

He obediently wrote down the parameters of the spell, his brow furrowed in concentration. Jessie studied the paper after he handed it back to her. She shook her head as she passed it to Greta.

"This is just a modification to extend the reach of a portal and prevent a target from being able to use it. Someone else must have come up with the spell that made it cross worlds. I figured as much, but I hoped we would get lucky. Witches who are spirit walkers can walk the spirit plane, but as a whole, witches usually can't build portals to entirely different realms. Nor should we. There's no guarantee we'll end up somewhere that can support life or that we won't let something very bad into our world."

"The fae who cast the glamour over the ogres probably keyed in the portal's destination," Greta agreed. "The fae can travel to different realms, and it makes sense that one of them would know the best world to use. They clearly had plans for the ogres, or they would have killed them right off the bat. I bet they would have brought the ogres back way before now if the Witch Council hadn't confiscated Theo's portal."

"Okay, Jared you are not to go back to your apartment. Make a list of everything you need, and we'll send someone to get it for you. Stay at your parents' house for now until Mara gets a place set up for you and Christopher," Jessie said.

Jared nodded and took a second sheet of paper from her. While he wrote, she turned back to Greta.

"Can you get in touch with Isabel and let her and Riza know about the redcap in Jared's apartment and that they got to the spell book? I'm going to see if the boys are free for a little recon at Jared's. Jared, how did the redcap get through your wards?" Jessie frowned.

He looked ashamed.

"I forgot to set them," he admitted.

Jessie bit back the lecture on safety and protection and always watching your own ass and decided to save it for another day. A day that would come very quickly.

"Then give me your key. I'm going to have Annie's brownies go through and make sure that you'll get your deposit back and that there aren't any other surprises."

Brownies were very resourceful when it came to dismantling everything from listening spells to boobytraps, as Jessie found out the last time her bar was attacked. Jared pulled the key off of his keyring and tossed it to her.

"Caroline said you're bringing Chris here tonight with that Zach guy. I want to go with you to wherever you're taking him," he said.

"Sorry, honey, but no. You're the one who gets to stay behind tonight. This is between Caroline, Chris, Greta, and me."

"But–" he started to protest.

"No, Jared," she said more firmly. "This part of the journey is not yours to take, and that's final. You can support Caroline and Chris when it's all said and done."

"Look at it this way," Greta spoke up. "Would you rather go with us and have to stand outside alone, in the dark faery wood, while we do our thing and then come back here to clean up the epic mess Nicky will leave behind the bar since there won't be anyone else around who can bartend–"

"Nope, I'll stay," he cut her off, shuddering at the mental image of a night with Nicky behind the bar.

"Why didn't I think to put it that way?" Jessie looked at her best friend.

"Because I'm more pragmatic," Greta shrugged smugly.

"You wish," Jessie gave her a withering stare.

17

The sun lazily sank deeper toward the horizon, gilding the autumn foliage with golden light while Greta waited on the porch swing for Jessie to finish giving Mikael and Nicky the list of things Jared needed from his apartment. Jessie joined Greta, who had one leg slung over the armrest as she lazily drifted back and forth in the crisp air. A ribbon of wood fire smoke from down the road curled through the air, winding its way around the witches. Jessie pushed Greta's leg off the armrest and sat down.

"How are you feeling?" Greta asked, running her fingers over the back of Jessie's neck and wrists, sensing the healing progress from Jessie's injuries in the battle against Theo and his allies.

"Very glad that long ago I gave you consent to use magic on me when I couldn't speak for myself," Jessie admitted.

"Yeah, you need to stop getting hurt. I am not a fan," Greta pursed her lips.

"Neither am I," John strode up from around the corner. He must have run to the bar in wolf form.

He had stayed with his pack the night before, holding

their equivalent of a memorial service. Then he spent most of the day with his dead pack mate's widow discussing funeral arrangements and making sure she would be taken care of. Sadness shadowed his eyes as he bent to kiss the top of Jessie's head before settling next to her on the porch swing. Greta reached across to pat him on the arm.

"I'm sorry," she said.

"Thanks. That sucked. He had a little one at home. The pack will take care of his family of course, but now his mate's all alone. We have to figure out what to do to help her."

"Funny you say that," Jessie said, glancing up at the door to the bar. "I need to hire someone to help out here. I need a server who can jump on the bar, especially now that Caroline and Jared are growing up."

"Really?" John brightened at the thought. "I'll run it by her tomorrow and let you know. She's really sweet. Her name is Shania, and she's a smart lady."

"Great! Send her to talk to me or give her my number," Jessie felt relieved at the thought that she might not have to recruit Nicky after all. She had been more and more worried about what she would do when her fledglings left the nest. Not that anything was wrong with Nicky. He was just a bit of a showboater, and she didn't think her liquor costs could afford the waste.

Jessie nestled into the crook of John's arm, and the three of them sat in companionable silence watching the glory of the sunset.

"I love this time of day," Greta sighed in contentment.

"What's on your agenda for tonight?" John asked.

"We're working on something else with Mara," Jessie

hedged. She knew he wasn't going to like the plan, especially the part where he would have to get left behind.

"Is she doing okay?"

"As well as can be expected. Dain was like a son to her. This really sucks."

"No shit," John sighed. "What's next?"

Jessie twisted around until she could look at him.

"Greta and I have to go to the Hill. We can't tell you why."

His brow furrowed, and his mouth hardened.

"What are you about to do?"

"I can't give you the details right now. You're going to have to trust me."

"I *do* trust you, Jess. I just don't trust everyone else."

"Hey," Greta protested.

"Well, *obviously* I trust you," he pointed out. "You keep putting her back together. It's the people who try to take her apart that I have a problem with."

"And that's understandable, but it also only happened twice," Jessie reminded him.

"That's twice too many times. What do you need me to do?"

"When we tried to go back to Jared's apartment and retrieve his uncle's spell book, a redcap was there waiting for us. The apartment was also tossed," Jessie climbed to her feet and hauled Greta up along with her. Why did all of the big people insist on making the small people help them up?

"I'll be right back," Greta opened the door to the pub, briefly flooding the porch with golden light and the cawing sound of LaSalle's laughter. Their friends were ready to kick some redcap ass, as Nicky had so succinctly put it.

"I need you, Mikael, Nicky, and LaSalle to go to the

apartment and get everything you can find on the list I gave Mikael. If you happen to annihilate any redcaps while you're there, I won't be too heartbroken about it," Jessie handed him Jared's key. While Jessie didn't particularly mind turning two vengeful vampires and a pissed-off Nain Rouge loose on a couple of redcaps in Jared's apartment, John's sense of smell and voice of reason could come in handy in case anything worth noting turned up.

"What are you going to do in the meantime? And how do you know the stuff we bring back will be safe?"

"A super secret mission you can't know about yet and I'll get Annie to send a brownie to help you," Jessie said. "Any brownie can detect and dismantle a boobytrap."

"Fine, I can do that," John sighed. "But I don't like it. I'm serious. It's not that I don't trust you or think you can't take care of yourself. This thing is big, and whatever you're doing is probably not going to be very safe. But I'll stay here. All alone. By myself. Wondering if my partner is going to come back to me in one piece. Speaking of, what do you want me to tell the others?"

"That you all get to go on your own big adventure without me," Jessie grinned.

They were interrupted when headlights flashed at the entrance of the parking lot. Four figures and two small dogs spilled out of a Subaru.

"Emma's here," Jessie said with some satisfaction as Greta rejoined them.

"Emma!" Greta launched herself off the porch and ran to the hedge witch. Jessie and John followed at a more decorous rate. The dogs sniffed John's shoes, and he gave them a solemn nod in return.

"Hey, honey," Emma laughed, squeezing Greta and Jessie. "Who's this?"

"This is my partner, John," Jessie introduced them. "John, this is Emma and her husband, Frank. Why don't you take him and the dogs inside and grab him a couple of beers? And send Caroline and Cassie out while you're at it,"

Frank pushed his shock of white hair out of his hound dog eyes and gave Jessie and Greta warm hugs before he followed John into the bar.

"So! This is fun!" Emma smiled brightly, her short ash-gray curls bouncing around her face, blue eyes twinkling with malicious mischief. "These are the kids, Christopher and Zach, as requested."

"I am twenty-five, not a child," the one who could only be Zach sneered.

Jessie immediately disliked him. He looked like an entitled, spoiled brat with a soft face and soft hands. His highlighted blonde hair was styled in an intentionally messy, shaggy cut that probably cost more than Jessie spent on her hair in a decade. He had dropped a lot of money on artfully ripped and distressed clothing designed to look street savvy, and the cunning, appraising look in his hard, brown eyes put her on high alert.

On the other hand, Christopher hadn't had to spend a dime on his impoverished appearance. He was bone thin. Jessie couldn't tell if it was genetics or starvation, but either way, she was pretty sure a good wind would blow his threadbare clothes to shreds and then blow him into Alabama. His black hair hung over his sunken, dark eyes, and his white skin pulled across the bones of his face like paper that was stretched too thin. Where Caroline was tan and athletic with an hourglass figure, he was all angles and bones.

"Is this going to take all night?" Zach continued in a gratingly annoying nasally drone. "I can't leave the Porsche double parked forever, am I right?"

"*Will anyone notice if he has an... accident?*" Greta projected in Jessie's and Emma's heads.

"*I won't notice as long as you let me do it. You're not the ones who had to deal with this fucking asshole for the last hour,*" Emma shot back.

"*Deal. I am so sorry,*" Jessie agreed.

To Chris and Zach, it just appeared that the three witches stared at them in grim silence. Christopher looked like he was ready to bolt, and Zach's nasal drone rose in pitch. He just would not shut up. Luckily for his life expectancy, Jessie heard the door slam shut behind her and felt the breeze as Caroline ran past to grab her brother in a fierce hug. Cassie came to stand by Jessie's side.

"I'm going too," she said in a voice that brooked no argument. "Caroline said I could, but I want to make sure that fact is established."

"Cool. You can stop us from doing something nasty to *that* one," Jessie nodded to Zach.

"Do I have to *actually* stop you? Or can it be more like, 'no, don't, stop, oh no, too late'?

Jessie grinned.

"Whatever makes you happy, Cass."

Caroline and Christopher stood in a close hug, foreheads

touching while Zach looked Caroline up and down, pursing his lips in crude approval. Jessie's skin crawled.

"I changed my mind. You get first dibs," she patted Cassie on the shoulder and went to Caroline's side, where she gently laid a hand on her apprentice's arm.

"Hey, we need to get going. We're going to meet someone who wants to talk to Chris. You guys can catch up with each other when we're done, okay?"

"Okay, let's go," Caroline sniffled, wiping away a tear. She refused to let go of Chris' hand.

Cassie grabbed Caroline's other hand, and they stepped through the portal Greta opened to the cathedral parking lot with Zach right behind them. He stopped to examine the portal appraisingly as if to figure out how it worked. Greta let it start to slip, and he darted through with a yelp when it began to close around his outstretched finger.

"I'm going to go see what my husband's up to," Emma told Jessie.

"Cool, thank you, Emma. If we need you, I'll call." Jessie hugged Emma back. "And your drinks are on me! I didn't tell Jared yet, so now you have to stay until we get back so we can catch up."

"Bitch. Okay, love you!" Emma waved a perky goodbye before disappearing into the bar.

18

Despite the clear, star studded, sky over the bar, they were greeted with heavy, almost ominous darkness in the cathedral parking lot. Even their witches' night vision had trouble penetrating the gloom, and Jessie suspected that the absolute blackness came more from fae magic than natural causes.

"There," Jessie pointed at a single light that hovered at the edge of a barely visible hawthorn grove on the far edge of the parking lot just past the cathedral.

They crossed the lot and joined a cheerful will o' the wisp who beckoned them along a path that opened up at their feet. The path became increasingly brighter thanks to the pixies and more wisps that joined the first, dancing around Jessie and Greta's heads in welcome. Their merry guides led the witches deeper into the grove.

Behind her, Jessie heard the soft hissing sound of a vape pen and sighed when the perfumed smell of poorly masked weed hit her nose.

"Dude! What the hell, man? Put that away!" Chris tried to keep his voice down, but it carried to her ears anyway.

"I strongly advise you to stay sober for what's about to come next," she warned over her shoulder.

"Whatever," Zach sneered. She didn't even have to see the smirk on his face to know it was there. She felt the hair on the back of her neck stand up as it always did in the presence of the fae's wild magic, and she let her own smile spread. Zach was going to be in for quite a night.

The path lightened as the wisps and pixies created an aerial dance while they wove among the hawthorn branches. Jessie was so caught up in their light display that she almost tripped over a tree root in surprise when she heard a yell behind her.

"I am the king of the forest! I will become the next Oberon!"

"Wait, stop, don't," Cassie deadpanned as Zach ran past them, ripping off his shirt and trying to unbutton his jeans. He tripped and landed on his face, but it wasn't long before he was back up and stripped down to a pair of silk boxers. He began to dance around a sycamore tree, whooping the whole time. Cassie immediately took a picture. Caroline squinted at him.

"Does the king of the forest know he's dancing in poison ivy?" she asked her brother.

"Chris, how did you get mixed up with this guy?" Jessie asked over her shoulder.

"Wait, stop, don't eat that," Cassie's face was stoic.

"Eat what— oh for Goddess' sake, take that out of your mouth, you fucking idiot!" Greta snapped in exasperation. Zach had found a mushroom and stuffed it in his mouth— and it was not a mushroom found in the mortal world. He turned a weird shade of green.

"I don't feel so good," he mumbled right before he threw up, spinning around in the process so that he made a ring of vomit. Immediately more mushrooms grew in the mess, and he froze in place.

"What just happened?" Cassie came to a stop, blinking in surprise.

"We decided to take care of this little 'lord of the forest,'" Mara's voice came out from the trees. She stepped into the moonlight, and Chris drew a sharp breath. Jessie guessed he had never come face to face with one of the high fae before.

"Jessie, what did you bring into my woods? I thought you were just bringing a witch and a human," Mara couldn't keep the exasperation out of her voice as she lifted the edge of her black velvet gown and stepped around the newly formed fairy ring holding Zach prisoner with some distaste. Annie followed behind, shaking her head with a vast amount of disapproval.

"Hi, Annie," Jessie greeted the brownie. "I need you to send one of your brownies to help the boys get Jared's stuff out of his place. We tried to get his uncle's spell book, and a redcap beat us to it. He boobytrapped the book. We lost it when Jared tried to bring it back through the portal."

"Consider it done," Annie popped out of sight. Jessie would have felt bad about ordering one of the fae around if she didn't pay a small fortune for Annie's cleaning services.

"Sorry about this, Mara. We didn't realize the forest king over here was going to be such a piece of obnoxious, entitled shit," Greta wrinkled her nose in disgust.

"He certainly is. The ring will hold him until we release him. He can't see or hear anything unless we put it directly into his mind. Now, child, let me look at you," Mara had reached Chris by now and, putting her fingers under his chin, gently tilted his head back until he looked into her eyes. He quailed back against his sister.

Cassie came to his other side and took his arm, looking up and whispering, "It's okay. She's a friend."

"I'm not crying, you're crying," Jessie muttered to Greta.

"Shut up," Greta surreptitiously wiped her eyes. "When did Cassie get so sweet and protective?"

"She's always been that way, but I think it really came out when she decided to bust through the door and save all of our asses when the witches attacked us."

Mara looked deep into Chris' eyes in silence. He remained frozen, helpless under her emerald gaze. While a fully grown witch would have been able to protect themselves from the fae glamour holding him captive, he was too young and untrained to be able to withstand her probing.

When the tears began to well in his eyes and spill over to cascade down his sharp cheekbones like diamonds in the strange werelight in the grove, she let him go, taking him in her arms and holding him. He didn't make a sound. He just clung to her shaking. She finally gently gave him over to Caroline and Cassie and walked to Jessie and Greta, shaking her head just as Annie reappeared.

"Dirty pool, Jess," she said with a shadow of a smile at the corners of her mouth.

"What?" Jessie looked up, wide-eyed.

"Don't play innocent with me. I know what you did. You

brought me a broken foundling to distract me from my grief, knowing I wouldn't be able to resist him once I saw his story. Well, it worked. I'll help him. The house I picked out for him will be ready tomorrow. We can find a way to combine witch and fae magic into a powerful ward, and he's going to need it. But you have to take him in too, Jessica. You have to take over his training. I suppose you know his element is fire?"

"Yeah, I know. But what's the deal with Zach?"

"And can we just leave him in the ring?" Greta, who did not share Jessie's more altruistic and wholesome nature, piped up.

"Christopher has to be the one to tell you about his history with Zach, and absolutely not. I don't want that thing in my grove any longer than he has to be."

"What are we going to do with him then?" Jessie grimaced. "I don't want to get stuck with him either."

"I have an idea," Mara's lips twitched. "What if we imprint the ideas that witches and the fae are sacred and their magic cannot be siphoned or harnessed deep in his mind, wipe his memory of Chris and tonight, and leave him in his father's front yard?"

"That's so bad," Jessie started to laugh.

"Um, quick question, what are you talking about, siphoning our magic?" Greta cut in sharply.

"Oh, you have quite a bit to discuss with Christopher. But first, let's attend to our unwanted guest, shall we?" Mara raised an eyebrow.

"After you," Jessie gestured.

"You never let me do stuff like that," Greta objected.

"Greta, there's a big difference between delivering someone

home with no memory of what happened and burying them up to the neck by a fire ant hill."

"I don't know. At least you know the fire ants are coming. Deep down, Zach's always going to suspect that something about his world is a little bit off, and he's going to wander around trying to figure out what happened to him until it makes him wind up paranoid and probably half crazy. He'll question his existence for the rest of his life until he drives away his loved ones, burns through his fortune trying to chase a memory he can't quite reach, and winds up in a worse place than Chris."

Everyone stared at her. Jessie sighed.

"Mara, make sure he vaguely remembers Chris as some human kid he used to hang around and partied too hard with one night. As a result of the partying, Chris decided to get clean and left the party scene. And all the siphoning and harnessing stuff is bad. Don't forget that."

"Fine. You're no fun," Mara objected, stepping delicately over the ring of vomit and mushrooms.

"See? That's what I said," Greta folded her arms, satisfied that she had made her point. Jessie chose to ignore her.

Mara put her fingertips at Zach's temples with a moue of disgust at having to touch him. She concentrated while a high-pitched and nasal keening sound came from his throat. Whatever Chris had shown her had instilled quite a bit of enmity in her for this kid, and she did not try to be gentle.

When she finished, she stepped outside the circle and snapped her fingers. A portal opened on a quiet street in Buckhead. Jessie could see the Atlanta skyline rising over the mansions of Argonne Forest, where houses started with the low, low price tag of $1.5 million. A satyr stepped out from the trees, grabbed Zach, and tossed him through the portal where he rolled to a stop on the verge. As the portal closed, Jessie could see him sit up and shake his head, looking down in confusion at his boxers.

"The portal is hidden from even the humans' surveillance systems. He'll think he got a ride from someone he didn't know and was dumped on the street when he couldn't remember his address," Mara said with some satisfaction.

"Is it going to be enough though? Someone planted the idea of how to harness energy in his head," Greta asked, chewing on a fingernail out of worry. "Chris, how rich is this kid? Like how powerful is his family?"

"According to Zach, they're some of the richest and most influential people in the country. Probably the world," he shrugged.

"We would be unbelievably naive to think that the humans who had a lot of money and power were completely unaware of the supernatural before witches, cryptids, and the fae came out in the open," Jessie pointed out. Greta nodded.

"We're going to have to keep an eye on this lovely new development," Mara sighed.

"But how can humans do something bad to the fae and witches? We don't even understand how your magic works," Cassie objected.

"Humans can handle metals we can't, and you made most of the advancements in this world," Mara reminded her. "Also I doubt a rich, powerful family lacks the resources to experiment at will. No, I think we need to be on the lookout for missing witches and fae."

"Yeah, I'll say something to Emma. The homeless and transient witches will be the ones no one except the hedge witches miss. Not to change the subject, but are you still up for a visit to the ogres' world?" Jessie asked.

"Yes, especially now that we know Zach's intentions. I want to know everything the cabal has planned. But I think we should bring Christopher. I want him to see what he helped open a door to, not as punishment, but as a way to understand the necessity for a teacher and the consequences of unfettered magic."

"Agreed," Greta said.

Jessie turned to Chris, who finally started to calm down.

"Hey, Chris, I think we should head back now. I need to talk to Emma, and Mara's got a great place for you to stay."

"He can stay with me tonight until it gets set up," Caroline offered.

"Thank you, dear. I'll have it ready for him by tomorrow evening," Mara said with a gentle smile.

"Mara, your help is invaluable," Jessie said, reaching for a hug. Mara returned the embrace.

"As is yours, my friend," Mara whispered into Jessie's curls. She stepped back and snapped her fingers again, the hawthorn grove fading away until they were left standing in the parking lot.

"Okay, let's go home, kids," Jessie said as Greta opened the portal to the Library.

"Do they ever stop calling us kids?" she heard Christopher whisper to his sister.

"Nah. They're ancient, so they automatically think everyone else is a child. You get used to it."

19

After giving Christopher as gentle a rundown on the dangers of entering the Library under false pretenses as they could and almost having him run away again, they finally settled him into a chair by the fireplace with Spot in his lap and a cup of tea in his hand. Jessie leaned against the arm of the sofa where Greta perched.

"First things first," Greta leaned forward, fixing Chris with a piercing stare. "How did you get mixed up with Zach?"

Chris looked down, his face flushing with red spots high on his cheeks. It was the first similarity to Caroline they had seen.

"It's okay to tell us," Jessie added. "You're not in trouble. We just have to make sure that we know the whole story in case he returns."

"I had started coming into my fire powers, but I couldn't control them," he said, his voice low. "They were just too bright and too strong. I was on my own by then, and I had this apartment with some crappy roommates. One day they stole my stuff to sell for drugs. I was so mad that I just felt like I was burning up. I tried to get away and blow off steam, but

I accidentally set an old building on fire. Zach saw it happen. I don't know if he was in the wrong place at the wrong time or if he followed me, but him being there seemed awfully convenient. I didn't know he was around, or I wouldn't have done it. I never did magic near other people because I was too afraid I would hurt someone. Anyway, he told me he would turn me in for arson if I didn't do more magic after that. He never left me alone. He kept talking about his father's money and connections and prestige and how easy it would be to harness the power of magic and use it himself."

"Where did he come up with that?" Jessie asked, exchanging a worried look with Greta.

Christopher shrugged. He wouldn't look up from Spot, who purred in his lap, occasionally making a biscuit or two which caused him to wince. Caroline came to stand behind him with one hand resting protectively on his shoulder. They reminded Jessie of Jared and Tug.

"It was something he heard his father talk about to his friends. So Zach kept bugging me to do magic for him and telling me he could make it hard for me if I didn't do what he said. He said I would never last in jail, and I just had to do him this favor in return for my freedom. I had a really bad feeling, so I kept making excuses not to do magic around him. But he was always there, watching, so I just stopped doing magic altogether."

Caroline's eyes glittered in anger.

"That's really fucked up," Cassie spat. Her hands were clenched into tiny fists.

"Hey, Zach can't hurt Chris again," Greta reminded them. "Only a faerie king or queen can reverse Mara's glamour."

"Honestly, I'm not sure how reassuring that is considering that we now know a king or queen of faery was probably partially responsible for the ogres' disappearance," Jessie pointed out. "Not to scare you guys, but I think a reality check would be very good right about now."

She pushed off from the sofa and crossed to the tea table where she poured water over rose hips and hibiscus petals. She noticed the way Christopher hungrily watched as she gently heated the water with her natural magic. He desperately wanted to learn, and if everything he'd said was true and he really *had* suppressed his powers for this long, he was probably starving to feel his magic again.

"We need to look into this some more," Jessie continued as she turned to face the group. "I think you should stay in the apartment over the bar tonight instead of at Caroline's. It's in good shape, and the wards will protect you. Tomorrow you should be able to move into your permanent home under Mara's protection. Caroline, go ahead and get him settled in. Greta, we need to go to the witch council and pay Isabel a visit."

"Agreed. One question though, if you stopped doing magic, how were you able to help Jared build the portal?" Greta stood up and looked at Chris. It wasn't an accusation. She was genuinely curious.

"Oh, he didn't need my magic for that. I'm really good at putting stuff back together. Someone had messed up the gears, and I just had to fix it," The tension left Christopher's shoulders when he started talking about the portal's mechanics. "See, magical devices use gears and mechanisms like clockwork to operate, so all you have to do is figure out what's stuck, and then bam! It's working again. What are you all looking at?"

The witches and Cassie stared at him in amazement before Greta started to laugh.

"So your secret power is that you're an engineer? I love that! Jessie, either he's going to make this place run like, well, clockwork, or you're going to walk in the door and find everything dismantled."

"As long as you leave all of Cassie's equipment alone. That's all I ask," Jessie hastily cut in. The last thing she needed was her entire security and phone system to go down because of a young witch's curiosity.

Still chuckling, Greta opened the portal to the bar for the younger witches and Cassie. After they were gone, she turned to Jessie.

"Just out of curiosity, why don't you have him stay here indefinitely? Tug's not likely to come back; that way, you could keep an eye on him."

"Because Mara needs him as much as he needs her, and if we've learned anything so far, it's that we probably shouldn't keep all of our magical eggs in one basket. The eggs being everyone we have to keep safe and the basket being this bar," Jessie explained.

"I figured out the metaphor, thanks," Greta's lips twitched.

"Plus this is the perfect chance to see if we can combine our magic with Mara's. I know we could do that here, but I would rather not experiment with the bar, thank you very much. Besides, I want Caroline to move in here and Jared to stay with Chris. Mara and I don't want the twins to live together."

"Very smart," Greta agreed. "So what's next?"

"I think we have a couple of witches we need to get back from the ogre's world, and we need to do it soon, but first I want to check in with Emma and let her know what happened."

"Do you want to talk to her here or in the bar?" Greta asked.

"Let's talk to her in the bar and maybe feed some misinformation to anyone who might want to listen in," Jessie led the way back through the portal and into her office.

They heard Emma's glorious laugh down the hall and came out into the bar in time to see LaSalle pass the goblet to her. It looked like the mission to Jared's apartment was a success, although John and the vampires sulked at one end of the bar.

"What's wrong with you?" Jessie asked, leaning in for a kiss from John.

"Well, we finished at Jared's and tried to check on all of you," John admitted.

"When we got to the Hill, it was like the entire wood was wrapped in a shroud that we couldn't get through as if it was warded against us," Mikael complained. He did not like being told what to do.

"It was," Greta said. "And anyone else who might be listening."

"We told you that you couldn't go with us," Jessie reminded them.

"Yes, but we didn't think you really meant it," Nicky objected.

"Well, we did. I have to talk to Emma for a second. I'll

be right back," Jessie didn't bother to hide her grin at their distress.

"Hey, honey, how did it go?" Emma greeted her as she came closer.

"Fine. I have a question for you," Jessie answered. "Have you noticed any witches go missing? Maybe ones no one would really notice were gone?"

Emma stilled, her bright eyes searching Jessie's face.

"Witches always come and go," she finally said. "What's going on?"

"It's probably nothing," Jessie shrugged. "I was just thinking about Christopher's situation is all. It would have been so easy for him to slip through the cracks, and we never would have known."

Emma gave Jessie a look of sheer disbelief.

"Uh-huh. Hey, you haven't shown me your new books in your Library. Let's go check it out," Emma hopped off her stool. "Frank, we'll be right back."

"Okay," he nodded at them and scooped up the dogs before they could follow Emma down the hall.

"Okay, what's really going on?" Emma asked once they were in the Library.

"Zach seemed to believe that his father had found a way to harness the magic from witches and the fae and planned to use it. That's why he hung around Chris so much. Can you find out if any of the transient witches really just moved on? I want to try to make sure everyone is accounted for," Jessie said.

"I'll do my best, but we don't keep tabs on anyone. You know that."

"I know. Maybe if you haven't seen anyone in too long or someone disappears earlier than they normally would. That seems the best place to start," Jessie suggested. "I want to learn more about Zach and who his family is too. Let me know if any other humans start to show up. I expect the curious ones to seek out witches like me who are in the open, but none of them should know about you. The hedge, hearth, and hood witches stay hidden too well."

"Yeah, I'll try. Jess, if this is really happening, how am I supposed to protect my people? You know we can't trust the Council."

"None of us can trust the Council," Jessie shook her head. "There is definitely at least one spy there. Probably more than one. Talk to the leaders of the hood and hearth witches and let them know what's going on. Tell them I'll back it up. Maybe if you all work together as a community, you can protect yourselves. Greta and I will assist you all in any way we can, and I'll ask John to talk to the local wolf pack down there too just to give you some added security."

Emma sighed.

"Goddess, there is not enough alcohol for this. Not even in LaSalle's goblet. I need to get Frank on the road so we can get home and call a conclave. Thank you, Jess. I mean it."

"Let me know if I can help," Jessie hugged her friend before leading them back to the bar.

Emma took one last swig from the goblet before corralling the dogs and her husband. As they pulled out of the parking lot, Jessie waved goodbye.

"It's like we take one step forward and two giant steps back," Greta joined her friend.

"Yeah," Jessie sighed. "Come on. Let's go enjoy some time with our friends while we can."

20

The next day Jessie slept in and then treated herself to a luxurious (for her) early dinner and coffee from the cafe down the street. The Naga family who ran it waved goodbye as she walked back toward the bar, enjoying the warmth from the late afternoon sun on her shoulders.

Greta waited on the porch swing again, idly pushing off with one shoe. John's slightly decrepit red Jeep pulled into the parking lot behind Jessie, and he joined her, wrapping an arm around her shoulders. He was already on board to go with them to the ogres' world, and so were LaSalle and Nicky. Mikael had to sit this adventure out due to Alliance business.

"Chris is inside with Caroline and Jared, and Annie said that Mara's house is ready whenever we get back from the ogres' world," Greta told them as they walked up. "We just need to grab Chris, and we can head to the Hill."

"Why Chris?" John looked between the witches, puzzled.

"It was Mara's idea. She wants him to see what he helped Jared do when Jared decided to make a portal without talking to any of us first. Sort of a nice way of explaining the consequences of his actions kind of thing," Jessie explained.

"I see. And what if there are any dangers?"

"Then he gets a crash course on how to defend himself with magic," Jessie shrugged.

Greta laughed at the look on John's face before ducking inside the bar to grab Chris, Nicky, and a book wrapped in brown paper. They followed Jessie to her car while the sun slipped out of sight, leaving a few gilded puffs of cloud to adorn the glowing horizon. LaSalle gave them a cheeky wave before porting on ahead to the Hill.

Porting everywhere was nice and all, but it was best to save the charges on their portal keys for emergencies when they could help it; plus, driving to the Hill gave Jessie and Greta a chance to go over the plan and work out all of the details without any unwelcome eavesdroppers. Jessie's beloved, ancient Prelude was warded within an inch of its life.

"I like it," Nicky's grin was feral and sharp.

"I grabbed Theo's journal," Greta said. "It's mostly full of narcissistic, stupid rants about how the whole big, bad world is unjust, but we can use his language to recreate the intent of the spell."

"Does that mean I have to actually read it?" Jessie groaned.

"Absolutely not. I read enough for both of us," Greta shuddered.

By the time they pulled into the cathedral's parking lot, the sun was down. Chris hung back nervously before steeling his nerve and joining the rest of the group as they strode toward the cathedral door. John slung a comforting arm around the young witch's shoulder and gave him a smile of encouragement.

Jessie paused to swallow against the lump in her throat

as she looked at the empty steps. There was no Dain there to give her the ceremonial greeting and smile shyly when she praised his efforts.

Robin, Annie, and three elves Jessie didn't recognize but who wore Oberon's armor stood in the foyer. Annie led them through a small side door that opened into an ash grove where Mara waited for them. Jessie was surprised when Melodium stepped through the trees on the other side of the clearing to loom over them.

"He refused to get left behind," Mara shrugged. She looked better than she had the last time Jessie saw her. Apparently rescuing a lonely witch was exactly what the doctor ordered.

"Nor should I be," Melodium crossed his arms across his barrel chest. "The fate of the witches who fought so bravely to free my brethren and myself is as much my responsibility as it is yours. I also am eager to learn what became of the treacherous fae who sought an alliance with the cabal."

"Hey, I'm not going to say no if he wants to come with us. We have no idea what we're walking into, and he knows the world. Plus he gets bonus points because he's almost in-destructible," Greta said. "I brought Theo's journal, but I have to be honest, I don't know if it will be much help. It mostly consists of the ravings of a narcissistic imbecile. A redcap waited for us at Jared's apartment when we went back for the spell book that had the actual portal spell, and the book was destroyed. I hope the journal will let us recreate his language and intent enough along with whatever fae magic still exists on that side of the portal to get through to the ogre's world."

"Very well, then. We believe we have the means to reach the ogres' world, but we must go deeper into Faerie and visit my uncle's court to find the portal I want to use. Are you ready?" Mara gestured them forward into the fairy ring.

"I guess," Jessie tried not to let her nervousness show. The fairy portals opened into vast, cosmic vistas and faraway kingdoms and courts on the other side of the world. It was not going to be an easy ride.

"Here, chew this," Annie thrust pieces of ginger root, peppermint leaves, and chamomile blossoms into their hands. "It will settle your stomachs."

Jessie paused, getting a good look at the brownie for the first time. She was used to seeing Annie with her nut-brown hair twisted into a sensible bun and her neat little apron smoothed over a clean, well-made dress, but tonight Annie wore full chainmail armor. Jessie didn't even know brownies had armor. The chain link looked like it was made for a slightly bigger person, but Annie still wore it with ease.

"Didn't know I could fight, did you?" Annie chuckled at the looks on their faces. "This is my Ian's armor. Mine is getting some dings knocked out of it."

"Dings from what?" Jessie asked, fascinated.

"Oh, some little skirmishes here and there. Nothing serious," Annie waved off their curiosity. "Now chew those plants. I didn't bring my apron, and I'll not have you throwing up on His Majesty's floors."

"Your apron?" Christopher asked.

"Where did you think a brownie's magic came from?" Annie sounded as confused as the witches felt.

Jessie had never realized that Annie's apron was the source of her hearth magic. It made as much sense as anything else about the fae.

"Chris, I'm going out on a limb and guessing you never used a faery portal. Just because witches can travel through them doesn't mean it's easy. Expect a lot of nausea and vertigo," Jessie warned.

"Aye, so you'd best be eating that ginger, mint, and chamomile," Annie scolded.

The witches and John exchanged a glance full of trepidation before obediently popping the herbs into their mouths. The ginger was potent; Jessie's eyes started to water almost immediately. She wiped them dry as Mara opened the fairy ring portal, whisking them away to Oberon's court.

Supernovas, planets, ancient forests, deep oceans, and sweeping mountain ranges all spun around them in a dizzying array of sight and sound before they came to a stop on a marble and flagstone platform. Melodium surreptitiously nudged Jessie and Greta upright when they staggered against him.

"Next time I choose the method of transportation," Jessie sat down rather ungracefully on the floor. Greta joined her, head between her knees. She was slightly green. Chris collapsed in a bundle of limbs.

"I think I'm going to throw up," he moaned.

"But I was right about the herbs, now wasn't I?" Annie nodded sagely. Jessie chose to ignore both Annie's wisdom and Mara's open grin.

"That wasn't so bad," John said to Nicky, who looked as much at ease as if he had just strolled through the door. Jessie and Greta ignored them.

"Your Majesty, I would like to present the witches Jessica and Greta, the werewolf John, the vampire Nicodemus, and the apprentice Christopher. I believe you already know the Nain Rouge, LaSalle," Mara said.

"Oh for the love of the Goddess," Jessie groaned, looking up.

They were in the middle of Oberon's receiving room, surrounded by openly staring high fae. Some looked as amused as Mara while others whispered behind their hands. Jessie elbowed Greta and Chris in the ribs.

"Get up, we're not alone."

"I hate everything about this," Greta climbed to her feet.

Oberon, in his high elf persona, radiating blinding beauty and power, leaned against the arm of his stately throne with his chin resting in the palm of his hand. He looked bemused.

"I thank you for coming, especially as I know that the journey from your world to ours is fraught with peril and leaves much to be desired. Should you require anything from the court physicians to counter the effects of travel, you have but to ask. My resources are yours."

The titters and whispers around the court ended pretty much immediately. When the High King of all Faery showed mercy and restraint, it was not a good idea to keep laughing at his guests.

"Your Majesty, we appreciate your kindness and the warm welcome to your court," Jessie recovered enough to incline her head and look at least semi-presentable.

Oberon stood up and gestured for them to follow as he turned and led them from the throne room. They walked along a rich path made of thick, vibrant, green grass that ran down the center of the marble floor. The walls were thickets of hawthorns, foxglove, bluebells, and clover, and ash trees interwove their branches to create a soft ceiling overhead. The air was clean and sweet, and the light that filtered through the trees glowed a soft, luminous, green.

"I have a portal that our smiths created quite a while ago. It laid in disuse for centuries. I have no idea if it will work, but for the moment, it suits our needs," he said as they walked along the path, the thick grass muffling their footsteps.

"Here's Theo's journal," Greta passed the paper-wrapped book to him. "Like I told Mara, it's mostly the ravings of an idiot. Unfortunately, we weren't able to retrieve the spell book with his original spell. At least one redcap beat us to it."

"We might be able to retrieve Theodore's essence from the pages and use it as the key to unlocking entry into that world," Oberon unwrapped the book and studied it as they walked. His form began to slowly shift, turning back into a beautiful dwarf by the time they reached the door at the other end of the corridor.

"That's what I thought too," Greta said.

They passed through the door and entered a small, simple stone chamber. Jessie felt a pang as she realized it was the same room from which Oberon had to watch Dain die, helpless to do anything to stop the attack. Mara's back stiffened and pain flashed through her emerald eyes. Annie gently patted the Duchess on the arm.

A very familiar black disc lay on the floor, and Jessie froze. Melodium let out a curse. They had destroyed the portal, so why was it here?

"What the hell?" Greta had the same thought.

"It is not the portal from whence you traveled to and from that world," Oberon's tone was dark. "But your reactions confirm my suspicions that the original portal must have been a fae design."

"It certainly explains how Theo was able to suddenly travel to another world," Jessie said. "He was a shitty witch before he wound up trapped there. He never could have made a portal like that by himself. But I am sorry that you keep finding evidence of betrayal from one of your own."

Oberon gave a bitter laugh.

"Oh, I am certain that the betrayals come from more than one of my subjects. I appreciate the sentiment nonetheless."

He continued to read the journal, his lips curling into a more and more pronounced sneer.

"Quite full of himself, wasn't he?" Oberon finally said. "Still, I believe this book has served its purpose."

Jessie felt the hair on the back of her neck tingle right before a beam of light shot up from the center of the portal. Oberon threw the journal into the light where it flared in a burst of white flame and went out just as suddenly. They stared at the empty, stone huts waiting for them in the doorway that stood where the column of light had been just seconds before.

"Here we go," Jessie gritted her teeth, and they stepped back onto a world none of them ever wanted to see again.

2 1

The portal opened up into the center of the village, and the small group looked around, getting their bearings.

"How long will this portal stay open?" Jessie asked Mara.

"We have an hour and a day," Mara replied.

"Our time or this world's time?" LaSalle asked. "Because they are very different, and I, for one, would like to be able to go back home."

Mara paused, exchanging a glance with Melodium.

"Perhaps we should err on the side of caution and accomplish our goals within the time constraints of this world," Melodium suggested.

"Smart," John agreed. "Shall we?"

They fanned out, cautiously moving through the village. Annie magically produced a sword and shield, and she and LaSalle, who had his axe at the ready, flanked Mara. Greta cast an earth shield around the witches, and Jessie's fire burned at her fingertips. Christopher hovered close to the two older witches. John shifted to wolf form and drifted silently behind them, while Nicky bared his fangs and talons. Melodium's skin glittered as it grew diamond-hard, and his eyes glowed red. He was ready to go into full rampage mode at the slightest attack.

They found Charlotte along the path leading into the dark woods on the other side of the barren fields. The air witch's eyes stared sightlessly up at the sky. Her body was bent and twisted at angles it should never have been able to achieve, and deep claw marks scored her face and laid her throat open. Melodium knelt and inspected her body.

"She is marked by claws and serrated teeth, and the putrid reek of an unwholesome sea clings to her skin," he said, getting to his feet.

Jessie looked around.

"I don't see any sign of Victoria. Is there any way one of you can pick up her scent?"

Melodium's nostrils flared, but he shook his head.

"Your wolf companion will have better luck than I. I will keep trying, but the reek of the monster responsible for this carnage overpowers all else."

John whined and planted his nose to the ground, snuffling around for the scent.

"This malodorous smell shall be our guide," Mara said. "For the creature is most likely on the trail of our missing witch."

Jessie did a double take. Mara's dress was now leather armor. Mara smiled in amusement at the look on Jessie's face.

"Brigandine armor," she explained, lifting the hem of her hauberk so Jessie could see the metal discs riveted to the armor underneath.

"I figured that much, but where did it come from?"

"Our garments provide as much protection as we wish," Mara shrugged. "They simply adjust to suit our needs."

"I wish I had clothes like that," Greta marveled.

"Yeah, me too," Jessie agreed.

"That's because you hate shopping. Now come on, we tarried enough already. Your wolf has the scent we need," Mara pointed at John who led the way further into the woods. Melodium followed, sniffing the air like a giant, gray-green bloodhound.

The path wound under the dark trees, sometimes crossing the tranquil river with well-built bridges that were clearly the work of the ogres. Melodium smiled in pride when Jessie commented on the craftsmanship. However, it wasn't long before they all smelled the brackish, rotting odor Melodium had picked up from Charlotte's body. Right at about the point where the trees began to thin, they also smelled the sickeningly sweet scent of burning flesh.

"That can't be good," Jessie broke into a run, Greta on her heels.

They burst from the cover of the woods into a field similar to the one next to Melodium's village, only this one was green with corn and wheat– except for the gaping hole in the middle of the crops where a smoking corpse lay. As the group drew closer, Jessie could see that it was a skeletal horse with a man's torso attached to the back. The torso had long, dragging arms, and a jutting snout like a pig's protruded from its face. Probably the worst part was that it had no skin. This was truly a creature of nightmares, the Orcadian demon of the sea.

"Nuckelavee," Mara hissed.

"But they're sea monsters! What are they doing here?"

Greta demanded. "They can't cross freshwater, and there's a river right there."

"Clearly another portal to this realm is in use," Melodium said grimly. "For there is no other way for this creature to reach this place."

"Shit, we really need to find Victoria and get out of here," Jessie couldn't keep the worry out of her voice.

"Maybe she's alive and in the village," Nicky knelt by the Nuckelavee's corpse. "This creature was killed not that long ago."

"Let's go, but be careful. She's a fire witch, and she probably doesn't expect any help. She'll attack first and check to see if we're friend or foe later," Jessie waved them forward.

Greta recast her shield, and the group doubled up behind it with Melodium at the rear of the little column. If anyone tried to attack them from behind, Melodium would be as good a shield as anything Greta could construct. They edged forward until they reached the village. Jessie felt extremely exposed.

"Victoria, honey? It's Jessie and Greta. We found a portal in the faery realm, and Oberon let us use it to try to get you home."

A blast of fire darts shot from the roof of one of the abandoned huts in the village and scored the ground at the edge of Greta's shield.

"Prove it," Victoria called out. Jessie could see her peek out from behind the chimney, the fire ready in her hand.

"We met in 1893 when you came from Egypt to join the Council, and you were shocked because I said 'fuck' three times in one sentence," Greta yelled back.

"And why was that?" Jessie grinned.

Greta shot her a dirty look and then sighed.

"Because I tripped on a brick and fell up a flight of stairs and ripped the skirt off of my dress in front of the Council," she snapped.

"Okay, I'm coming out. No one else would admit to something that ridiculous," Victoria slowly edged around the chimney until she faced them. "Holy shit, it is you! I can't get down. I burned the ladder when the Nuckelavee tried to follow me. How did it get here?"

Melodium stepped forward, arms outstretched.

"Jump, and I will catch you, Madame Witch."

Victoria cast a doubtful look at Jessie and Greta who smiled encouragingly. She took a deep breath and leapt off the edge of the roof and into Melodium's waiting arms. Jessie and Greta ran to her, folding her into the tightest hugs they could. She started to cry, shaking so hard that she couldn't stand up.

"Charlotte... that thing killed her. I couldn't get to her in time. We had split up. We should have stayed together. I could have saved her."

"You don't know that," Jessie comforted the other witch. "You might have died too."

"Yes, you had the advantage of height when you destroyed the monster, and it was weakened when it crossed the river. Freshwater rivers and lakes are poison to the Nuckelavee," Mara added. "We need to discover how it arrived in this world if we can."

"Victoria, do you want to come with us or have us send

you back? We still have an open portal," Jessie turned to the still-shaken witch.

"I'll come with you," Victoria said, a note of determination strong in her voice. "I will never forgive myself if you die too."

"How much time passed between when you were left here and now?" Mara asked.

"About three weeks, maybe more. There was nothing for days. We went from village to village together searching for any sign of the cabal, and we saw nothing. So we decided to split up and check the villages again before going back to the mountain. I had just gotten back here to meet Charlotte when the Nuckelavee came out of nowhere. One minute everything was fine, the next there was a goddessawful smell, and it grabbed Charlotte from behind. It bent her backward and killed her. It was like watching a malicious child destroy a doll, and I was too far away to help her."

Greta put a comforting arm around Victoria's shoulders.

"Let's go back to the mountain," Annie suggested. "We know that Theo used it as his base of operations. Melodium, do you still have the amulet?"

"Always," the ogre pulled the necklace from under his jerkin.

"Leave it out," Mara decided. "The light helped you once before, maybe it will do so again."

They turned and headed back toward the mountain, giving wide berth to the place where Charlotte still lay, broken and tossed aside. To Christopher's credit, he only flinched, although his jaw was clenched tight. Jessie briefly spared a thought for what he must have endured to make him so capable of looking at horrors that would send most people to their knees in shock.

"I will make sure your friend reaches her home so she may receive the proper burial and rites," Melodium reassured Victoria.

"Thank you," she murmured.

As they crossed back through Melodium's former village, Jessie couldn't help but notice that the ogre's face grew dark. It wasn't her imagination when he gained a couple of inches in height and girth either. Nothing jumped out to attack them, and they continued toward the one lone peak rising to the sky.

"The mountain is the anomaly," Mara said. "The rest of this world is too flat for it to exist naturally in that state. It reeks of cosmic manipulation."

"It feels wrong," Greta said. "Was it always there, Melodium?"

"Aye, as long as we were," he said.

"My guess is that the cabal planned to use this world from the beginning and made the mountain before Theo brought the ogres here," Nicky, who had been a military advisor when he was alive, shrugged. "That's what I would do."

They continued on, crossing the rope bridge over the river and making the arduous climb up the mountainside until they were in front of the shallow cave at the peak. John scouted ahead of them, still in wolf form.

"There has to be more here. There's no way Theo would be content in just a cave like this," Jessie said. "Greta, do you pick up anything from the earth?"

"Yeah, I do, actually," Greta walked forward. "Melodium, can you shine the amulet back here?"

He obliged, and she squinted against the glow that lit up the back of the cave wall. They all watched as she ran her fingers over the wall with a frown.

"It's not here... maybe on the other side of the cave, come on!"

Melodium chased after her as she spun on one foot and took off running out of the cave, the rest of them close behind. Just at the very end of the narrow path, she found what she was looking for: a crack in the mountainside shaped like an arch. She concentrated and pressed her fingers against a spot that was a shade darker than the rest of the surrounding rock.

LaSalle swore, axe at the ready, when the arch rumbled open and revealed a much more spacious room that was opulently decorated with some of the most garish and ridiculous furniture and bedding Jessica had ever seen. The cave was thick with dust, and rotting scraps of food littered the floor.

"This was Theo's alright," Greta's nose wrinkled in disgust. "No one else would be this tacky."

"Look," Chris pointed to a spot along the far wall. Sure enough, a black disc sat on the floor. Footprints led from the disc to the entrance where they huddled. A lot of footprints.

"Someone's been busy," Jessie said.

"I count at least four different kinds of tracks that come and go," Melodium told them as he hunched down to get a better look. "And see, here are the hooves from the Nuckelavee. They have the same scent."

"Let's get rid of this thing," Mara said with some distaste.

"LaSalle, when I tell you to, hit it with your axe as hard as you can."

She, Victoria, Jessie, and Greta combined their magic into a stream of pure energy that she directed into the portal. It began to quiver under the attack, glowing red.

"Now," she snapped sharply, and LaSalle shattered the portal with a mighty blow. The piercing shriek as it splintered into pieces made them gasp and cover their ears. When the ringing stopped, they looked at each other in alarm. A new sound reached them, one of angry shouts.

"Everyone ready?" Nicky called out before he fully turned, causing Chris to stumble backward, panicked.

John threw back his head and howled in a challenge, and Melodium towered over them in full battle rage before he led the group in a charge down the mountain and to the rope bridge. The redcaps and elves on the other side took one look at the rampaging ogre, terrifying vampire, huge wolf, axe-wielding Nain Rouge, and the fire streaming from Jessie's and Victoria's fingertips and then skidded to a halt, turned tail, and ran.

"After them," Melodium thundered as he barreled across the bridge and plunged headfirst into the wood on the other side, the rest of the group close on his heels.

It really couldn't have worked better if Jessie and her friends had planned it. The fleeing enemy panicked and ran for the first escape route they saw– the portal Oberon himself had opened in the middle of the ogres' village. And, unbeknownst to them until it was too late, Oberon and his guardsmen waited on the other side.

"Never let it be said that redcaps were known for their

intelligence," Annie remarked as their little group rejoined Oberon.

"No, I suppose not," Oberon agreed. He looked at the redcaps and the two elves who still wore his armor. His guardsmen surrounded the renegade fae and held them at spearpoint.

"We destroyed another portal, Uncle," Mara told him. "We didn't have time to see if there were others."

"I must return and claim the body of your friend. Hold this open but a moment more," Melodium didn't wait for an answer before he ducked back through to the world he wanted to leave behind.

"Your friend?" Oberon looked the group over, noting the addition of Victoria, who looked very shaken as the shock of everything she endured set in.

"Yes, we lost Charlotte to a Nuckelavee. These fucking assholes brought one through and set them on the witches," Greta's fingers twitched, and the ground under the redcaps rumbled alarmingly.

"Perhaps we could avoid opening holes in my demesne," Oberon hastily cut her off. "How much time passed for you there?"

"But a few hours," Mara replied.

"It seems as though no time passed for us," he said, looking sadly at Melodium as he came back through with Charlotte's broken body hanging limp in his arms. "Melodium, if you would be so kind, please carry their friend to their home so she may be laid to rest following their customs."

"I'll show you the way. Victoria, you come too," Annie opened a portal. Jessie saw a warm hearth with a cauldron bubbling over a roaring fire before Victoria, Annie, and Melodium stepped into the portal and blipped out of sight.

Jessie turned back to Oberon.

"Jared figured out the formula for how much time passes in that world as opposed to this one," she said. "We need to get that from him. I'm sure it will come in handy."

"Don't destroy this portal," Greta added. "We didn't have time to explore the whole area, and I'm sure there is much more beyond the ogres' villages and the mountain. But these assholes came running as soon as they heard the portal in Theo's lair crack. Maybe we'll get lucky and that will be the last one."

Oberon's face darkened like a thundercloud, and his eyes turned stormy and black.

"I understand. I shall place wards that no fae can break around this portal and keep it safe."

"Come on," Jessie turned to her friends. "Let's go home."

22

They rejoined the rest of their friends in a corner of the bar just as Robin's own portal opened and he stepped through. Caroline and Jared took turns waiting on customers and checking in on the conversation.

"I have news on the poison used to hurt Rupert," Robin did not smile.

"How bad is it?" Jessie asked, a knot forming in her stomach.

"He will heal, but I fear the psychological damage will be extensive. This is the same poison that destroyed most of his kin. It neutralizes the proteins that cause the Matagot's coat to become impenetrable. For obvious reasons, I will not list the ingredients out loud here, but they are difficult to find. Very few people even knew this recipe existed."

"I wonder if someone made a new batch or if they found what was left from the attempted extermination of the species," Mikael said.

"That I do not know," Robin admitted. "I understand Madame Blanche's decision to destroy the arrow, but I wish we had it nonetheless."

"If the poison was made for the Matagot, then that means the enemy came to the fight with the intention of specifically hurting him," Jessie realized.

"Maybe. Do you know if it works the same way on ogres?" Greta asked.

"It does not, but to your point, the enemy may have coated their arrows with the poison in hopes that they might penetrate a rampaging ogre's skin," Robin told her.

"Yeah, well, it was also a pretty good bet that he would be with us," Nicky shook his head.

"And as the one invulnerable member of our party who is always present at every fight and capable of inflicting pretty crippling damage, if they had a chance to take him out, they would have been stupid to pass it up," John added.

"How can we help him heal?" Jessie asked.

"For now let him remain with Madame Blanche. He is safest there," Robin said. "Try to visit when you can. It will do him good to be reminded that you are also his family."

"That makes sense," Greta nodded. "Do you know what happened to the remaining Matagot?"

"Rupert was able to send word to them. They have gone to ground, and all seem to be accounted for."

"So what now?" Nicky asked.

"Caroline, can you break your lease? I would really rather have you over the bar in Tug's old apartment."

"Sure, I'm already packed. I saw this coming from a mile away," Caroline gave a grim nod.

"Good. Chris, you and Jared can move into your new home tomorrow. We'll also start your training. Be here at noon,"

Jessie said and then paused, considering. "No, make it two. I want to sleep."

"Do I need to get or bring anything?" he asked, nervously twisting his hands together.

"No, we'll take care of all of that tomorrow. And we're going to get you some new clothes," she told him. "I hope you understood why we wanted you there today."

"I think I get it," he nodded. "Doing spells like that when you don't know what's waiting on the other side or what the possible consequences could be is dangerous."

"Hey, can you teach Jared that same lesson?" Greta asked from Nicky's other side. Jared scowled.

"Do you think Astrid knew about the portal?" Nicky asked.

"I doubt it. She seemed clueless about anything important," Jessie said. "But I wonder if she had dealings of her own with the fae."

"Might be worth it to ask," LaSalle belched. He had the goblet again, but Jessie noticed he was much more careful about slinging it around.

"Yeah. You guys hold it down here. Greta and I need to go have a long talk with Isabel and Astrid," Jessie pushed off from the bar and shrugged out from under John's arm. He grumbled in protest, and Jessie gave him a kiss before she followed Greta down the hall to the Library where they opened the panel that led to Isabel's office.

Isabel sat behind her desk in an airy tower room lit by stained glass skylights. A horned owl rested on a perch next to her. Jessie cocked her head and looked at the owl.

"Where did the barn owl go?"

"He's in the owlery," Isabel replied, reaching up to gently

stroke the horned owl's feathered chest. "I can have more than one owl, you know."

"I know that, silly. I just really like the barn owl. Don't get me wrong, you're very nice too," she soothed the indignant owl's metaphorical and literal ruffled feathers. He had not taken kindly to being compared to a *barn* owl of all things. The very idea!

Isabel was not alone. A tall witch with silver hair that hung to her knees and runes tattooed on her face rested gracefully on a chaise lounge against the wall. A small fae perched next to her. Olav was a Nisse, a Norse fae similar to the Celtic brownies. Only the single eye in the middle of his forehead gave away the difference.

"Greetings, Olav and Gertrud," Jessie nodded to them.

"Hello, Jessica. It is nice to see you again. I appreciate the effort you have put forth to help my daughter, even if I fear your efforts might be in vain," Gertrud returned the nod and rose from the lounge.

Gertrud was older than Jessie, Isabel, and Greta by a few hundred years or so. As a *völva*, she could traverse the spirit planes. No one to Jessie's knowledge was more powerful— or had been before Gertrud's daughter Astrid ambushed her mother for the cabal. She tricked her mother into creating a necromancer, thus draining Gertrud of all of her power until Gertrud repaid the karmic penalty for such an act to the universe. Gertrud had moved into the Witch Council towers to try to speed things along, even going so far as to help create a magical prison for her daughter that only she would be able to dismantle once her powers returned.

"Isabel, thank you for your time as always. I will leave

you to your discussions. Please let us know if we may be of assistance," she said as she glided out of the room. It was still very disconcerting to hear one such as she defer to them, and Jessie and Greta exchanged a quick uneasy glance.

"What's up?" Isabel asked, looking from one to the other.

"We wanted to fill you in with everything that's going on and ask you some stuff about what happened with Jared," Jessie explained as they sat down in cozy armchairs in front of Isabel's desk.

Back when she had been Jennet and Isabel had been Ysabell in a tiny Scottish village long lost to memory and dust, they had never imagined that one day they would sit across from each other in one of the most powerful offices in the world. It took a surprisingly short amount of time to tell Isabel everything that had happened.

"We also have proof that the cabal might still have access to that world– at least the fae did until earlier today. I wish we had a chance to look for more portals," Jessie finished her story.

"Speaking of, how's Victoria?" Greta asked.

"With the healers. She will be fine. I wish you had discussed leaving witches behind with me though. We're already running short of allies we can trust."

"We didn't have any other way to destroy that portal," Jessie said. "Trust me, it was the last thing we wanted to do."

"I know," Isabel sighed. "Poor Charlotte."

"In light of everything we've learned, we can't discount the possibility that a king or queen of faerie is helping the cabal too," Jessie added.

"I wonder if that's why they targeted Mara," Isabel stared thoughtfully into the distance.

"Targeted?" Jessie and Greta exchanged a startled look.

"Well, first her own child is killed right before the ogres were taken, then she's attacked on her grounds and loses the one who is essentially her second child. One of two things was going to happen as a result of that attack. Either she would be killed or she would be incapacitated by grief. As long as Dain stood by her side, he would take the blow for her. That was never in doubt. He was loyal to the end. But she's the grounding force of the Fae in the Southeastern U.S. Only four others in the Americas are on her level, and they're spread out pretty thin. If she goes down, that will open up an awful lot of doors for the cabal."

"Crap," Jessie blew out an explosive breath. "That didn't even occur to me."

"Yeah, well, you probably need to discuss this with her and Oberon," Isabel's tone was very dark.

"What about Jared's abilities on the ogres' world?" Greta asked.

"He's right. Illusion is the province of air magic. An earth witch twisting the air to do his bidding caused it pain and turned it against its purpose. It saw that Jared was its rightful master and went out of its way to help him. We can always nicely ask for assistance from an element that is not our own, but we don't have the right to force it. If Theodore hadn't abused the air the way he did, Jared would have had a much harder time. In a way, his uncle gave Jared more power and leverage than anyone could have imagined. It's a shame that

Sharon was dragged into this again. We need a way to tell her that she's not being looked at."

"The hood witches are working with her," Jessie said. "She's one of their own."

"That's good then. They'll help her heal," Isabel decided. "What else?"

"Are you positive your chambers are safe from spies?" Greta asked with a hint of nervousness as it occurred to her that they were openly discussing some rather sensitive topics.

"Oh, yes. That's another thing air does really well. I can erase, distort, and even recreate sound waves. There's a bubble around the three of us, and the air changes our words. I'm sure the walls are riddled with spies, just from council members who want my position. But they're hearing a completely different conversation than the one we're having now. I can even change the movement of our mouths in case anyone tries to read our lips."

"That's so brilliant," Jessie laughed.

"You probably shouldn't laugh. The spies think that you just told me that one of the cats died," Isabel grinned.

"Oh, I'm sorry. How's this?" Jessie looked up with her blue eyes full of crocodile tears. Greta groaned.

"While we're on the subject of things that are safe," Jessie said in a more somber voice. "We're moving Caroline into Tug's old apartment. Mara provided a house for Jared and Christopher, and she's going to reinforce our wards. I want to be absolutely clear that when word gets out that we have a pair of twins on our hands, they will *not* be turned over to the Council. I will do whatever I have to do to keep them safe, and they will not be safe here. You know it as well as I do."

"Oh, I was not going to suggest that," Isabel shook her head vehemently. "I'm not taking that risk with a pair of twins."

"One more thing," Jessie continued. "Charlie and I talked to Madame Blanche. The compound on the arrow that penetrated Rupert's wing in crow form was the same that the original cabal used to hunt down the Matagot and try to take their pelts. The remaining Matagot are hidden, but we need to find a way to protect them."

Isabel sat back in her chair and huffed out a sigh.

"Poor Rupert. If he loses the rest of his clan then that will devastate him more than anything else the cabal could do. We probably need to get eyes on every race of cryptid and fae they targeted in the past. We should have done it sooner."

"Yeah. Let us know how we can help with that. I also want to talk to Astrid and see if there was anyone she talked to before she disappeared from her mother's house," Jessie added as she reluctantly got out of her chair. She loved Isabel's chairs. More than once she had fallen asleep in one and woken up hours later to Isabel working away at the carved desk while an owl stared at Jessie in disapproval.

"Do you think she'll tell you?" Greta shot her a sideways glance.

"Probably not. But if someone is spying on her, and I am still convinced that's the case, it could light a fire under that person's ass, and maybe they'll make a mistake."

"Or it could get someone killed," Isabel reminded her.

"I'll be nice. I'll let Greta go in with me. That will freak her out."

Isabel grinned at her friends.

"Yeah, you're right. But I also think you should have Olav

there too. He'll keep her in check if she starts to lie. Apparently, none of Gertrud's companions trusted Astrid and did quite a bit of spying of their own."

"That's what I'm counting on," Jessie was smug.

Isabel looked at the owl who took off, gliding on soft, silent wings out a small door that opened in the wall.

"He'll get Olav to meet us at Astrid's cell."

She rose from the desk and led them out of the room and down a wrought iron winding staircase that looked like it was plucked right out of the French Quarter.

They came around a corner and saw Olav waiting outside a heavy oak and iron door. He wasn't alone. Riza stood scowling, arms crossed across her chest.

"Get this shit," she said as they approached. "Someone definitely broke into the vaults. Spell books, artifacts, and the records of everything we recovered after we captured the leaders of the first cabal are all missing. Some stuff's still there, but we have no way of knowing what's gone."

Jessie felt the color drain out of her face.

"You can't be serious," she gasped in dread. They had confiscated so many dark artifacts and spells that should have never seen the light of day– artifacts like Jared's uncle's portal.

"As a heart attack," Riza's tone was as dark and grim as her mood.

"This is bad," Isabel hugged her arms to her chest and rocked back and forth on her heels.

"Hey, Isabel, can you do your little air bubble thing again?" Greta asked with a vague wave.

"Yes, just because you made it sound so elegant. Why?"

"Because I still have the copy of the vault records that you gave me."

Isabel and Riza stared at her.

"Does anyone else know?" Isabel demanded.

"Fred and Sharon unless someone spied on us at Jared's house when I blurted it out. I told them I could prove that Sharon had turned over the portal. The records are hidden in our Library vault. I don't want to bring it here, but you and Riza can come to study it there, or we can move it to one of your Libraries. I don't think it will last long in the Council towers."

"No, it definitely won't," Isabel started to pace in excitement. "You keep it for now. But if anyone asks you about it, let me know immediately. I mean, it, Greta. Don't assume that anyone is safe outside the four of us."

"I won't," Greta promised.

"Olav, can you tell us anything about Astrid's activities before she disappeared that we don't already know? Did she talk to any of the fae?" Jessie asked the little Nisse.

He was startled by this question. It simply had not occurred to him that something of that nature might be important. The fae tended to be both very literal and not of the moment. Their gaze was so far-reaching that they often did not think to include little details that would make a witch's life easier, as Jessie had learned many times with Mara. Apparently, this was one of those times.

"Well, yes. She frequently spoke with the dark elves."

"The dark elves? And you didn't feel a need to share this with us?" Riza was incredulous.

"Just because an elf is dark does not mean they're evil,"

Gertrud said from behind them. "Dark elves are called so due to their skin color and their world under the ground. At most, they believe, and perhaps rightfully so, that Oberon's rule should not extend to them. Several of the fae from my homelands feel that he is too entrenched within the Celtic fae circles and that the Erlkönig should be given full rule over the northern fae."

"I know that," Riza snapped in exasperation. "But I kind of think that regular consultations with a group of fae who did not live on your farm or regularly interact with you or your fae assistants would have been useful information in light of her activities."

"True," Gertrud admitted. "Perhaps you should ask her yourselves."

"I think we should do just that," Jessie marched to the door and pushed against it. The heavy wood swung open at her touch; it was used to her by now.

When the cabal swayed Astrid to join them, the voluptuous, blonde-haired, blue-eyed poster child for Viking culture had envisioned wealth, power, and recognition that would go with her rightful place as one of the leaders of the world. Never mind that she was still in her twenties with no understanding of her power and no interest in self-control.

Instead of world domination, she now lived in a wormwood cell that blocked her magic and drained her beauty, and she had to endure the daily lectures of a Nisse of all creatures. The Nisse were mere servants in her eyes, not good enough to speak to her much less scold her for her actions; the humiliation she was forced to endure never ceased.

Her own mother refused to speak to her. The few times

Gertrud entered the room to bring food or clean clothes, she wouldn't even look at her daughter. Astrid didn't want to admit it, but that hurt more than anything else she had experienced since she was taken prisoner by Jessie and the Council.

At least Jessie broke up the monotony. Astrid, convinced that she could play the older (and much wiser) witch like a fiddle, begged Jessie to come back as much as possible. But Jessie's stonewalling when asked for information on the cabal's progress and what the Alliance planned to do to stop it frustrated the younger witch. Deep down, Astrid was forced to examine the thought that maybe she wasn't as skillful a manipulator as she thought.

She looked up when Jessie entered the room, the beginnings of a simpering smile appearing on her sallow face that was framed by limp, lifeless hair. The smile froze and drained away along with whatever was left of the color in her face when she realized that Greta was right behind Jessie. She had not forgotten how Greta had casually buried half of the cabal's forces alive and then pouted when Jessie made her let them go.

"Hi, Astrid. I know I was just here, but I figured I could always come back for another visit. And look! I brought company!" Jessie's smile did not reach the icy coldness of her blue eyes. If Astrid needed any confirmation that Jessie never believed her redemption routine, this was it.

"Hey, Astrid. Long time no see– oh, right. Because you're stuck in here, and I'm not," Greta waved. "Question for you: why on earth would you, who clearly think you're better than the rest of the world and believe that only witches are pure and good enough to rule all, want to fraternize so closely with dark elves?"

That was the last thing Astrid expected to hear. They watched as she began to frantically look around for help. Her eyes involuntarily turned toward the shadows.

"I didn't!"

"For shame," Olav pushed forward, hands on his hips. He shook his head in admonishment. "I saw you many times."

"They wouldn't leave me alone! They wanted me to... to... talk to my mother!"

"About what?" Riza was very skeptical.

"They wouldn't say. I swear I don't know what they wanted. I swear by Freya."

"I would leave Her out of this. I don't think She's as bothered by the wormwood as the rest of us," Jessie said with a little snort of amusement. Greta openly grinned.

"So you're going to stick to this story?" Isabel raised her eyebrows.

"It's the truth!" Astrid wrung her hands together.

"Well, I guess that's all we're getting today. Let's go," Isabel turned on her heel and strode out of the room, leaving the rest to follow in silence.

They looked at each other and then at Gertrud, who had waited for them.

"Did you hear that?" Jessie asked.

"Aye, I did," Gertrud said. "It would be easy to verify or disprove her story, whichever the case may be. The dark elves and I always respected each other. They brought me metals for my work, and I gave them treasures from the surface for theirs. They are skilled craftsmen who specialize in jewelry steeped in magic."

"I take it she doesn't know you had a working relationship with them," Greta jerked her head toward the door.

"Presumably not. She was very intelligent and loving as a child, but we drifted apart as she grew older and more resentful that I chose to remain isolated from the world. It seems her precocious nature had not left her, for she took the initiative to make her own connections, however poor they were."

"Okay, thanks, Gertrud. I'll keep you posted if anything turns up, but can you or Olav verify that the dark elves weren't actually trying to reach you? Just so we can get that out of the way," Jessie asked the tall witch.

"Certainly. Olav comes and goes between here and my farm quite frequently. After all, a huldra and a keiju are not the world's best farmers or land keepers. And, thanks to both my daughter and you, I seem to have picked up a peikko as a tenant," Gertrud said with an amused quirk on her lips.

"Ah, yes. Sorry about that. We were in a hurry. He seemed perfectly nice though once he decided not to kill us," Greta said hastily.

Ingrid was the huldra with the beautiful face of a woman and the hind legs and tail of a cow, and Sharaya was the rainbow-winged, scatterbrained sprite of a keiju. They and Olav had helped the witches get past the farm's defenses to save Charlie and Madame Blanche when Astrid kidnapped them and hid them at the back of a cave in a mountain. Grubben, the vicious peikko, was one of Astrid's traps, for she had imprisoned him and set him on the witches' path to kill them. Instead, they set him free– and it looked like he decided that the farm was as good a place to settle down as any.

"It's fine," Gertrud laughed. "If anything, I no longer have to worry about trespassers. Just their bones."

They all shuddered.

"Isabel, Riza, please let us know what we can do to help and if you find anything else about the missing artifacts and records," Jessie hugged them both.

"We will, and I'm going to search the layers of time to see if we can find anyone going into the vaults. We know when Jared found the portal, so that's a good start," Isabel told them. She was quite proud of her time-searching trick. It involved intricate gestures in which she peeled back layers of time and space to see what had occurred in the past.

"Oh, that's a great idea," Jessie brightened up before stepping through their portal.

They walked into the bar's main room. Caroline made drinks while Jared restocked the ice and rinsed the glassware.

"Great, so now we have to figure out who helped Theo because you know damn well he didn't get that portal into Jared's parents' garage by himself," Greta blew her bangs off her forehead with a frustrated sigh and took a seat by the newly-returned Mikael. He sipped a twenty-one-year-old Macallan, something he thought he deserved after dealing with Alliance politics all day.

"Yeah, and I don't know how to start narrowing that down," Jessie plopped down on a stool next to John.

"What's going on?" Nicky asked.

"Well, it turns out Astrid got cozy with some dark elves before she ran away from her mother's farm, and someone broke into the Council vaults and stole artifacts and spell books that were confiscated during the uprising. They stole the records too, so we don't know what the thieves took or when," Jessie told them.

She felt a little curl of guilt at the lie by omission, but she had to admit that even she couldn't guarantee that there weren't ears in the walls of her bar. She made a mental note to ask Annie to take a look for listening spells again after the fae completed their mourning rites for Dain. Almost nothing could get past a brownie.

"Isabel has her little time reveal trick she's going to try to use, but the only marker we have is when Jared found the portal. There's no telling how long it was in his parents' garage if they go in there as little as he says they do. Or if it was kept somewhere else and then moved," Greta added.

"That sounds extremely bad," John shook his head after kissing Jessie on the temple.

"It is," she replied.

"What do we do now?" Jared asked as he sanitized a stack of newly cleaned pint glasses.

"You are going to ramp up your lessons with Isabel. She confirmed that the air worked harder for you because you 'rescued' it from torture. But we have to consider you to be a target now. You pretty much orchestrated everything that undermined the cabal this time, and I know they'll be coming for you," Jessie told him without trying to sugarcoat it.

"You need to add your own wards to the ones Jessie, Mara, and I will place on your house and do not *ever* forget to set them again," Greta added.

"Understood," he nodded. "I can hang out more with my folks too."

At least he took this seriously, which was a huge relief for Jessie.

"We need to be extra vigilant," Jessie looked at all of them. "I'll say this again, if anyone knows young witches who don't have a teacher, try to convince them to come to one of us for protection. Or tell them to go to any full-blown witch who you trust. Also if you see anything that looks like a talisman, artifact, or spell book that you don't recognize, don't touch it. Let Greta or me know. Most of the stolen items are really ugly and used for nasty things. I don't want any of you getting hurt."

"We'll be careful," Jared promised.

"Jared, how are the ogres?" Greta asked.

"Oh, they're doing great," he smiled. "The place where they live by Oberon's castle is amazing. Oberon did a great job restoring it so quickly. It's beautiful. Everything's carved out of marble, and there are these trees I've never seen before all over the place. The houses are really nice too. Everyone has their own bedrooms, they have real furniture, and they have kick-ass uniforms and armor and nice clothes."

"How bad was their village on the other world?" Jessie asked. She had been too busy almost dying and trying to rescue her friends to take a good look around.

"It wasn't terrible," Jared shrugged. "It was just simple, and they didn't have a lot to work with. Now they have these huge forges, workshops, and kitchens and they even have a place where they can set up a market. They're pretty amazing craftsmen, you know. Tug's happier than I've ever seen him."

"Is there anything we have to worry about right at this moment?" Nicky asked a touch plaintively. "Or can we breathe for five minutes?"

"I think we can breathe for five minutes," Jessie gave him a sideways hug. She still worried about him and probably would be for a while.

"That's a nice change," he hugged her back.

She looked around at her friends and loved ones. They all met her eyes, old acquaintances and new, and all showed worry, new pain, and determination. This was going to be a long fight, but she was glad that this was her army.

Epilogue

"Well, that was a great Halloween. I'm exhausted," John slung his arm over Jessie's shoulders and let himself slowly go deadweight until she squirmed away, giggling.

The last kids had just been bundled into their parents' cars and were on their way home to get hyper on obscene amounts of sugar. Witches had been out in the open for a while, but they were still new enough for local kids to get extra excited about having one in their backyard at Halloween. Jessie hoped, as she did every year, that the sentiment held true at Christmas.

"It was," she agreed. John's son and daughter had enthusiastically joined in the fun, dressing in the scariest costumes they could find and jumping out of the bushes at the entrance to the parking lot to scare everyone who walked down the street. Shania had taken them home with her to keep her own son company. He still reeled from the loss of his father.

Shania was a strikingly lovely woman with an Afro, light, golden eyes, and smooth, cocoa-colored skin. She had only worked at the bar for a few days before she admitted to Jessie that her little boy woke up crying for his daddy every night, and she didn't know how to grieve for both of them. It had broken Jessie's heart, like so many other losses she had watched women suffer throughout her long years.

"Shania's going to work out great," Jessie said.

"Yeah, I figured she would. This will be a good distraction for her. Her son can stay with my kids if you need her at night too."

"Hopefully that won't be too often, but I appreciate it. She said they're good for him."

"Well Maisie can't stand to watch anyone suffer, so she comforts him when he cries. Trevor tries to bring him toys and candy to make him feel better. He's right in between their ages, and I don't think my cubs will let him go. They're their own pack now," he said with a fond smile. "But don't tell Shania he's getting sweets at my house, or I'll never hear the end of it."

"Do your kids remember their mom?" Jessie asked. John rarely talked about his dead wife.

"Maisie does. I think Trev's starting to forget."

They went back inside and sat down at the bar next to Cassie. LaSalle and Matthias had taken up posts at the door as Jessie's semi-new security.

"Still no word from Tug?" Charlie asked. Charlie had never been a fan of change, and losing the constants in his afterlife didn't sit well with him.

"Not as such, but Jared said he's still doing well," Jessie told him.

"Yeah, he and the rest of the ogres seem to be thriving. I think Tug's getting bored, though," Jared added.

"So do we still call him Tug or what?" Cassie reached for the electric pink drink Caroline sat in front of her.

"I've been calling him Elisian when he's with his tribe, but I don't know what he would like us to call him," Jared frowned thoughtfully. It hadn't occurred to him to ask.

"Tug is acceptable from you. It is a poor memory from a world I thought was mine but a happy one from the world I joined," Tug's voice rumbled from the door.

"Tug!" Cassie squealed, flying off her stool and into the startled ogre's arms. He was swarmed in seconds by his friends and the bar regulars alike, both supernatural and human.

"Okay, give him some air," Jessie yelled, laughing. "Just kidding, it's my turn."

After Tug put her down, he gave her a shy smile.

"If it's okay, I would like to continue my employment. I discussed this with my brethren. We feel that in light of the attacks aimed at the bar and you as well as your involvement in this fight, I would be better served by your side."

"Tug, that is the most wonderful thing you could have possibly told me. You are welcome to work anytime you like."

"My thanks," Tug gave her a bow.

"Come on, Tug, let's get you situated and get you a beer. I want to hear all about your life," Charlie sort of guided Tug to a stool. "Caroline put it on my tab!"

"You don't have a tab, Charlie," Caroline objected.

"Pretend I do," he waved her objections away.

"That's amazing," Cassie came to stand by Jessie and watched Tug and Charlie. "We spend so much time together and know so little about each other. I didn't even know Tug had a family. Hell, I forgot John has kids!"

"Yeah, they're good kids too. They're protective and nurturing, just like their dad," Jessie looked up at John fondly and nudged his shoulder with her cheek. He smiled down at her.

"What happened to their mom? I mean, if you don't mind me asking," Cassie asked.

"A manticore somehow got loose in our territory a few years ago, and she died trying to fight it. Our daughter was five, and our son was three. They were too little to defend themselves, and I was out dealing with a case. I didn't know until the call came in," he looked at the floor, his voice trailing off.

"A manticore is a Persian cryptid," Jessie explained after catching the puzzled look on Cassie's face. "It has the body of a lion, a human head, and a scorpion's tail that has venomous spines. Some can fly. We think it was part of someone's private zoo. They're extremely dangerous and not native to this area."

"Oh, I'm sorry, John. I didn't know about that."

"Thanks, Cass. It's okay," He gave her a reassuring smile over Jessie's head.

"What about you, Jessie?" Cassie asked, her legendary curiosity whetted.

"I have a brother who returned to Scotland, and Greta has a brother and a niece who had a daughter about sixteen years ago. Greta's sister was killed in the first uprising right after her niece was born. Both of us lost our mothers over the years."

"You don't know your fathers?"

"No, the witch gene always breeds true, but male witches are sterile. Before artificial insemination became possible, witches just used human men for breeding purposes. It was hard to stay with someone when he aged and you didn't, especially for those of us who were born in the late tenth century."

"What about you?" John grinned at Cassie over Jessie's head.

"Well, my parents aren't thrilled that I wound up dating a witch, but they're coming around. And they love Caroline, but they wanted lots of grandkids. It's hard for them to give up that dream even though I never planned to have kids," she explained. "My oldest brother is at UGA. He wants to be a vet. All of my other brothers and sisters are in high school and middle school. There are seven of us."

They stayed quiet for a moment, watching their friends. The vampires were at a Halloween masquerade ball, and Jessie didn't expect to see them for several days.

"Come on, let's stop being antisocial," Jessie broke the contented silence, leading John and Cassie back to their small family and home.

Astrid huddled on the floor against her cot, shivering. This time, it wasn't from the ever-present damp chill of wormwood that permeated the air and seeped into her bones. She had messed up badly, and she knew it. It had been several days since Jessie confronted her about her activities on her mother's farm, and the presence who lurked in the shadows around her cell had been ominously absent. The one who slipped through the pools of darkness to taunt her and remind her of her failures didn't fear wormwood. Her mother's protective spell may stop Astrid's tormentor from actually touching her, but there were other ways she could be hurt.

"Astrid..."

She whimpered.

"You were very naughty," the voice hissed. "And you're a terrible liar."

"I'm sorry, Mistress. Please–"

Her head erupted in white, blinding pain. She screamed, a high, thin sound no one heard, clutching at her skull as her eyes rolled back in her head. The voice chuckled and faded away as she collapsed, unconscious, blood trickling from her eyes, ears, nose, and mouth.

She was still like that when Olav checked on her an hour later. He immediately alerted Isabel and Gertrud. They looked at each other grimly as they crouched next to her.

"Magical aneurysm," Isabel shook her head.

"Aye," Gertrud gently, sadly, touched her daughter's hair. "She must have given away more than we thought when Jessica spoke with her last. Can we remove the trigger?"

Isabel gently probed Astrid's skull.

"If I can get Greta and Ivan to work on it, then there's a very slim chance. But it's in there pretty good. There's a high risk that we would set it off," Isabel warned.

Gertrud bowed her head.

"So it's come to this," she said in a voice so soft that Isabel almost didn't hear her. "I lost my magic and my daughter in one fell blow due to my hubris and refusal to meet the world and her changes head-on."

"Stop that," Isabel snapped. "The last thing we need is for you to beat yourself up. We have all made mistakes in our lives, and I defy you to show me one witch as old as we are who can raise a perfect teenage daughter."

Gertrud gave a reluctant, small smile.

"You are right. Olav will stay with her for the remainder of the night. I imagine she will have a nasty headache when she awakens."

"I'll arrange for some basil and thyme tea to be sent in," Isabel reassured the *völva* as they rose to their feet. Between them, they were able to get Astrid on her cot.

"Do you know how this happened through your spell?" Isabel asked as she locked the door of the cell behind them. Olav stayed behind, but he had his own key.

"My spell stops many things, but if she willingly let someone into her head, then they have a foothold that can be accessed from anywhere in the world. No spell can stop them. Her mind is a door to which they already have all the keys, and we can never lock it."

Isabel shook her head and held her tongue. This was something else Astrid should have learned at her mother's hand.

"You cannot stop me from 'beating myself up' as you say over this," Gertrud sounded numb. "I should have taught her better, and you know it. I can see it in your eyes."

"I'm not going to try to stop you. Come on. I'll make you some tea. I think I have a bottle of scotch stashed somewhere around here too," Isabel gently guided the other witch out of the cell and to the tower's stairs, leaving Olav to clean up the mess Astrid left behind when she began to thrash in the throes of the aneurysm. He never saw the faint yellow gleam in the shadows– a gleam that looked like eyes before they vanished in the darkness.

www.ingramcontent.com/pod-product-compliance
Lightning Source LLC
Chambersburg PA
CBHW071240300726
48975CB00002B/497

About the Author

Eli Rainwater moved to Durham, NC from Atlanta where she lives with her three cats and drinks way too much coffee. When she's not playing in her garden, she can be found draped over furniture reading a book, throwing a temper tantrum when she plays video games, yelling at the television during football season, or sleeping through one of the many movies and TV series she keeps meaning to watch.